ELLIE

Jackie Mills

ELLIE

BRANDON

A Brandon Original Paperback

First published in 2000 by
Brandon
an imprint of Mount Eagle Publications
Dingle, Co. Kerry, Ireland

10 9 8 7 6 5 4 3 2 1

Copyright © Jackie Mills 2000

ISBN 0 86322 275 7

Cover design by id communications, Tralee, Co. Kerry
Typesetting by Red Barn Publishing, Skeagh, Skibbereen
Printed by ColourBooks Ltd, Dublin

For Lyn and Marie
remembered with love

PROLOGUE

Birds chirped in the garden, the gentle sunshine of a May evening maddening them with joy.

I stared at Matt, stunned.

Part of me wanted to laugh – from shock, I suppose, or that sense of unreality that goes with utter devastation. I became aware of the cast-iron dish in my hands (Le Creuset – a wedding present from his cousin Mary) and stared at it as if it held the secret of life.

I remember thinking: if I put this down very carefully, I'll have achieved something. I will have accomplished my first act as an un-married woman.

Instead, I threw it at him.

I suppose it was lucky I missed. Cast-iron hurtling through the air impelled by such betrayal could have been lethal.

The pot hit the wall, its contents glistening down the tiles like vomit. A single bay leaf stuck in the grout and hung there, irresolute, before sliding down to rest on the Beef in Guinness it had been flavouring.

"Jesus, Ellie."

Matt, like me, was mesmerised. Three of the hand-painted Italian wall tiles had cracked.

I reached for the antique iron and took aim. Matt ducked. It crashed into the wall with a satisfying thud and the tiles shattered.

"Your dinner," I announced, stepping over the mess and closing the door behind me.

The night he informed me his girlfriend was pregnant I did what wounded parties do in the movies – told him to pack a bag and leave. And he did. I heard him moving round the bedroom, then his steps on the tiled floor of the en suite as he gathered whatever a man being thrown out of the marital home might need to see him through the first couple of days.

I was tempted to call out to him, to put an end to the drama. I would fix him eggs and we'd sleep on it. But something stopped me. At some level I knew there was no going back. Better to let him go, then face whatever had to be faced.

Telling Charlie was the hardest thing I'd ever had to do.

He tried to act cool, but the shock in his eyes winded me. At eleven he was bright and perceptive, unusually aware of his world. I wanted to be straight with him, I just could not find the words to tell him about Bethany's pregnancy. I could barely entertain it myself. When it flashed through my brain I saw the distended belly of full term rather than the squiggle it undoubtedly was in her well-toned uterus.

Bethany. The name made me want to spit.

I'd leave the pregnancy disclosure to Matt.

Charlie listened, very tense, very still.

"It's okay, Mum. We'll be okay." He hugged me quickly and was gone, back to whatever global destruction he was wreaking through the PC in his room.

Days merged and became weeks. The sense of unreality deepened even as I became aware that I needed to pull myself together, to take some control over my life.

The 'Des. Res. in Executive Surround.' bought for us by Matt's father would have to be sold.

I would have to find a job.

I would have to find a place to live.

And I would have to break it all to my mother and the aunts.

CHAPTER ONE

AT FIVE-THIRTY ON a freezing November morning I was wakened by an ominous grinding noise. With a growing sense of alarm I followed the sound to its source. There, in the tiny hallway that separates my kitchen from the garden, my good-as-new boiler appeared to be having a convulsion. As I watched, disbelieving, it thumped and fell silent.

I sat on the stone floor with my head on my knees. There was no escaping the fact that I would have to call Mr Flynn, the builder to whom I had been metaphorically joined at the hip since buying the house four months earlier. It was one short, glorious week since I had paid him off and thought my life was my own.

Arriving at work, I found the library steps unusually crowded. An ambulance yawned towards the building, a young garda and two ambulance men hovered, nervously eyeing a mongrel dog who bared his teeth at them, growling. Miss Tuohy, every inch the librarian with her balletic bun, spectacles, tweed skirt and matching cardie, gestured fiercely at the men to stay back. She approached the dog carefully, avoiding its eye, talking gentle nonsense all the while. The dog continued to growl, though with less conviction. It leaned into something that looked like a bundle of rags wedged into the handrail at the side of the steps, sniffed Miss Tuohy's hand and waited.

Slowly, calmly, Miss Tuohy took hold of the animal's string lead and edged towards the street.

"You will not," she hissed at the young garda, "send for that cretinous warden. I shall take the dog myself."

She coaxed the mongrel into her car and returned to organise the men as if they were unruly infants.

"Mind his head! There's a lot of blood."

The ambulance men exchanged a look as they knelt by the dark mass, checking for vital signs. When they reached for their stretcher I glimpsed the bloodied, battered face of Tom, the tramp who came on occasion to warm himself in the library. His clothing was soaked. He must have lain there all night.

I joined Miss Tuohy who was looking down at Tom, her expression grim.

"Bastards," she said, for maybe the first time in her life.

A fine, misty rain hung over the street. Everything was still and grey. That Tuesday it was Miss Tuohy's turn to open up the library. In the six months I had worked with Miss Tuohy I had never before seen her angry. Her hands shook as she handed me the keys.

"See to things, Ellie. Keep the main doors locked until nine-thirty. I'll bring him to my vet and come straight back."

The ambulance men passed us, manoeuvring their

stretcher. Tom's neck was secured with a brace, the blood on his face already congealing to a dirty brown.

"Will he make it?"

"He'd better," she replied, heading for her car.

Martina, unusually animated, and Paul arrived together.

"What's going on?"

"Is he dead?"

I shooed them inside.

"No, Paul, he's not dead. I hope."

The ambulance lamp flashed through the reading room windows. An urgent *nee-naw, nee-naw* signalled its departure. The young garda banged on the outer door.

"Garda Gerard Murphy," he said as I locked the door behind him. "Any chance of a cup of tea while I wait for your woman?"

I led him to the large cupboard that did service as a staff kitchen. Our breath smoked the air.

"And you are . . .?"

"Ellie Pierce. I'm assistant librarian."

He nodded, chafing his hands. "It's colder in here than out."

I lit the Super-Ser as we waited for the kettle to boil. "You get used to it." I felt oddly defensive. "It takes a while for the heaters to kick in."

"So, you know this fellow, do you . . . this Tom?"

As Paul and Martina turned on lights and coaxed gas heaters to life, the library was revealed in all its gloom. The reading room was damp, shabby, Dickensian. The wooden desks were scarred from years of schoolboy penknives, the chairs uncomfortable and mismatched, the floor worn and uneven. Several lamps were bereft of bulbs. The shelves sported gaps that allowed what books there were to tumble over one another in a free-fall of neglect.

Garda Murphy, stamping his feet to get warm, looked around in awe.

"I thought this place had closed."

From habit, I shushed him. Such talk was not encouraged in the Blessed Oliver Plunkett branch of the municipal libraries.

"Should be. It's a dump." Martina handed him a mug of tea and sniffed. "One of these days the Health Board will close it, if the place doesn't fall down first. Them books," she pointed, "are riddled with disease."

She glared at the policeman. Drawing on white cotton gloves she started to shelve volumes from the trolley with malevolence.

Paul hovered, fingers worrying a spot on his neck.

"What do youse think then?'

Today he spoke pure Dublin. His accent was unpredictable, ranging from Cockney through New York Jewish to African-American, depending on which TV programme was uppermost in his psyche.

"Junkies, was it? From the Valley?"

Garda Murphy shook his head.

"Don't know, son. Time will tell."

The Blessed Oliver Plunkett, administered by Proinsias Ó hUiginn, librarian, was dying on its feet. Erected at the turn of the century on the main street of what was then a thriving village ten miles from the capital, it had been swallowed up in the forward march of urbanisation. One of the few original buildings still standing, it was surrounded by massive housing developments known locally as the Valley. At the foot of the mountains, box-like semis huddled around high-rise blocks that looked as if they were giving heaven the finger. Built as starter homes and apartments for young city commuters, they had fallen into disrepair as families traded up and out as fast as they could. Teenage gangs roamed the

Valley at night, drinking cider from plastic bottles. The fighting, which made headline news only when weapons were involved, effectively imposed an after-dark curfew on women and on old people who had been rehoused here from city centre flats earmarked for demolition.

Three years earlier the Council had secured money from Europe to build a new library, a superstructure housing community information services and the latest technology. It was staffed by bright young things on first-name terms with their public. The chief librarian, William R. Pender, wore aftershave. He was energetic and ambitious. The only person in the municipal system to have achieved this rank below the age of forty, he was known as Billy the Kid. He was a thorn in the side of Proinsias Ó hUiginn whose personal crusade it was to keep the Blessed Oliver Plunkett – his fiefdom – staggering on for as long as possible, hopefully until his own retirement in eighteen months' time. Ó hUiginn had enough clout with the Council to have got his way so far, but the Blessed Oliver had been starved of cash and resources.

For me it was an ideal route back into the library world. The pace was slow, the work undemanding, the readers mostly elderly people looking to put a structure on their day by having somewhere to go. My contract stipulated that I could be sent to do relief work if another branch was understaffed, and on the two occasions this had happened I had been glad to get back to the jaded gentility of the Blessed Oliver Plunkett.

Our boss, Mr Ó hUiginn, had little to do with his staff, preferring to deal with us through his deputy, Miss Tuohy. He spent most of the day holed up in his office, the door shut.

Miss Tuohy was efficient and acerbic. She was also kind. She lived alone with her dogs in the seaside town where I had grown up and to which I had returned after my thirteen years in the Des. Res. Having nursed her mother through terminal illness, she had found herself, aged fifty, with a large house, a magnificent garden and an unusual dedication to her work. She played bridge, was active in the local historical society and idolised her dogs.

Martina, now, was something else. So young, so grim, she had a natural rudeness that was breathtaking. However black my mood, it always lifted on seeing Martina in action. Her dream was to be a hairstylist – she saw herself as *coiffeuse* to the rich and famous – instead of which her Da, who had been with the Council all his working life, had put in a word on her behalf and she found herself here, in the pits, biding her time.

Young Paul was stranded on the brink of adulthood, his hormones in a state of turmoil. Tall and gangly, he picked at his spots and spent long periods closeted in the lavatory. Miss Tuohy had forbidden him to touch anything in the kitchen other than his tea mug and had warned me never to send him out for food.

The Blessed Oliver was not a chatty place: the staff rubbed along without needing to socialise after work like the crowd in Billy the Kid's. The elderly readers could be cranky, but Martina or Miss Tuohy soon sorted them out. And so far the library had been spared the vandalism which would probably be its death warrant.

It had the advantage for me of being within walking distance of home. I could leave my cottage, the sea sparkling at the end of the road, and within thirty minutes find myself in this grey hinterland. It made me feel quite smug: I was managing, I was doing okay by Charlie, which was all that mattered.

Miss Tuohy saw Garda Murphy off. Yes, the man's name was Tom. No, she knew nothing about him other than that he had been in the library on occasion. No, she had no reader's card that might give his address – it was a fair bet that he was homeless. And no, absolutely not, under no circumstances did she want that deranged dog warden involved. She would keep the animal until Tom was well enough to care for him.

She then called the hospital from Mr Ó hUiginn's office. The doctor who'd admitted Tom told her he had concussion and mild hypothermia but should be out and about in a few days. He too was anxious for a name and address for hospital records. Miss Tuohy left her work number and suggested he get administration to ring around the hostels.

She took a sheet of headed paper from the desk.

Dear Mr Tom, she wrote,
I have taken the liberty of minding your dog while you are indisposed. He will have the run of an enclosed garden and the company of other dogs. You can contact me here when you are well enough to take him back.
The library staff wish you a speedy recovery.
Yours sincerely,
Agnes L. Tuohy.

She brought the letter to the counter. I read it while Martina looked over my shoulder.

"Agnes! What a lovely name."

Miss Tuohy turned pink.

"See that it goes out with the morning post. We don't want the unfortunate man fretting."

The clock struck ten. At the door, on cue, stood our Mystery Reader. Mr Carolan was beautifully turned out, down to his polished shoes and pigskin attaché case. Nodding a greeting, he made his way to the table farthest from the counter and laid out his papers with precision. I had suggested that he move close to a heater, but he left me in no doubt that he valued privacy over comfort.

Mr Carolan was a lot younger than most of our readers.

Miss Tuohy reckoned he had lost his job and needed the dignity or discipline of putting in hours away from home. She left word that the appointments sections of the national dailies were to be left by his desk. He had never been seen to read them. He was quiet and courteous and made a point of reshelving the material he consulted.

The regulars started to filter in, seating themselves around heaters. Some came to read the newspaper, some for warmth and company. Once in a while researchers appeared but these never stayed, opting instead for the multitudinous sources available to them at Billy the Kid's.

"Steps!" The thin squeak was followed by a fierce rattling as Mrs Clark, at ninety-odd our eldest regular, banged her walking stick on the iron railings outside. It was our cue for one of the staff to help her up the steps and into the building.

Martina jerked her head at Paul.

"Boy. You're wanted."

With a sigh, Paul headed out the door. Mrs Clark could be contrary. She was not beyond thumping a person with her stick if she felt it would get results. Her spine curved so that her neck and shoulders craned outwards, parallel to the ground. In addition, she was tiny. It was no easy matter for a person of Paul's stature to move her with grace.

Her passion was local history. She had perfect recall and could spend hours poring over photographs of people and places she had known. She had a special chair which was padded out with cushions to anchor her so that she could read. She had to be lifted into it, but could sometimes get down herself.

As Paul and a grumbling Martina settled Mrs Clark on to her throne, I removed a drawer from the card catalogue and continued to check entries against stock. It was a largely pointless exercise given the rundown of acquisitions, but was considered good library housekeeping. It was oddly soothing in its monotony. On a really good day you might turn up a volume listed as missing which had simply been misshelved.

"*Dia daoibh!*"

The Irish greeting, delivered to the room at large, announced the arrival of Proinsias Ó hUiginn, librarian.

Martina's lip curled. She considered the Irish language to be the province of bogmen and culchies.

"*Bongjewer.*"

Mr Ó hUiginn turned to her, the smile not reaching his eyes.

"*Agus conas tá tú inniu, a leanbh?* In good form, are we?"

He strode to his office to be briefed by Miss Tuohy on the morning's events.

Martina scowled at his back.

"Silly sod," she said.

To me, Proinsias Ó hUiginn epitomised the legacy of de Valera and John Charles McQuaid. His moral home was the Catholic Ireland of the fifties with its certainties, its absolute values, its code of good and evil. He had witnessed the demise of Church authority in every area of Irish life. He did not take this lying down.

He and his wife, Nóra Bean Uí hUiginn, raised five children and buried another two. Irish was spoken in the home. Family rosary was said on the evenings they were all together. A regular Mass-goer, Ó hUiginn supported his local church but found at its heart a vacuum in this new, liberal age. Even the priests were wishy-washy, their authority undermined by the sexual and financial scandals in which so many clergy had lately been implicated.

This lack of leadership caused Ó hUiginn and a number of like-minded individuals to band together. They set up a study group where over the years the agenda had become more militant. They saw themselves as a think-tank for a Catholic Church that had lost its way. It was their aim to educate and inform the Catholic flock to ensure that any tweaking of the 1937 Constitution would not lead to a further erosion of moral law.

They were professional men and women – though mostly men – and had access to the law, to the medical profession and, significantly, to politicians. Well briefed and adept at anticipating future referenda, they fought hard. Where necessary, they fought dirty.

Much of this I had gleaned from newspaper articles about the various factions involved in recent referenda on abortion and divorce. Such issues were not discussed at work. Mr Ó hUiginn, in turn, did not force his politics on his staff. And he was respected in the community for making a difference. He was a member of a private task force which worked at night with the homeless on Dublin's streets. Nóra Bean Uí hUiginn had fostered a number of teenagers for the Health Board and had put manners on them in short order.

Miss Tuohy paused at the counter on her way out. Tuesday was her half-day and she was off to collect Tom's dog from the vet's.

I nodded towards the office.

"How did he take it?"

Miss Tuohy was thoughtful.

"I think he's relieved there's one less indigent hanging around. It's odd, you know," she went on, "in spite of the mercy missions, I don't think he cares very much for Tom."

"Ma says it's shigh'."

Miss Tuohy sighed and looked into the belligerent twelve-year-old face of Bobby Phelan from the Valley. His widowed mother had raised six children and seen three of them turn to heroin. The eldest girl had full-blown AIDS and was not expected to live long. Mrs Phelan found herself rearing her daughter's children while still trying to cope with her own, of whom Bobby was the youngest.

"Shite, Robert. Shite. You must try to enunciate."

Miss Tuohy led him to the most heavily used section in the library – Romantic Fiction. She had set up a separate classification to facilitate the women who devoured these books. It was the only area of Blessed Oliver stock where acquisitions were still actively made.

Bobby's stage whisper whistled round the reading room.

"She said for you to give me that Lav-in-ya whatsit."

"Lavinia Mosse? I think she's read them all. Tell her there's a new one due soon."

"Doesn't matter. They send her to sleep inanyway."

Miss Tuohy had a sixth sense when it came to romantic fiction. The women from the Valley, many of them stuck at home with small children or aging relatives, looked to her to feed their dreams and indulge their fantasies of colourful, exciting worlds where good and beauty always carried the day. The women consulted her and her alone for advice on new titles and writers.

"We offer a service," she would say, "and that means giving people what they want. So long as it's legal."

By five o'clock it was snowing. The gloom outside had not lifted all day, but by mid-afternoon it had taken on a yellowish hue. The temperature rose, the streets held their breath, then the first fat flakes fell.

Miss Tuohy called and told me to close up early. Our elderly readers should get home before a freeze set in.

Martina was out the door before I had finished speaking. Paul offered to stay but I sent him off. The Library Committee in its wisdom had ordained that a postgraduate qualification in Library Studies was a prerequisite for opening or closing the building: a Professional on the Premises at All Times. Mr Ó hUiginn had already left.

Ellie

I walked slowly down the street, savouring the beauty of a world gone silent. There was something about snow that conjured up childhood. It was more than memory. It was the joy and expectation that children feel in the face of something beautiful and unforeseen. The grey bulk of the Valley was shrouded in swirling white, the dark shape of the mountains looming behind. Like a glass ball that a child might shake sending a flurry of white up through liquid to descend and settle, covering everything like a benediction.

The wind picked up, my face went numb.

I hurried on home.

CHAPTER TWO

THE COTTAGE WAS dark. Muddy footprints leading from the kitchen to the back hallway indicated that Mr Flynn, true to his word, had made his initial assessment of the boiler. Mr Flynn had his way of doing things. He sucked on his pipe and declined to be rushed. It could take any number of assessments before the solution to a problem could begin to be envisaged. I had left a key with my neighbour before calling him from work.

"The thing of it is," he had opined on the phone, "to be calm. Worry never got a person anywhere. It's probably just a gasket."

A gasket it may well have been. It was hard to say, given that the boiler had been reduced to its component parts, none of which was now functioning. I shut the door on the hallway.

"Worry never got a person anywhere," I reminded myself through clenched lips.

A note on the fridge announced that Charlie was going to his Gran's from school and would be home by seven. It was my one house rule: I needed to know where he was at all times. He understood that things were different now that I was working and on my own.

I fed Beethoven into the CD player and wandered into the sitting room, belting out the "Ode to Joy". I sat on the hearth and looked around the small room. Like the rest of the house it was furnished with pieces from my mother's place. The battered leather armchairs were worn down the centre where I used to slide off them as a child. In spite of Matt's offer I wanted nothing from the marital home. Apart from the antique iron, which had symbolic value, I took away only what I had brought in.

Almost seven months had passed since Matt left. Seven months since he announced that Bethany was pregnant. Seven long months during which I had been forced to look to myself for resources I did not know I had.

And somehow, step by step, I had managed to make a life for myself and our son. I was now the sole, proud owner of a century-old cottage with enough character to make an estate agent weep. I had a job. I had friends. But there were days when I had to force myself out of bed, when the effort of going on seemed overwhelming. Again and again I asked myself why Matt had done it, why he had thrown it all away. We were happy enough, we suited one another, he loved Charlie.

In my hurt and humiliation I sensed he sometimes asked himself the same questions. And the sheer betrayal of his impregnating a younger woman, having convinced me that we were lucky in the child we had, left me breathless.

Bethany was a very determined individual, used to getting her own way. When she set her mind to having a child it was only a matter of choosing the father. Clearly, she was interested neither in single parenthood nor in men her own age. She wanted comfort and stability. Unluckily for all of us, she settled on my husband.

Matt was a grown man. He chose to screw her and if he was duped he had only himself to blame. But it was hard to see your partner abandon a marriage for a situation that seemed to leave him bewildered. I wasn't generous enough to feel sorry for him, but I did feel tremendous anger. And I dreaded the baby's birth. It would be the irrevocable end to this hiatus in which we were living where nothing seemed quite real or decided.

Our Des. Res. had appreciated enormously in value. Its sale had allowed me to buy the cottage outright. Matt muttered about the advantage of having a mortgage for tax purposes, but I was adamant. The sense of security I had taken for granted as his wife had turned to dust on that evening in May. Logic now came a poor second to the need to be safe and in control. No matter what my financial circumstances, no bank or building society could claim an interest in my home, and that was how I liked it.

In fact, I wasn't doing badly. Matt took care of Charlie's school fees and was good about child support. The library paid quite well, and quitting smoking had made a big difference to my finances. Unfortunately, over the past months most of this had gone to Mr Flynn. I had to be careful, and luxuries like holidays were a thing of the past, but we got by.

At one level, I was used to Matt's absence. His work as a software installation consultant had involved a lot of travelling. He could be gone for up to a week at a time. I had liked the space and delighted in Charlie's company. When the split came I convinced myself that the disruption to Charlie had been minimal. I read up on children of divorce and watched for the signs – denial, grief, anger, the whole bereavement package. But Charlie, always a self-contained child, resisted all my efforts to talk about his feelings. I could only hope he would open up to me when he was ready.

With Matt away so much we had decided that I should stay at home. My job as director of information resources in a small academic library was interesting but not something I felt passionately about. Despite the grand title it boiled down to doing searches of journal literature for researchers in the field of technology. Matt earned a good salary and made it clear that he didn't want more children, so it made sense to spend as much time as possible with the one I had. I never regretted the years at home but the idea of returning to work had been daunting, which was why the somnolence of the Blessed Oliver suited me so well. And I loved the independence of earning my own money.

I gave thanks to Miss Tuohy. This extra hour at home was like a gift. Ignoring the boiler, I opened the back door to leave out food for the stray cat which had taken to calling, and a blast of freezing air stung my face. The garden was still and strange under its blanket of snow. The old fruit trees looked as if they had been swathed in cotton wool.

I warmed myself at the Aga before clearing the breakfast things and setting the table. Dinner was just a matter of reheating yesterday's casserole and throwing a few potatoes into the oven to bake. The kitchen was our haven. The Victorian stone tiles were chipped and the presses sagged, but there was something welcoming in its shabbiness. The Aga had come with the house. It was old and eccentric but ensured that one room, at least, was always warm.

I lowered the wooden airer and folded the towels. Then I slung up clothes from the washing machine. They would be rock-hard and dry by morning.

On impulse, I opened a bottle of cheap red wine and left it by the Aga to warm. It might just have breathed its way to drinkability by the time I got back from my mother's. The evening stretched ahead like a treat I had earned.

"Eleanor, is that you?"

I picked my way through the darkness of my mother's glacial hall to the sitting room where my aunts, Dorothy and Lillian, were sipping sherry by a mean-looking turf fire.

"For heaven's sake. It's freezing in here."

I raked the fire and threw on a couple of logs. Lillian eyed me prissily.

"We have to economise, dear. May said so."

"It'll be a false economy if you get pneumonia."

Lillian, smirking, pecked my cheek. Dorothy continued to crochet as she raised her face for a kiss.

"How was work, dear?"

"Oh, you know, the usual." I stopped, gobsmacked. "What am I saying? Miss Tuohy found a man beaten up on the library steps."

Dorothy shook her head, tut-tutting. Lillian was still smiling. She would catch up in a moment.

"Poor Agnes. Not a nice thing to happen."

I looked at Dorothy, surprised.

"I didn't realise you knew her that well."

"Everyone in town knew the Tuohys. The dreadful mother with her notions. Agnes didn't have much of a life. Still," she shrugged, "at least she has a good job."

"Any word from May?"

Dorothy shrugged again. "She's due home tomorrow. Why would she call?"

Because, I thought, it's not like my mother to be out of touch for five days. Come to that, it's not like her to have gone off to stay with an Old Friend. But I knew better than to argue.

I went upstairs to look for Charlie. He would be in George's room. My only brother had been gone for years. The electric train set given to him by my father was now laid out for my son. It provided an illusion of continuity.

Our family home, Cedar Hall, was shambolic. Dark passageways at drunken angles led to largely unused rooms. It was bitterly cold and afflicted with rising damp, and its upkeep was becoming a serious problem. As structural problems arose my mother simply turned the key on yet another room.

She could probably have been persuaded to move were it not for the gardens. The grounds extended over almost four acres and swept in terraces right down to the shore. At night the place was a magnet for local kids. The cemetery and the public park closed early in winter. Apart from the beach and sports grounds, there were few open spaces available to them. No harm had been done as long as they were quiet and stayed well away from the house. Lately, though, they were getting bolder. The door of the tiny gate-lodge had recently been forced, a downstairs window broken.

My mother and Dorothy were keen gardeners and the grounds had something of beauty for every season. More than one developer, his mind's eye on townhouses and penthouse apartments with sea views, had sipped May's sherry and tried to relieve her of the burden of it all. She would listen, her expression unusually vague, and thank him for his concern. Then she would note the revised value of the land in a ledger kept for the purpose in her roll-top writing desk and show him out.

She acted as if it were a game, but I was worried. It mattered to me that she and her sisters should live out their days here, in the home they loved. But the house was big and impractical with only Beattie to help for a few hours on weekdays, the sisters no longer young.

On the landing outside George's room there was a framed photograph of the Lord children, dating from the late 1930s. The girls stood to attention around a seated figure in starched uniform. May would have been about ten, Dorothy eight, Lillian six, their sister Fanny just a toddler. Three little boys in sailor suits sat on the floor and an infant slept in Nurse's arms. Within three years, the boys would all be dead: Albert and James of a virulent strain of measles, Edwin of a post-operative infection having had his tonsils removed and baby Harry of what would now be known as Sudden Infant Death Syndrome. Their mother, Edith, was bewildered by her inability to sustain life in her male offspring. Her withdrawal from the girls was already well established by the time her husband upped and caught pneumonia, leaving her a widow in her fortieth year.

Apart from a brief spell in their twenties when they had done clerical work in London, my aunts had been dependent all their lives. First on their father, then on Edith, finally on my parents. An only child himself, my father had insisted that Dorothy and Lillian come to live at Cedar Hall when their mother died. Edith took her time about dying. She lolled against the pillows of her sickbed in a fug of cigarette smoke, and the fire brigade had to be called on a regular basis.

Dorothy was a fine needlewoman and Lillian was just Lillian, a natural phenomenon who could find joy in any situation. May, being older and more practical, had an authority over them that was reinforced by her status as woman of the house. The youngest sister, Fanny, had died tragically. On the rare occasions she was mentioned they would smile: a closed, private memory.

The aunts were as much a part of my life as my mother. I loved them all fiercely even when they drove me to distraction. At times, when I was doing something mindless like weeding the garden, thoughts would pop unbidden and unwanted into my head. What if they became ill? What if one of them were to fall and break a hip? What if – and here I would have to get to my feet, go inside, do whatever it took to put physical distance between my brain and the notion – one of them were to die? My only defence against these questions was to chant a nonsense rhyme from childhood, over and over again until my mind was empty. I didn't want to dwell on Lillian's increasing eccentricity and her habit of constantly repeating herself; or on why, over the past weeks, I had noticed Dorothy sitting alone, staring into space, her face unutterably sad.

My father, Edward, was a solicitor with St John Carey, the firm founded by his grandfather. My memory is of a kind, ironic man surrounded by doting women. I was five when he keeled over into his bread pudding: a massive heart attack. May must have been devastated when she learned that he had been so busy making provision for his clients he had neglected to do so for his family. Or maybe at forty-four he had not got round to considering his mortality. Whatever the reason, money was tight and May had turned her skills to practical use and had started to teach piano, first in pupils' homes, later at the Academy.

The house, at least, was mortgage-free, having been in Edward's family for three generations, and was at the time relatively sound. And there was always the option – as a last resort – of taking in lodgers. Somehow, May managed. And if she fretted, if worry kept her awake at night, we never knew.

She adored my brother George. He was twelve when I was born and left home soon after my father's death, so my memories of him are vague. But I sensed that his going had left a gap in my mother's heart that I could never fill. It must have seemed the bitterest irony that she, as surely as her own mother, had been fated to lose the men in her life.

I had a happy childhood in this house of women survivors. There was music and laughter and a great deal of inquisitive affection. Where children at school would run things by their parents, I had to contend with my mother, the aunts, and their friend and mentor, Dr Saul.

Discussions were heated and tended to digression so that I would find myself, none the wiser, creeping up to bed while the grown-ups continued to argue at full throttle.

I was surrounded by beauty. Every window to the rear of the house looked out to the horizon and the lights that encircled the bay. The old oaks and cedars, the shrubs and flowers, the sloping grass terraces and the beach with its boathouse and tiny wooden jetty – these were heaven for a child. It gave me huge pleasure that my son now had the run of them, even if the vegetable garden was no more than a memory and nature was inexorably reclaiming the rest.

I had done the garden centres in my years with Matt, had planted out shrubs and bulbs and spring flowers, but after Cedar Hall that small patch of earth skimmed over builders' rubble had never seemed quite real. When Charlie was six, Matt took a notion that we needed a dog for protection. The German shepherd ate the plants, dug up the grass, shat over everything and was dispatched to the country. The garden was paved over and became a patio. At weekends we would sit on our hammock and look over the walls at other people's foliage.

I found Charlie on the floor in my brother's room, wrapped in an eiderdown and so immersed in George's old comics he did not hear me come in.

"How's it going, pal?"

He grinned, shrugging off the eiderdown. His teeth started to chatter. "You couldn't turn down the heating?"

I knelt beside him and rubbed his hands between my own.

"Right, that's it. One more minute and you'll be frozen rigid."

"I'd defrost by spring."

I hauled him up.

"No arguments. Home, now."

Lillian was waiting at the foot of the stairs with a balaclava which she insisted Charlie put on.

"There," she pinched his cheeks. "That'll keep your ears snug."

We walked down the centre of the deserted street. The sky was heavy with stars. Charlie hung on to my arm as he tried to slide on the impacted snow. He was small for his age and thin, with ash-blond hair that framed the most luminous grey eyes. He was sensitive about his height and refused to believe that his long legs were already pushing him into an adolescent growth spurt.

"Mum, why doesn't George ever come home?"

"I don't really know. I suppose because he's made his life somewhere else."

"Well why don't we go see him, then?"

It was a fair question, and one to which I had no simple answer. When George first went away, I gave him pride of place in all my artwork. The subject was irrelevant – I could work his stick figure into The Night Sky, My Favourite Animals, A Day in the Life of a Tadpole. I would sift through my drawings at the end of each month and send him the best. When the adults weren't around I would talk for ages to the telephone tone, carrying both sides of the conversation, imagining his delight at hearing from me. When he did actually ring, at Christmas or on my birthday, our conversation was stilted. As time went by we had less familiarity to ease awkward silences. Eventually, I stopped writing and he dropped the birthday calls. He rarely came home, and when he did I felt shy around him. He never stayed more than a couple of days.

"If I had a brother I'd stay in touch. I wouldn't let him become a stranger."

"Maybe you will," I began, but Charlie strode on ahead. I called after him. Ignoring me, he let himself into the cottage with his key. I followed slowly. The impending birth was like an open wound. Charlie resorted to angry silence when the subject came up, but this infant would be his half-brother or -sister and he needed to separate that fact from his resentment against its parentage.

Charlie went straight to the sitting room to practise his cello. He studied at the Academy on Saturday mornings and was showing serious talent. He also did piano, but had to practise on my mother's. His teacher at the Academy was quietly excited.

"He could really make it," he had said more than once. "So long as he doesn't lose interest. Girls and pot and so on," he would add vaguely. "It's in the genes, you know."

I myself was a competent, if uninspired, pianist. It had been an ongoing battle between us when I was growing up: the more May nagged at me, the more I dug my heels in, refusing to practise. I would do so only stealthily, when she was out of the house. But I loved to sing and looked forward to my Thursday evenings with the local choir. We were working towards a benefit concert for the district hospice in early December.

The answering machine on the hall table was winking. There were two messages, one from my pal Liz, the other from Matt, asking me to call him on his mobile. I assumed he didn't want Bethany to know he was on to me any more than was necessary. I took a deep breath and adopted my most neutral tone. I was way past getting the shakes on hearing his voice, but he could still unnerve me.

"Ellie!" Then, softly, "Ellie. It's good to hear you."

"You did ask me to ring."

"Oh yeah." There was a pause. I stood there, the connection between us buzzing. I felt myself get irritated.

"Was there something . . .?"

"No. No. Just wanted to know how you are. And Charlie of course."

"We're fine. Did you want to speak to him?"

"No, I won't disturb him." He became abstracted again, finally adding, "I wanted you to know that I think about you. Both. That I care."

"This isn't helpful, Matt. Save it for your girlfriend."

I hung up, gritting my teeth.

"Grow up," I hissed at the phone and poured myself a glass of wine.

Liz's message was delightfully terse.

"Tomorrow evening. Food. Here. Bring Charlie if you like, he can bugger off upstairs to the computer."

I kicked off my shoes and put my feet on the Aga. I desperately wanted a cigarette. Stay Off the Booze, I'd been warned by reformed smokers. It will be your Downfall.

Well sod that, I protested to my absent counsellors, we all need our little crutch. I considered sneaking a smoke in the garden. Virtuously, I resisted, pouring more wine instead.

I thought back on the day. Mr Flynn philosophising on the phone, the aunts freezing in that huge house, my mother effectively AWOL, poor Tom worked over and left for dead with only a mongrel to care. There was something about Tom, something worn out and sad, as if he were just going through the motions until his time was up. A bit giddy from the wine, I vowed that we would take better care of him in future – keep track of where he was staying, give him something warm at lunchtime, generally look out for him.

Pleased with myself, I committed the staff of the Blessed Oliver Plunkett to Tom's welfare.

CHAPTER THREE

THE SNOW DIDN'T last. By mid-morning it had turned to greasy slush under a low, grey sky. Only the mountains stayed white, as if to distance themselves from the Valley below.

The Blessed Oliver was quiet. Mr Carolan was punctual as ever but the old folk were slow to appear and each new arrival cursed the slippery paths. Mr Ó hUiginn called to say that he wouldn't be in until after lunch, he was working on his presentation for the Library Committee meeting the following week.

Miss Tuohy arrived late. She had slept badly. Her dogs had not taken kindly to their guest and she'd been forced to separate them during the night. The mongrel had peed all over the kitchen – probably nerves, she said. She had tried leaving him outside, but he whined so piteously she became nervous the neighbours might complain.

I clucked in sympathy.

"Could you leave the stock control, Ellie, and work on user statistics? They'll be needed for the librarian's report."

User statistics was library-speak for counting readers' heads at given hours of the day and totting up the weekly lending figures. As an argument for keeping the Blessed Oliver open, it seemed to me they could only work against Mr Ó hUiginn, but he insisted on having them. I could do them at my leisure in the staff kitchen.

"Wipe your feet," bellowed Martina, as she had been doing all morning.

A young woman, no more than eighteen, hovered in the doorway. I looked up. Everyone in the reading room looked up. She was exquisite, with flawless olive skin and dark eyes. Tall and slender, she wore a leather micro-skirt over black leggings that seemed to reach up to her neck. Martina was speechless.

The young woman approached the counter and shook out a mass of auburn hair from under a baseball cap.

"I'm looking for Frank," she said in a soft, lightly accented voice.

"Yo," said Paul, emerging from the Gents'.

Miss Tuohy took charge. "Frank, dear? What makes you think he might be here?"

"He works here," she said simply. "Frank Higgins."

It took a moment for the penny to drop.

"Higgins. Ó hUiginn. Proinsias," I intoned, unable to stop, "Francis."

Miss Tuohy looked at me over her glasses. Martina chewed her gum, riveted.

"Mr Ó hUiginn, would that be who you want?" Miss Tuohy, like the rest of us, was floored. To each of us occurred some variation on the image of elderly men groping nubile innocents.

"He's my . . ." she hesitated, as if searching for the right word, ". . . uncle."

This creature bore no earthly resemblance to any blood relative of our boss that I had seen. The look on Paul's face defied description.

"Well, you can't see him." Martina was snapping out of it. "He's not here."

Miss Tuohy reached for a notepad. "He's due in this afternoon. If you'd care to leave a name I'll tell him to expect you."

"Sylvie Toulon." She wrote it on the page Miss Tuohy held out to her and smiled. "Thank you so much."

"Well," said Martina in the kitchen as she munched her Philadelphia on rye. "I don't believe a word of it."

Miss Tuohy looked up from the soup she was pouring into plastic cups. Bilingual signs on the reading room walls warned of dire consequences should food, drink or tobacco be consumed on the premises. Miss Tuohy's law stipulated that the old folk should be given something warm in winter, as long as Mr Ó hUiginn was not around to see. The powdered soup was paid for out of library fines.

"What you believe is neither here nor there. The matter is no concern of ours."

Martina pulled a face, but she waited for Miss Tuohy to leave before adding, with grudging admiration, "Dirty old man."

I took the user statistics out to the reading room, reasoning that the kitchen table was too small to lay them out properly. In truth I was intrigued, hoping for some action.

I was disappointed. We all were. When Mr Ó hUiginn arrived he made straight for the office. Miss Tuohy, as usual, followed him in. Her expression when she came out gave nothing away.

Paul was on his half-day and I was downstairs in the bookstacks when Sylvie returned. Mr Ó hUiginn left with her immediately, saying he would be back. Martina raked his countenance for some trace of debauchery, but had to concede that he appeared his usual self.

From mid-afternoon when the librarian returned, it was dark and humid. A storm was forecast. Every light in the building was on.

Just after four I headed for the office. As I raised my hand to knock, I heard Mr Ó hUiginn's voice inside. He sounded angry. Then there was the thump of a receiver being put down with some force. I knocked anyway.

"Tar isteach."

Relative to the reading room the office was quite grand. Mr Ó hUiginn sat in a high-backed leather chair. His walnut desk stood on a faded Persian rug that extended for three feet on every side. Across the desk, for the use of visitors, stood a more modest version of his own chair. More than one guest and the plastic stacking seats piled drunkenly in the corner were called into play.

A small fire burned in the Victorian cast-iron grate. The flowered tiles surrounding it were pretty in spite of their cracked glaze. Mahogany shelves lined three walls and held bibliographies and back issues of periodicals like *The Bookseller* and *Books Ireland*. The section nearest the door contained publishers' catalogues and flyers in open box files. Ranged on both sides of the fireplace was the librarian's pride and joy – a collection of old and rare leather-bound books, some of them in Irish. Very occasionally, these were made available to researchers or to collectors like himself. A rosewood cabinet inlaid with shallow drawers of the kind used to store maps housed the old photographs of local interest for which he sometimes bid at auction. Mrs Clark would have given her eye-teeth to view them, but they were held under lock and key and never left the office. Two sash windows gave on to a back alley used locally and illicitly for dumping rubbish.

Chapter Three

The ceiling was high and corniced. From its centre, suspended by a heavy chain, hung a wonderful light fixture of brass and frosted glass. It was probably an original gas fitting.

On the desk, beside the leather blotter and crystal inkwell (Mr Ó hUiginn wrote only with a fountain pen), stood a framed photograph of Nóra and the children. None of them was smiling.

It was an unspoken rule that staff, with the exception of Miss Tuohy, came to the office only when summoned or on urgent library business. It was like being back at school. I half-expected Reverend Mother to materialise.

"Dia dhuit, a Ellie."

"Dia is Muire dhuit," I replied obediently. "I've brought you the statistics. They're up to date to last Friday."

"Maith an cailín."

I was about to leave when I thought: What the hell. I shook off the ghost of Reverend Mother.

"Your niece is charming."

No response. Embarrassed, I started to edge towards the door.

Slowly, he looked up. His eyes, behind the gold-rimmed glasses, were unreadable.

"Yes," he said neutrally, "she is."

He continued to stare at me, then lowered his gaze to the papers on his desk.

I was dismissed.

Miss Tuohy elected to wait for Mrs Kelly, the cleaner. Martina and I left a few minutes before six and went our separate ways.

The first boom of thunder came as I reached the end of my street. By the time I got to the front door I was drenched.

I rang Cedar Hall and was relieved to hear my mother's

voice. Yes, she'd had a nice time. No, there was no need for me to come round – the weekend would be time enough. Charlie was doing homework and wanted her help with a difficult Brahms piece. Would it be easier if he stayed the night since I was going out?

I agreed that it would, and thanked her. She was good about minding Charlie and I tried not to take it for granted. He loved sleeping at Cedar Hall – he got to keep on most of his clothes and snuggle up to a hot-water bottle in George's lumpy old bed.

I would have killed for a bath. I made my way slowly to the back passage and peeked around the door. The repositioning of boiler parts on the floor indicated that Mr Flynn was still in assessment mode.

Maybe Liz would let me use her jacuzzi.

By seven-thirty I was securing the back tyres of my yellow Mini with two lumps of granite I carried in the boot. Ideally, I needed to park on the flat as the handbrake was dodgy. Where Liz lived everything sloped gently or steeply, depending on whether it was garden or street. The views were magnificent. The whole exclusive area was built like an aspiration – the higher you were, the more valuable your home. And Liz's house was very valuable indeed.

She opened the door with a cigarette in one hand, a drink in the other, and gave me a bear-hug without upsetting either.

Liz had recently turned forty. I had known her all my life. Striking rather than beautiful, she had wonderful, expressive eyes. She was Charlie's godmother and spoiled him rotten. Liz worked in her partner Christian's estate agency and sometimes, when the property season was at its height in late spring and early autumn, she would rope in myself and Charlie to help with weekend viewings. Charlie worked "security" and she paid him ridiculously well. He took it very seriously and regarded every house viewer as a potential felon. When he was saving for something special he would call and ask if she needed help. She never let him down.

"You sly thing, you."

"What?"

I followed her to the kitchen.

"What?" I asked again.

She parked her cigarette and leaned on the table, eyeballing me.

"Boots is home. He's been looking for you."

"Boots." Stupidly, it was all I could say.

Robin Schumacher, aka Boots, was my first boyfriend. He it was who rescued me from the horrors of my first teenage disco. He who had brought me on my first proper date and kissed me. He who had groped me – nothing below the waist – in the back seat of the cinema. We had gone out together, on and off, from our mid- to late-teens. He was scruffy, diffident, without grace or physical coordination, and I was mad about him.

It was only when I decided that my virginity was a burden I needed to lose that things went badly wrong. Boots was involved with yet another woman at the time, but I figured the deed was better done with someone I could trust. He came by my bedsit one night, pondering some crisis with his girlfriend. I plied him with Pedrotti and argued him into bed. It was a disaster – for both of us. Mortified, we stopped being friends and eventually he went to live in Australia. I'd heard nothing from him since.

"Boots," said Liz with relish. "I met Mrs S. in town and she asked for your number."

Liz was determined to fix me up with someone, anyone. She wouldn't accept that I was happy as things stood, that I liked my own company. "Depression," she'd say. "You're clearly depressed."

And try as I might, I could not convince her that I really, truly, was not looking for Another Man in My Life.

She poured me a large gin and tonic and shoved two ceramic dishes into the oven.

"*Voilà*. All done."

Liz didn't believe in cooking. She had an Italian woman who came twice a month to bake, stew and roast delicacies for her freezer. Any shortfall came from Marks & Spencer.

"God. It must be twenty years."

"What's half a lifetime between friends? Anyway," she went on, "just so's you know, he's on the prowl."

It was a lovely evening. I felt like a movie star sipping my gin in the jacuzzi while Liz sat on the edge and chain-smoked, yakking away. Dinner was delicious, the wine only distantly related to the plonk at home. And I resisted the urge to smoke. As usual I lost track of time and was shocked to see it was nearly midnight.

She walked me to the car.

"Any word from Dogbreath?"

"Actually, yes. I spoke to him this evening."

This was our no-go area. I knew what she thought of Matt. I knew she was angry that I hadn't crucified him – financially and every other way. We had more or less agreed to disagree.

"He sounded, I don't know, a bit lost."

"Really," her voice dripped sarcasm.

I was about to shut the car door when she said, over her shoulder, "By the way, you're invited on Saturday week. Just a small dinner party. Seven-thirty for eight."

"Can I bring Michael?"

"No, you cannot. He was outrageous last time. The Cooneys still haven't forgiven me. But," she added generously, "I promise not to play Cupid."

With a little wave, she disappeared into the house.

Damn, damn, damn. I banged my head off the steering

wheel. I could cheerfully go the rest of my life without gracing another dinner party, and I knew that Liz would be incapable of keeping her promise. Saturday week loomed like a death sentence.

CHAPTER FOUR

I LOVED THURSDAYS: my half-day from work, followed by choir practice in the Methodist church. I ate early with Charlie, then set off on foot, taking the sea road as far as the post office. Drizzling rain obliterated my view of the bay and gobbled up the boom of a foghorn.

Choir was tremendously important to me. My voice wasn't exceptional and I would not sing solo to save my life, but I loved being part of a group of people, individually unremarkable, who together could produce a sound that could gut you with its beauty.

I first met Michael through choir, when we were both members of the College Singers. He qualified as a solicitor and had worked for a time at St John Carey before specialising in criminal law. Michael hovered at the edge of the Dublin gay scene. His only long-term relationship had broken up when his partner emigrated to Canada two years earlier, and he tended to go in for casual affairs punctuated by long periods of celibacy. Michael was my ideal man. We could hug, kiss, laugh, cry, go to the movies, rescue one another in couple-type situations and never, ever worry about becoming romantically involved.

His elderly parents still lived in the midlands town where he had grown up. Highly protective of them, he fretted about how traumatised they would be if they found out he was gay. Michael knew that his father's sister, Aunt Bea Brophy, delighted in putting the wind up his mother by asking when he was going to settle down. Aunt Bea treated his bachelor status with contemptuous incredulity. She pointed out, frequently, that no girl in her right mind would pass up a professional, unattached male with prospects, not to mention his own penthouse apartment.

In an effort to reassure his mother, Michael sometimes brought me down home when Charlie was staying at Matt's. We would arrive on Saturday evening and stay for Sunday lunch. It was tacitly assumed that I was his girlfriend.

The church smelt like the top of a bus on a wet Monday. The radiators were covered in steaming coats by the time I took my place on the stands. Philip Preston, our new director, tapped his baton for silence. There was some shuffling from the thirty-odd choristers, then total quiet.

"We'll take the "Benedictus" first."

He paused, listening, then slowly raised his baton. The opening notes of the "Benedictus" from Mozart's *Requiem* rang around the church.

This break with tradition made some people nervous. We had always performed Handel's *Messiah* in December. We all knew it backwards, as did most of the paying public who came to hear us. But Philip Preston was made of stern stuff. At the end of his first evening as director he told us we were lazy and complacent. He would work us hard, and if we gave it our all he could mould us into something promising. There was no room in his choir for slackers. He further ruffled egos by threatening to engage professional soloists for our public performance.

The practice was fraught. Over and over again Philip made us repeat the same difficult passages. Some of the older women were close to tears. At one point I caught Michael's eye and he mimed strangulation – first on Philip, then on himself. By nine we were exhausted. The mood was flat as people gathered up their scalding coats and headed for home.

"Lift?" offered Michael.

A small group was gathering in the church porch. Rebellion was in the air.

". . . I mean to say, a requiem at Christmas?"

"Never mind Christmas. A requiem for the hospice? A mite tactless, to say the least . . ."

I took Michael's arm and waved goodbye to the disgruntled choristers.

His MG sports car pulled up at the cottage in under five minutes. The car made me feel middle-aged and ridiculous and I prayed the neighbours wouldn't see me struggling to get out of it, but Michael was a good driver, fast and confident. I myself saw children lurking behind every parked car, small animals at every gate, joyriders at every intersection, and accelerated only with a view to having to make an emergency stop. I was the worst back-seat driver on earth, but with him I felt safe.

I left Michael in the sitting room, where Charlie was playing the prelude to Bach's *Cello Suite No. 1 in G*, and went to the kitchen to make coffee. I sat at the kitchen table, my mind empty, waiting for the kettle to boil. As Charlie's music filtered into my brain, I felt a kind of incredulous pride that that gifted, complex human being should be my child.

When the music ended, I needed a moment to pull myself together before bringing in the coffee.

"Not bad for a beginner," Michael was saying. Charlie took a swipe at him. They started to shadow-box around the sitting room.

"Stop it, you two. Next door will think someone's being murdered."

"Now there's a thought." Michael throttled Charlie who lashed out, aiming for the groin.

Michael howled in mock agony and hopped around the room, hands clasped between his legs.

"I hope you realise you may, at a blow, have annihilated the next generation of Steltons. You cad."

"Bounder."

"Lowlife."

"Girl's blouse."

"Mummy's boy."

The fight went out of Charlie. It was as if someone had thrown a switch. He pecked my cheek.

"Night, Mum. Night, Michael."

At the door he paused. "Dad called. He wants to pick me up straight after school tomorrow. Said to tell you he'd have me back by seven on Sunday."

The door closed.

"Sorry," said Michael. "Spot of both large feet bang in the middle there."

"You were only messing."

"He's a kid, Ellie. I, by virtue of my years, am supposed to be mature – you know, as in thoughtful, attuned, bloody copped bloody on."

We drank in silence for a while.

"How's he doing, anyway?"

"Okay, I think. He doesn't say much."

"In my vast experience of human nature, that may not be so healthy."

"But what can I do, Michael? I can't force him to talk to me."

He put his mug on the floor and kissed my forehead.

"In this instance, you may not be the person he needs to talk to."

I thought about that long after Michael had left.

Friday was busy at work. It was pension day and many of our borrowers called in on their way to or from the post office.

Martina was in an unusually good mood. She had requested a half-day to give her time to get ready for some dress dance she was going to.

"Think half a day will be enough?" quipped Paul.

The look she shot him would have split a stone.

"Some people," she said, "some people are pure fucking ignorant."

Miss Tuohy, groggy from lack of sleep, tut-tutted half-heartedly.

"Language in the library, please."

I spent Friday evening at home, doing the ironing with Radio Four for company. I decided to get to bed early and read – I had a mound of books stacked on the rocking chair to catch up on.

I must have dozed off. At three-thirty by my clock I woke suddenly. The bedside lamp was still on. I sat up, heart pounding, and listened. Besides the normal creaking of the house there was only silence. I turned off the light and closed my eyes, but could not get back to sleep.

I cursed heartily and went to the kitchen to make tea.

The night was still and clear. I pulled on boots and wax jacket and spent an hour wandering the garden, thinking about the things I would plant in spring. I'd talk to Dorothy about cuttings from Cedar Hall.

At five, wishing I could take a bath, I put my feet on the Aga and gave myself a severe talking to.

This restlessness tended to come over me on the nights

Charlie was away. It wasn't that I was nervous, exactly, just very aware of being alone. And you are, I thought, alone. Your marriage went down the toilet and now Charlie has to spread himself between two households. This is a fact, and you need to deal with it. It's not fair to invest all your well-being in him. Those skinny, twelve-year-old shoulders should not have to support your neuroses. Get a grip. Get, as Martina would say, a life.

This should have been my Saturday off but, with Miss Tuohy dead on her feet, I had offered to swap. I hoped she would sleep in, or at least do something that didn't involve dog urine.

The morning passed without incident. Paul offered to clear the backlog of shelving in the bookstacks. It was a messy job, the bound volumes being heavy and dusty. Martina would slit her pretty throat before she would volunteer to do it. Paul was an obliging kid, and easy to be around when Martina wasn't there to give him the evil eye. I reckoned that he fancied her and was terrified of her in roughly equal measure.

Ten minutes before closing time Mr Mulhern, who had read every thriller in the building at least twice, chose to query the Council's policy on sexism.

"Why is it," said he, "that every man Jack of them Mills & Boons is provided for the ladies, and not a decent new detective story in sight?"

I promised to pass his observation to the appropriate authority and sent him off with a biography of modern serial killers. At least I had made someone happy.

On the way home I stopped off for groceries, having decided to use the afternoon to cook for my freezer. I was determined to stay on my feet, knowing that if I took a nap I wouldn't sleep that night.

Martina's spiritual sister was on the checkout: perfect make-up, manicured purple nails, the epitome of disdain.

"Twenty-six forty."

"Thank you."

She held out my change. "Coupons?"

"Excuse me?"

She looked at me as if I were brain-dead, and enunciated slowly, "Are you collecting coupons for our special on a bedside table at nineteen ninety-nine?"

"No, but thank you for asking."

"Next," she snarled.

By six o'clock I had made and stored a couple of short-crust pastry cases, two pizza bases, a lamb casserole and some leek and potato soup. The freezer was full and I wouldn't have to cook for a week. I loved preparing food for special occasions, or when the mood was on me, like now, but I loathed the daily drudgery of it.

I rewarded myself with a Chinese takeaway and switched on the portable TV in the kitchen. I flicked through some game shows of numbing stupidity before chancing on Fred MacMurray and Barbara Stanwyck in *Double Indemnity*. By eleven I was ready for bed, and this time I slept through the night.

"You look peachy, darling. Doesn't she look peachy, Dr Saul?"

"Lillian. Please."

"I'm just saying . . ."

"We heard you," remarked Dorothy.

Sunday lunch at Cedar Hall. The guest was young Dr Saul, no longer so young, but not to be confused with his late father, the Dr Saul of childhood.

Lillian loved company. She especially loved the company of men. She was wearing her best skirt and a gay, multicoloured blouse fastened at the throat with a diamond pin, her one good piece of jewellery. Her eyes were shadowed in blue and her mouth was painted a vivid red.

She was getting on Dorothy's nerves.

"Let the man eat."

"Let the man eat? Let the man eat? Am I somehow preventing the doctor from eating?" She fluttered her eyelashes at young Dr Saul. "Am I?"

He kissed her hand and turned to my mother.

"The lamb is delicious."

"You see! He finds the food delicious. Now how could he do that if he were being prevented from eating?"

May cut in. "Jane and the children are back tonight?"

"That's the plan. She'll be very touched by your kindness in having me."

"It's always a pleasure, as you know. Do help yourself to potatoes."

Lillian held the dish for him. "A little more gravy? I made it myself, with wine."

"Thank you, I will."

Lillian sighed happily.

"Darling Eleanor looks positively peachy. Don't you think so, Dr Saul?"

Matt, true to his word, brought Charlie home just before seven. He lingered at the door but I didn't invite him in. Charlie seemed tired and disinclined to chat, saying something about unfinished homework. He trailed into the kitchen, schoolbag dragging on the floor. I shut the door to conserve some heat and went to my bedroom where I screamed long, hard and silently at the wall.

I wished to God I knew what was going on in his head.

CHAPTER FIVE

"MISS TUOHY," MARTINA'S tone was reverential, "you'd better come out here."

Miss Tuohy, halfway into the office, walked back to the counter without raising her eyes from the early evening paper. She was looking for an item on the postal go-slow that had left us without a morning delivery.

"Yes, Martina, what is it?"

Martina jerked her thumb. "Him."

And there, blushing and awkward, stood Tom. He was dressed in an odd combination of old-fashioned garments, all of them warm, all of them clean. They looked like a throwback to the forties. Miss Tuohy smiled with pleasure and I realised that was exactly what they were – they had probably belonged to her father. Tom doffed his cap and we stared at the long scar where his head had been shaved for stitches. His remaining hair had been washed and the facial bruises were all but gone. I noticed he had the most beautiful navy blue eyes.

Miss Tuohy shook his hand warmly.

"Mr Tom. You do look well. The rest has done you good."

He blinked, opened his mouth and shut it again. I couldn't bear to watch his discomfort.

"Paul, Martina. There's shelving to be done."

I started to tidy the reference section. I glanced across just as he was placing a bunch of wild flowers on the counter.

Tom reclaimed his place by the heater. Some of the elders came over to shake his hand and Mr Carolan saluted him from the far end of the room. It was as if he had come home. The staff were acutely conscious of him and at some point every one of us sidled past to see that he was all right. He suffered our attentions with patience and leafed through an illustrated encyclopaedia while he waited for Miss Tuohy to bring him to his dog.

Mr Ó hUiginn came and went. He was to accompany a visiting librarian from the North on a tour of the municipal libraries. Clearly, the Blessed Oliver was not on the itinerary.

He paused briefly on seeing Tom.

"He's back, is he?" He looked neither pleased nor put out, but there was resignation in his tone.

The afternoon passed slowly. I kept thinking about my aunts and the lunch at Cedar Hall. There was something brittle, almost maniacal, about Lillian these days. Perhaps it was overexcitement. A proper Sunday lunch in honour of young Dr Saul would cause great anticipation. Visitors now were rare. So many of the aunts' friends were housebound or in full-time care. They seemed to meet up mostly at funerals.

It must frighten them, this constant reminder of their own mortality. Whatever life had dealt them in the past, the future could not be reassuring. And they were vulnerable in other ways. Dorothy and Lillian, in particular, had barely spent a day apart. In the minds of those who knew them they existed as a single entity – Dorothy and Lillian this, Lillian and Dorothy that, the sisters the other. Did they, in their hearts, rail at the circumstances that had bound them together, eternally childlike? There must have been times when they dreamed of escape, from the despotism of their mother, from gratitude to their married sister, from one another. But escape with life ahead of you was one thing. At this point it would constitute abandonment.

They were fortunate at least in young Dr Saul. He played them well: deferential with Dorothy, mildly flirtatious with Lillian, open and sensible with May. He cared for them as friends of his father, refusing any payment, muttering about a fictitious account that was always in the post. And when May tried to balance things – as she had on Sunday – by inviting him for a meal, he would arrive laden down with sherry or wine. He and his wife, Jane, had them round every Christmas Eve and made the kind of fuss that was still being exulted over the following Easter. I sensed the day was fast approaching when we would have to consult him formally about Lillian's future, though I dreaded what he might say.

"Hello again."

I looked up into the warm brown eyes of Sylvie Toulon. Today she wore baggy dungarees over a man's white shirt, and still looked like a supermodel. She hesitated, then extended her hand.

"Sylvie. How nice to see you. I'm afraid your uncle isn't here."

"Ah." Her disappointment was plain. "I wanted to tell him my news."

I waited. She was obviously dying to tell someone.

"I have got the job I was telling him about. And another studio – well, maybe not a studio, but a room . . ."

She had found work in a nightclub in town, the Blue Bistro. It occurred to me that "blue" in association with a club could spell trouble. I would check it out with Michael, that great expert on the city's nightlife. She chatted on about her kind Irish landlady and the friendly tenants who greeted her on the stairs.

"How long are you planning to stay?"

"Ouf, for a while – you know." Again, she hesitated. "But you are busy. I am disturbing you."

"Not at all," which was true.

"A man came in, on my first night at work. He wants to shoot me – you know, photos."

"Lord."

"I thought maybe I should ask my uncle's advice."

We pondered this development. Any man with an eye in his head and a Polaroid in the cupboard would want to take her picture.

"Perhaps you should wait, talk it over with him first . . ." As if it were any business of mine. Auntie Ellie.

She shook my hand again.

"I will. Please tell him I came. And thank you."

The sweetest smile and she was gone.

Miss Tuohy returned in high good form. The reunion had gone well. She couldn't say who had been happier, Tom or his mongrel, but she was relieved to see the back of the dog. They had finally reached a compromise by which the animal would let her sleep only if he slept with her. Her own dogs were sulking and life on the home front had become quite unpleasant as they took their revenge where and when they could. The carpets would have to be steam-cleaned.

She had provided Tom's dog with a new collar and a name-disc giving the library telephone number, just in case the dog warden tried to pick him up.

I congratulated her on a job well done. She shrugged.

"He's such a gentle man, you know. And those hostels can be quite violent. I don't know what will become of him. I really don't."

Tuesday started like any other day. I arrived as Miss Tuohy was opening up. There was still no sign of a postal delivery. It was bitterly cold and I was turning on heaters when the counter telephone rang. Miss Tuohy got to it first. It was Mrs Phelan, wanting to know whether she should send Bobby down for the new Lavinia Mosse.

"I'm afraid it's not in yet. But I'll pick out something else and leave it at the desk."

She hung up and stared at the phone.

"Where does that woman get her courage?"

The doorbell rang, heralding the arrival of Paul or Martina, or both. Miss Tuohy asked me to fetch the cash box and went to let them in.

I was still thinking about Mrs Phelan as I walked to the office. Her eldest girl was dying; little more than a child herself, she was leaving two babies for her mother to rear. As if Lavinia Mosse could make a difference.

From force of habit, I knocked. "Idiot," I scolded myself and opened the door. The lights were on, Miss Tuohy must have been there ahead of me.

I reached up to the shelf on my left where the cash box was kept overnight. For such a small object it was remarkably heavy. I stepped inside to lift it with both hands and was almost out the door when something made me turn.

The box slipped from my hands.

"Holy Mother of Christ."

Facing me, suspended by blue nylon rope from the heavy chain of the light fixture, was Proinsias Ó hUiginn, librarian.

CHAPTER SIX

REALITY KICKED IN with a vengeance. Garda Murphy arrived in a squad car with Sergeant O'Brien, a big Kerryman with a battered face. They had to wait for the doctor on police call to view the body *in situ* before cutting it down.

Miss Tuohy handled it all with her usual efficiency. She offered to break the news to Nóra, but Garda Murphy assured her that a female garda was already on her way to the Ó hUiginn house.

We sat in the kitchen, unsure what to do next.

Miss Tuohy put in a call to Personnel. There was nothing in the Council handbook to cover Suicide on the Premises. The young woman in Personnel didn't believe her. Miss Tuohy demanded to be put on to the manager, Mr Condor. Even he was sceptical. Then he fretted about the reading room being closed.

"There are very specific guidelines . . ."

"If a body swinging from the ceiling doesn't qualify, I don't know what does." She hung up, drained.

It was a sad, sad business, she remarked. And poor Nóra. She didn't particularly care for the woman, but nobody deserved this. A man like Mr Ó hUiginn, always in control. He was the last person she would have expected to take his own life. But then, you never could tell. You just never knew what was going on in another person's head.

I printed up a notice and taped it to the front door: "CLOSED DUE TO SUDDEN DEATH". A number of our readers were outside, grumbling.

"What's going on?" Mr Mulhern clutched my arm and waved his murderers' biography in my face.

"What sudden death?"

"What about my returns? I'm not paying a fine, you know."

I looked at them, at their faces unaffected by that obscenity in the office.

It was a mark of the late librarian that he had not touched people through his work. His passion and energy he had invested in family and politics. He was powerful and, to my mind, dangerous. His absolute rectitude, his belief that he could impose his views on others less able than himself, people who would have to live out the consequences of his convictions, were chilling. There had been a certain contempt in his dealings with his elderly public. They provided his user statistics. He neither took an interest in nor particularly cared to provide for their needs.

The elders pressed in around me. In the distance I could see Tom approaching with his dog.

"Go on home now. You'll catch cold."

I disengaged my arm and went back inside.

Martina, initially bright-eyed and excited at being party to a scandal, turned grey and silent as the black body bag was carried from the building. Paul's face looked as if it had been subjected to the ministrations of a myopic acupuncturist.

Garda Murphy put his head around the kitchen door. "Almost done."

We must have been a sorry-looking lot. He put a hand on Paul's shoulder. "You . . . Paul, isn't it? Why don't you make a nice pot of tea for the ladies?"

Instantly, Miss Tuohy was on her feet, reaching for the kettle. The young garda beamed. It was clear that he approved of women taking care of little things like this – the nurturing instinct.

We were waiting for Mr Condor from Personnel. He spoke to Miss Tuohy before coming in to offer his commiserations. I had met him only once, at my job interview, and had not found him impressive.

"Ghastly business. Ghastly." There was something salacious in his manner. His red face was shiny with perspiration. The lick of sandy hair plastered across his pate had blown to the side and hung behind his left ear like a question mark. The gut that spilled over his trouser band seemed to move with a life of its own. Without warning, he dropped to one knee.

"Eternal rest grant unto him, O Lord, and let perpetual light shine upon him," he paused to let us catch up. "May he rest in peace."

"Amen."

And that, apparently, was the Council's response to the untimely passing of Proinsias Ó hUiginn.

I went to Cedar Hall. I didn't want to be alone. At some level I felt a need to keep moving, as if by doing so I could banish the gruesome image of the morning.

Beattie was in the kitchen, clearing up after lunch. A smell of baking lingered on the air. She hugged me and sat me at the scarred oak table with tea and rock cakes.

"Well, isn't this a treat? You're a proper stranger these days. I have to get my news through that boy of yours."

I kicked off my shoes and parked my feet on a stool.

"Beattie," I was guilty but desperate, "you wouldn't have a fag on you?"

"Charlie said you'd stopped."

"I have. Really." I watched her hesitate and knew that I was going to play dirty. "But I found a body this morning, at work."

Beattie's eyes widened. Her small mouth puckered in horror as she fished a pack of Rothmans from her apron and handed me one before lighting up herself.

Quid pro quo, I described the whole grisly business even as my head reeled from the nicotine. I savoured every drag, only slightly ashamed of myself.

Beattie had come to my parents in 1959, when she was sixteen. Young Beattie was large and placid and fitted in well. She kept the house relatively clean, if not tidy. The kitchen became a kind of confessional – everyone, from my father down, would tell her their woes over a cup of tea. She had never been known to break a confidence.

The only drawback was that she couldn't cook. May showered her with recipe books and sent her to demonstrations at the local technical college. To no avail. Beattie's response to any cut of meat was to boil it, firing in the accompanying vegetables for the last hour of cooking time. The family existed on boiled sheep for two months until Edward put his foot down. It was agreed that Beattie would prepare the food, but my mother or the aunts would cook it. It was a small price to pay for domestic harmony.

I was seven when she married Ignatius Reardon, our postman. I was inconsolable until she promised to have me as her bridesmaid. Looking back, I think she delayed the wedding as long as she could out of kindness, not wanting to upset a household already reeling from Edward's death and the defection of George. She continued to clean two mornings a week, bringing in time a clutch of shy, pretty daughters for the aunts to fuss over. Dorothy hand-smocked their frocks while Lillian played with them. Iggie sometimes lent a hand in the garden. Now that her girls were grown, with children of their own, she spent a couple of hours on weekdays at Cedar Hall.

"Lord have mercy. Isn't that just shocking."

I sneaked another cigarette while she thought about my boss's sudden demise.

"Are they sure it was suicide?"

I went upstairs and knocked at my mother's door. She had taken to lying down after lunch.

"Eleanor. Come in." She patted the blankets. I sat beside her and kissed her forehead. "You look tired."

Again, I told my story, though with fewer embellishments. May listened quietly.

"His poor wife," was all she said.

Her room closed around me like a mantle. It could have been oppressive, but the darkness and solidity of its furnishings were oddly comforting. As a child I had spent hours in the huge walnut wardrobe, loving the smell of lavender and the silky feel of my mother's evening dresses. I had anchored my skipping rope to the chest of drawers, paraded in front of the cheval glass in high heels and May's extravagant hats. If I was sick, or had a bad dream, my parents would let me snuggle down between them in the big iron bed.

"How was your week, darling?"

"Fine, and yours?"

She smiled. The silence between us was easy.

"You never told me about your trip."

"Didn't I?" She yawned and closed her eyes. "Some other time."

Perhaps she was sleepy. Perhaps she was being evasive. Either way, I had no option but to leave.

Charlie got home just after five, so drenched he left puddles all over the kitchen floor.

"I should have gone to meet you, I didn't realise . . ."

"Don't fuss, Mum. It's fine."

"Don't fuss? Look at the state of you." I reached for a towel from the airer and started to dry his hair.

He snatched the towel from my hand.

"I can do it myself."

"Charlie . . ."

"Don't, Mum. I'm going for a bath." He left the room before I could react.

Seconds later I banged on the bathroom door. I would have marched in had it been open. Charlie was extremely modest: he locked the door to wash his face.

"Charlie! Are you listening?"

There was no reply.

"You and I are going to talk. Do you hear me?"

I could tell from the sucking splash that he had pulled his head under water. I often did it myself. You could hear your heartbeat and the gurgling of the pipes. The rest of the world was silenced.

"Charlie! Get out this minute! You'll catch your death."

I ran to the back hall. The boiler had been reassembled and was humming discreetly in its corner. I could have kissed Mr Flynn. I slapped my wrist, hard, for all the nasty things I had ever thought about him.

I dialled his mobile. Unusually, he answered. A mobile could be a double-edged sword for builders being pursued by demented householders like myself.

"Mr Flynn, you are a wonderful human being." The stem of his pipe tapped against the phone. "This is Ellie Pierce, by the way."

He exhaled slowly. "Well now," there was a slight pause. "Well now, the thing of it is, it doesn't do to get too excited."

I waited, praying there was no more. I should have known better.

"That there is by way of being a temporary job. Should see you through the next couple of weeks while I order a new unit."

"A what unit?" Even to my own ears I sounded shrill.

"There's another one coming out of a job we're on at the moment, but given recent events you'd be safer with the new. That way, you'd have a guarantee."

This isn't happening, I told myself.

"How much?" I whispered.

The phone rang as I hung up. It was Miss Tuohy, calling to say the library would stay shut until after the funeral on Friday.

"There has to be a post-mortem, you see, in cases of sudden death."

"How are you bearing up, Miss Tuohy?"

"I'm grand, dear, thank you for asking. I brought my hounds to the mountains and ran the socks off them this afternoon. It did us all a power of good."

Back in the kitchen I rubbed the charred skins off my peppers with some violence. I flung together the makings of a quiche onto a thawed pastry base and banged it in the oven.

"Right." I squared up to my reflection in the window. "This is a minor setback. It's only money."

But it wasn't only money. It was having been warned by everyone, including Matt, especially Matt, that you get what you pay for. There wasn't a circumstance known to man that justified installing second-hand appliances that happened to come off another job. As for it being only money, it would mean renegotiating my overdraft, and just before Christmas.

I sat at the kitchen table feeling thoroughly sorry for myself. In the space of a day I had found a suicide, smoked two cigarettes and thrown myself under a builder's boots, begging him to walk all over me. The sound of water running out of the bath brought me to my senses.

For months now, I had waited for Charlie to talk to me. He was my child, he was hurting, and he had shut me out. Today of all days, life was just too short.

I always wanted to hug Charlie after a bath. He was sweet and rosy and looked very young in his soft tartan dressing gown. Sometimes he let me, sometimes not. This evening he pushed me away.

For the next hour he talked. Dinner lay forgotten on the table. Sometime during that hour I reached behind the clock for my hidden cigarettes.

"If he'd loved me more, if I'd been better, he would have stayed. It's all my fault."

"You couldn't be more wrong, Charlie. Your Dad loves you to bits – you know he does."

"Not enough. Not enough to live with us."

"But that's not because of you . . ."

"Shorty was telling us his parents can't stand each other, they only stay together because of the kids. He says they're always screaming and fighting. You never used to fight."

"Sometimes people fight without words." Saying this, I realised it was what we had done, Matt and I. We had grown apart quietly, finding a bit less to love and cherish in each other with every day that passed. Civilised, undramatic and deadly. "But that's not the same as what parents feel for a child. That love never changes."

"So why did he leave?"

"Because of me, because he didn't love me in the same way any more." I could see from his face I wasn't getting through to him. I felt my throat constrict as if trying to cut off the words even as I asked: "Would you rather live with Matt? Would that make you happier?"

"I don't know," he said, leaving the room.

CHAPTER SEVEN

I DIDN'T SHUT my eyes all night. The thought of losing Charlie left me numb. I wanted to believe that he was just punishing me, making me pay for his hurt, but what if he meant it? I chanted my nonsense rhymes to banish the image of Charlie ensconced in the love nest. When my mantra failed to work, I turned to prayer. I prayed fierce-ly, bargaining with God as I hadn't done since childhood days when I still believed He would come through for me.

Charlie was pale and quiet at breakfast, but he did hug me before leaving for school. I fisted that crumb of hope all morning.

It was early afternoon when the doorbell rang.

My hair was skewered on top of my head. I was wear-ing my House Attack gear – kneeless jeans, a paint-spat-tered sweatshirt and tennis shoes that pre-dated any notion of designer runners. I was trying to exorcise my demons by doing housework in the only way I knew how – with a vengeance. It was a chore I despised. It seemed so pointless to run yourself ragged getting everything clean just for it to get dirty again. I dealt with it by pretending I worked in a hotel. I was the cleaner of choice for management and guests alike at the Seaview.

"Send for Ellie," they'd cry. "She'll sort it out."

And in I would march with my hoover, polish, bucket and mop and set to with relish. It was pathetic, but somehow the notion that it was proper paid work made it seem less of a waste of time. My friends in the hotel were deeply appreciative of my energy and efficiency, whereas in real life I knew that cleaning was something that got noticed only when it wasn't done.

I was hanging out sheets from Room 205 when I heard the bell. The kitchen airer was laden down with underwear and garments I had virtuously hand-washed in the morning. I opened the door, still half-believing I'd been summoned to reception.

"Mrs Pierce?"

My impression was of a tall man, mid-to-late forties, slightly stooped, with dark hair turning to grey. He stuck a laminated card in my face but I pushed it aside and stared at his companion: young Garda Murphy, large as life.

"Detective Sergeant Nick Pinchon. Garda Murphy you already know, I believe."

I stared at them, my mind a blank.

"I wonder if we could come in for a moment."

I stood aside. Garda Murphy squeezed my arm.

"Afternoon, Mrs Pierce." He seemed excited in some weird, subliminal way.

The older man turned to look at me. I realised he didn't know where to go.

"Please," I said, waving in the direction of the kitchen.

They were inside before I remembered the underwear over the Aga.

"Damn and blast," I moaned. I decided to rise above the situation by ignoring it.

"About yesterday," Detective Sergeant Pinchon began.

Instinctively, I covered my ears. I had spent the morning outrunning that dangling spectre, along with my fears over Charlie. Between them, they accounted for my stint of overtime at the Seaview.

The men exchanged a look. Garda Murphy, as on both previous occasions we had met, cast around for a teapot. I put the kettle on.

"I'm sorry. I'm trying to forget . . ."

"I understand, Mrs Pierce, but we need you to remember," said Pinchon.

I looked at him then. He seemed restless, shifting round on his chair.

"If you could just tell me. In your own words."

I had never understood that phrase. Whose words could I use but my own? He was watching me with some irritation. I gave myself a mental slap; I needed to come down from this cloud I was on.

As clearly as I could, I told him. Miss Tuohy and I in the reading room. Miss Tuohy going to open the front door, asking me to fetch the cash box.

"From the office?"

I nodded. "That's where it's kept overnight."

"And then?"

"That's it. I reached in and picked up the box. I was on my way out when I saw him – it – him."

"The cash box was where, exactly?"

"Fourth shelf up, to the left of the door. It's so close I nearly didn't go in, I nearly missed him . . ."

"Hmm," went Detective Sergeant Nick Pinchon. "Think carefully now. Did you touch anything?"

"No. Well, the cash box, obviously . . ."

"Which you then dropped."

I wondered how he knew. Perhaps keen young Garda Murphy had made a note.

"And the doorknob. That's all."

"The outer doorknob?"

I nodded.

"You're sure?"

"I'm not likely to forget."

They regarded me in silence. Garda Murphy nodded sympathetically; his colleague frowned.

I made tea. Wisely, they refused Beattie's rock cakes. The detective was wriggling. I wondered if he had piles. With some embarrassment he popped a tablet and started to chew. I scrutinised the label: Bisodol Extra.

"Why do you want to know?"

Ignoring me, the detective wriggled off his chair and headed for the garden.

Garda Murphy leaned across the table. "Your friend the librarian?" he whispered, looking from me to the back door. "Either he was a bit of a Houdini or he was helped on his way. He was dead before he was hanged."

Through the window we could see the detective talking on his mobile. He seemed agitated.

"Bit of a cock-up, really," said Garda Murphy.

"Does Miss Tuohy know?"

"We had to get her in this morning, to open up for the scene of crime lads. It's a bit late, though," he added glumly, "what with all the to-ing and fro-ing and nobody thinking to preserve the scene. Still, those boys can work wonders."

Detective Sergeant Pinchon was pacing the garden, his expression thunderous.

"Is he ill?"

Garda Murphy made an agonised, vomiting-type gesture.

"Ulcers," he remarked with respect, as if these were the mark of a true professional. "Give him hell, I believe."

When they left I took my tea outside. I sat on the old rope swing that hung from the apple tree and lit up the cigarette I'd parked behind my ear. I had lost count of how many that made in two days. I was disgusted with myself, but everything was beyond me. I would give up giving up until this was over. That way, I wouldn't become discouraged.

Two days ago my boss had been conducting a tour of the municipal libraries. Then he had killed himself. Now he'd apparently been murdered. It beggared belief.

I needed to talk to someone. I went inside to call Liz.

She was waiting in the agency doorway when I pulled up in the Mini.

"Go, girl," she said, hopping in beside me. "I'd murder a G & T."

"Liz! It's barely three."

"Go on, be a devil. My treat."

We went to a pub on Main Street. Once an unpretentious local, it had been done over in Ye Olde Worlde nonsense at vast expense, but it was comfortable and served food all day. A television flickered in the corner, the volume mercifully low. Two old men sat at the bar, trying not to slide off the highly polished stools. They stared ahead without speaking. Otherwise, the place was deserted.

Liz ordered a large gin. I opted for white wine and the *"Potage du Jour"* – *jewer*, as the barman put it. Today's was veg, he told me, and not a tin or a packet in sight. It came with home-made brown bread. We settled ourselves at a table and he brought our drinks.

I started to talk and found I could not stop. I barely registered the barman when he put my soup on the table.

"And there's nothing else? You're not holding out on me?"

I took a moment to realise she was sending me up. I sank back into the velour banquette.

"What am I going to do?"

"About what? Your boss gets knocked off – this is unfortunate for him, but hardly your doing."

"But I found him."

"True. Not very bright of you." She put an arm around my shoulders. "Ellie, it was just rotten luck. It doesn't make you responsible . . ." She sat up straight. "Now, let's start with Charlie."

CHAPTER EIGHT

THE WHOLE AFFAIR was, as Garda Murphy had pointed out, a bit of a cock-up.

On Thursday morning the library staff assembled at Divisional Garda Headquarters, where Detective Sergeant Pinchon and the team investigating Mr Ó hUiginn's death were based. We were asked to bring in the clothing we had worn on Tuesday. We were fingerprinted and had hair samples taken, with a view to isolating us from any physical evidence found at the scene. Mrs Kelly, our cleaning lady, was interviewed. I couldn't help feeling we were being put through the motions. The crime scene had not been secured for more than a day after the event. Garda Murphy, Sergeant O'Brien, the ambulance men, the doctor, myself and later, when the body was gone, Mr Condor, Miss Tuohy and Martina had all traipsed through the office, shedding hair and fibres to beat the band. There were no signs of a forced entry and it was reasonable to assume that whoever had gone to the trouble of faking a suicide would have taken care to wipe the place clean of prints.

Detective Sergeant Pinchon was not happy.

"It's a horse's arse," he said, his mind apparently running along the metaphor of stables and doors being bolted. He glanced at Miss Tuohy. "Begging your pardon," he added.

He gave each of us a card with his work and mobile numbers, asking us to call if anything relevant came to mind.

"I worked with the man for more than twenty years," said Miss Tuohy. "I don't think I knew him at all."

Martina chewed on a nail.

"Are we in danger? I mean, if there's some loop out there with a grudge against library staff?"

"Let's stick to the facts. All we know at this point is that the librarian didn't die of natural causes. And no, we don't believe you're at risk."

"But you don't know for sure?"

Pinchon popped a pill and passed a hand over his face. He looked as if he hadn't slept for days.

"It is our professional judgement that you are not in any danger. Unless, of course, there's something you're not telling us."

I glared at him. Martina slouched, then brightened.

"What about the wan with the hair?"

"With the pins," Paul added helpfully.

Pinchon looked into their excited faces. "We have a person – a female – with hair and legs?"

"The librarian's niece," supplied Miss Tuohy. "Sylvie, Sylvie something. She came to see him a couple of times. What was her name again, Ellie?"

"Toulon. Sylvie Toulon. But she wasn't, she couldn't have been involved . . ." I realised they were staring at me. "She's only a kid."

"Ah well, there we are then," said Pinchon.

"Sarcastic prick," muttered Martina. Miss Tuohy pretended not to hear.

Pinchon leaned forward, fiddling with his biro. "If you could ascribe a colour to the lady's hair, a description to her person, and a list of the dates and times she called on her uncle, then we might get somewhere. In addition," he stared at Martina, "you would do well to remember that this is serious police business. Don't waste our time and we won't waste yours."

Unusually, Martina let me take her arm as we left the building.

By Thursday evening the scene-of-crime officers had finished in the librarian's office. I helped Miss Tuohy clear up before choir. There was surprisingly little mess: some blue and white crime-scene tape and a fine silvery residue around the areas they had checked for prints. The chair I had last seen lying on its side beneath the body had been removed for further examination. Only the light fixture showed signs of the violence that had taken place. The brass disc that secured its chain to the ceiling rose had given under the strain and hung askew, its wiring exposed.

Miss Tuohy followed my gaze.

"We'll get that fixed," she said. "First thing after the funeral."

"What do you reckon, Miss Tuohy?"

She made to sit in the librarian's chair, recoiled slightly and leaned against the desk instead.

"I don't know, dear. I really don't."

I could see she was tired. The press had been after her. For the first time I grasped the logic of those dogs – no reporter would be stupid enough to lurk around her home. She had warned us all, in the presence of Detective

Sergeant Pinchon, that any statements would be issued by the police or the Council's press office.

"Will they close us down?"

She looked around sadly. "Perhaps."

She stood up, smoothing her skirt.

"Probably."

Friday dawned, the day of the funeral. It was damp and cold, real graveyard weather. A large crowd attended the Requiem Mass. Mr Ó hUiginn's removal the previous evening had been a family affair. The burial would also be private.

I stood with Miss Tuohy towards the back of the packed church. It was one of those modern abominations that had been constructed from the late fifties onwards. Within its vast space the altar was surrounded on three sides by benches for the faithful who were, at this moment, busily sizing one another up. A couple of abstract stained-glass windows drizzled yellow light over featureless representations of the saints. It had more the atmosphere of an airport terminal than of the Divine Presence. By the altar, almost a distraction, stood the coffin of the man we had come to mourn.

Nóra Bean Uí hUiginn, shadowed by her offspring, sailed up the aisle, her head high. Whatever else, she had guts. The dubious circumstances of her husband's death combined with his profile as a public figure had generated heavy press coverage. The tabloids were having a field day. Every head in the building craned for a better look. She settled herself regally in the front pew as if she were at the theatre.

The priest droned on about a long life in the service of others. The minister for justice surreptitiously checked his watch. The Council chairman wore his chain of office and stood directly behind Nóra and the children, Mr Condor at his side. Perhaps it was the priest, perhaps it had to do with the large attendance of public representatives, but as a service it was curiously impersonal. The mood of the congregation was of anticipation rather than loss.

As I stepped into the aisle to let Miss Tuohy past for communion, I glimpsed a mane of auburn curls at the far side of the church. I peered around the communicants, trying unsuccessfully to make out its owner's face. By the time Miss Tuohy returned, the hair had vanished.

Outside, I looked again for Sylvie while Nóra and her children accepted the condolences of notables anxious to leave, but saw no sign of her. The Ó hUiginns climbed into their limo and set off after the hearse.

The show was over.

It was nearly midday when we opened up. Mr Carolan was waiting on the library steps. He reached into his attaché case and produced an envelope which he laid on the counter.

"A mass card, for his lady wife. Would you be kind enough . . .?"

"That's good of you, Mr Carolan."

He waved it off.

"A small gesture in her time of trouble."

Mr Mulhern hovered. He waited until Mr Carolan was seated before approaching the counter and thrusting the serial killers' biography into my hands as if it were contaminated. Ted Bundy leered up at us from the dust jacket.

"Not quite the business," he whispered. "I'll try something different."

A youngish man in biker jacket stood engrossed at Romantic Fiction. Then he turned his attention to Gardening and DIY. Three minutes later he was at Women's Health. He must, I mused, have a lovesick, green-fingered girlfriend with a gynaecological complaint who needed tips on rewiring. I breathed a sigh of relief when, having dawdled at Crime, he moved on to Anthropology. I did notice he was getting ever nearer the office.

Mr Carolan too was charting the stranger's progress. He coughed discreetly and beckoned me over.

"Gentleman of the press, I think you'll find."

I alerted Miss Tuohy who locked the office door ostentatiously and remained glued to the young man's side, offering help and advice on his varied interests. He pleaded for a statement. She escorted him off the premises.

By the time I went to lunch several bunches of flowers had been laid at the office door.

By Friday evening we were drained. There was a sense of anticlimax and of something coming to an end. The staff hung around, waiting for Miss Tuohy to finish locking up. We lingered a moment on the steps. Perhaps we should have gone to the pub, but what was there to say?

Our boss had met with a violent death and it had happened in our place of work; we could think of nothing else, but it was too much to grasp. And we had to deal with the guilt of not having liked him much when he was alive.

I walked home slowly. Usually the prospect of a Saturday off would fill me with glee. All I felt was rage that I had let myself get roped into Liz's dinner party. Still, it would take my mind off Charlie's being at his father's, with all that might entail.

CHAPTER NINE

CHRISTIAN WAS PROMPT as ever. By seven-fifteen when the doorbell rang I was giving myself the once-over. Face it, girl, I thought, you're no beauty and you're not as young as you were, but it could be worse. I gave thanks to Ghost for clothes that hid my stomach, gave me height and could still be thrown in the washing machine when the inevitable wine was spilled on them. I had been fiddling round for more than an hour. I was showered, shampooed, perfumed, made-up. I even had the dangly earrings. And, I vowed, if any drunk lays a finger on me I'll throttle him.

Dinner *chez* Liz was a funny business. She and Christian were wonderful hosts. The food and wines were delicious, and there was a lot of both, but things sometimes got out of hand. The last time but one, I had gone alone and found myself being pawed by a greasy individual called Terry. His wife sat directly across from us. She had a sad, pinched face and hands that were never still. Everyone was a little drunk.

Liz was arguing at the far end of the table, the noise level was high. I felt as if I were in a vortex. All around me people were talking and laughing, while I was getting colder by the second.

The first time Terry put his hand on my thigh I brushed it away. The hand parked itself on my chair back, stroking my shoulder. I shrugged him off and leaned into the table, trying to talk to Phil on my right. Phil was also without a partner and this was presumably what Liz had in mind when she seated us together. He was a nice man, a banker or something, but he was terribly shy. My own store of chit-chat is pretty limited and Phil was hard work. He was probably as miserable as I was, and I sensed it wouldn't be long before he pulled out the photo of the kids. Then I felt Terry's sausage fingers plucking at my bra strap through the fabric of my shirt. I doubt he even realised. His hands just needed to be kneading something. It wasn't going to be me.

I swung around, elbow raised, and clocked him in the eye.

"Jesus!" he roared, skidding backwards on his chair.

Conversation died. I watched dispassionately as he clutched his eye, tears seeping between his fingers.

"You are one crazy bitch," he spat, stumbling towards the door. His rage hung on the air. I looked around the shocked faces and felt totally disengaged. Someone started to laugh – a high-pitched, unhappy sound. It could only be Terry's wife. She got up, filled my glass with wine and raised her own.

"Cheers," she said.

Next time, I had refused to go without Michael.

"All set?"

Christian kissed my cheek and held the door open. It was a feature of these dinners that Liz sent him out on some pretext and he would just happen to be in the area to give me a lift. She would, if necessary, send me home by taxi.

I settled into his large Mercedes and watched him drive. I liked Christian because he made my friend happy, but we didn't have the kind of intimacy that would justify my usual back-seat hysteria. So I looked at him instead. He had a warm face, open and kind. His hair was receding and he was getting heavy. He must have been nearly sixty. I knew that after an unhappy start with his first wife he considered Liz the best thing that had ever happened to him.

They met through work and Liz had scandalised the office by moving in with Christian, her boss, within months of his wife's leaving him for another woman. The wife also left their children, Zoë and Dave, in the throes of adolescence. The kids had loathed Liz from the beginning, pulling every trick in the book to get her away from their father. But she loved Christian, she stuck it out and their hostility foundered. By their mid-teens they had come to accept her and now, in their early twenties, it was unconditional love. Liz was the first to point out that she wasn't especially maternal, that there had been times when she cheerfully wished them under the wheels of a bus, but as adults she could appreciate them. She fretted over their job prospects, their relationships, their health, and genuinely missed them now that they had moved out. She phoned them regularly and gave supper parties for their friends.

Christian seemed to worship Liz more with every year that passed. I found myself wondering if Matt would feel the same about Bethany ten years down the road.

"Who's coming, then?"

"Oh, you know," he hedged. This made me nervous.

"Christian."

"Ellie."

He grinned at me.

"All right. All right. Sandy from the office and her husband, Joe. They're expecting their first baby. Maureen and Will from two doors up. My brother Toby whose wife is in hospital, and some woman called Caroline. Liz knew her in London years ago."

"And that's it?"

"Hmm. Oh, that fellow you used to know, Shoes or Socks or something."

"Boots." I would kill her.

"Boots, that's the one."

The house looked amazing. The drawing room was lit by scores of candles and a huge open fire. We could have been in an observatory, the city lights seemed so far below. The scent of freesias and lilies lay over everything. A white-jacketed barman saw to the drinks. He had a heavy hand. The first hit of gin made my eyes water.

I stood with Joe, the expectant father, while Liz floated around being sociable. She looked stunning in a slinky number that caught and reflected the candlelight.

"Behave yourself, you," was all she said before thrusting me at Joe.

He was easy to talk to – delighted about the baby, mad about his young wife. They were planning a home birth, and while he thought highly of the midwife he admitted to being secretly terrified. Still, it was what Sandy wanted and he had to pretend he wanted it too.

Liz's shriek brought us up short.

"Wow. He's a monster! Get over here, Ellie."

Her diamonds glittered as Sandy's stomach undulated beneath her hand. She pulled me on to the sofa and laid my hand where hers had been. Her eyes were full of wonder. I twisted round, trying to introduce myself, thinking that Sandy mightn't care to be prodded by every passing stranger, but she smiled her consent, placid and proud.

And so it was that I was being kicked by an unborn child when Boots walked into the room. He half-waved, coughed instead. He flicked the blond hair from his eye in the way I remembered and jammed his fingers into his pockets. The barman materialised at his side and got elbowed in the chest as Boots struggled to retrieve his hand. Liz stepped into the confusion and he managed to kiss her without bumping anything else. Then the baby lashed out and I realised Sandy was staring at me.

"Are you feeling all right?"

"Fine. I just need some air."

I went out to the garden.

I cursed myself for not being more mature. I was a grown woman with a child, a child three years younger than I had been when I met Boots. My hands shook as I tried to light a cigarette.

"Let me." He reached around and took the lighter from me as he used to do all those years ago behind the bike sheds. I glanced at him, the flame flickering between us. He was still gorgeous, no doubt about it. Those long, sensitive hands that he never knew what to do with. The touch of salt and pepper at his temples was distinguished, his skin tanned and healthy. He had always been more relaxed out-doors where he was less likely to knock something over.

"So, Eleanor."

"So, Boots." I held out my hand, thinking that I had to stop acting like a parrot.

He threw back his head and laughed.

"Jesus, I haven't heard that in years."

"So what do we call you? Robin?"

"Boots is fine." He looked down at my hand in his. Gently, he turned it and brought it to his lips. Through the patio doors I could see the barman wandering the room with his drink.

He'd had a tough time growing up. His German father moved out when Boots was fifteen and set up house with a girl not two years older. His mother was manic-depressive. When she was high she spent vast sums of money they simply did not have. She ordered bizarre household items from magazine ads and bought clothes by the armful as gifts for her friends. She selected wines by the case until the off-licence cut off her credit. It fell to Boots as the eldest and the only boy to salvage what he could by pleading with traders to take the stuff back. It was hard to be always apologising for the mother he adored.

When she was down she took to her bed. She didn't wash. She didn't sleep or read or listen to the wireless. She just lay there, without hope. He would cook and clean, get his two young sisters out to school, help with their homework and do his own as best he could, all the time running up and down stairs with food that went uneaten.

Sometimes she was admitted to hospital. His sisters were terrified that she, like their father, would abandon them. Boots would bring them to visit, but the wailing of the other women in the grim, Victorian wards, the glassy drug-induced stare of their mother were too much for them. More than once the girls had stayed at Cedar Hall where even Lillian failed to break through their silent fear.

And through it all Boots managed a kind of adolescence. When his mother was well he would be out and about with the rest of us. When she was ill he stayed home. Her illness was not discussed. He wanted no sympathy, but a little part of him was always on guard and out of reach.

"No, *really*," squealed Maureen. "You're not in that place, the Blessed whatsit?" Gold bangles jangled up her arm, diamonds leaped about her ears, her neck was encased in a kind of chain armour that probably cost as much as a small house. Her skin had the leathery look of one who takes six foreign holidays a year and refuses to believe this nonsense about too much sun giving you cancer.

She turned to her husband, Will.

"Isn't that extraordinary?"

Will stared at me from hooded eyes. He didn't respond. There was something unnerving about him.

"Well I think it's extraordinary."

"So you've said."

Maureen glanced at him, took a sip of wine and looked around the table for support.

"It is," agreed Toby, the gentleman, "in so far as one would hardly expect one's stewardship of a library to end in violence."

"And did you *know* him?"

"That's a bloody stupid question. She worked with the man."

"You know what I mean. What was he like?"

I played with the venison, cutting it into tiny pieces in the hope it would magic itself away. In my mind's eye, Bambi frolicked across my plate, looking for his mother.

"I really couldn't say. He was a very private man."

I was seated to the right of Boots, Caroline to his left. I strained to catch their conversation even as Maureen was fishing for gossip. Caroline was one of those smart, confident women who know where they're going and how they plan to get there. She had beautiful hands and she used them, gesticulating and tapping Boots's arm with a manicured fingernail for emphasis. She worked as a talent scout for the London office of a creative management agency. Her work took her to theatres all around Britain. It was her aim to hijack some of the agency's more biddable clients and set up in business for herself.

"After all," the fingers brushed against Boots's sleeve, "I discovered them. They're mine."

"You discovered who?" asked Maureen.

Caroline mentioned people I'd never heard of. But then, by the time I heard of an actor he had usually made the cover of *Time* magazine. Maureen was enthralled. Given half a chance I suspect she would have noted down the names, just in case any of them turned out to be Someone.

"And you, Robin. How do you pay the mortgage or whatever it is in Australia?"

"I run a home," said Boots, "for the elderly."

Liz liked her guests to change places after the main course. The women stayed put while the men moved. It was hard work. Chances were that by then you had established some sort of rapport with the people each side of you, and here you had to start over. I excused myself and went to the bathroom. When I came back Will was in the seat next to mine.

"Interesting, is it, working in a library?"

I looked into his strange eyes and felt suddenly wary.

"I enjoy it." I fiddled with my dessert fork, digging little channels in the linen tablecloth.

"Must have been quite shocking, what happened."

I forced myself to meet his eye.

"Sad. It was very sad."

He considered me for a moment, then turned his attention to Caroline.

Toby spoke about his wife who had undergone surgery three days earlier. He was too delicate to say so, but the implication was that she'd had a hysterectomy. The surgeon had clearly put the wind up Toby by implying she might suffer emotional or psychological problems as a result. She was fifty-two, with a terrific appetite for life, and had never been one to mope. He spoke with affectionate pride.

Christian raised his glass.

"To Marge, and a full and fast recovery."

The evening was winding down. Caroline slipped a business card to Boots, then took it back and wrote on it – presumably the number of where she was staying in Dublin. I had gathered that she was divorced, childless and in an on-off, long-distance relationship. About the personal life of Boots I had learned precisely nothing.

"I can drop you on my way," she was saying to him across the table. "It's no trouble."

I was doing battle with the seatbelt in Toby's Volvo when Boots knocked on the window.

"See you around, Eleanor." Again, the little half-wave.

Toby gunned the engine and shot out the gates. I barely noticed. More than anything, I wanted to be alone in the dark and to howl with grief. For what, I was not sure.

CHAPTER TEN

L ILLIAN'S HAIR WAS an alarming shade of red.

"It said on the bottle: 'For younger, healthy-looking hair'."

"It said on the bottle: 'Not to be used on more than ten per cent grey'," supplied Dorothy.

"What grey? My hair was silver."

"It also said: 'Not to be used while taking certain prescribed medications. Consult your pharmacist.'"

"What prescribed medication?" I asked.

They glared at one another, then looked away.

"Dorothy. Lillian. What prescribed medication?"

Lillian regarded me coolly.

"Some matters are personal and not open to discussion."

Lunch was nearly over. I had brought the chicken, cooked, stuffed and wrapped in tinfoil. May had roasted potatoes with garlic and rosemary, Dorothy had defrosted the peas and Lillian had made a meringue confection of dizzying complexity.

Mention of my meeting with Boots led to a flood of reminiscence. They'd been fond of him as a boy. They were angry that he had, as they saw it, been robbed of his childhood. For his mother they felt only sadness. The German father had died the previous year from cancer.

"Only decent thing he ever did."

"Dorothy!" exclaimed May.

"It's true. Leaving that boy to deal with a sick woman and two little girls. And all because he couldn't keep his Thing to himself."

"Table!" we chorused automatically.

"Is he married?" asked Lillian.

"He didn't say."

We ate for some time in silence. I could almost hear Lillian's brain buzzing. Her eyes bored into the side of my head.

"I don't know," said Dorothy eventually. "From Robin to these young hooligans, and we call it progress."

There had been trouble during the week. Local kids were using the woods at night and a fight had broken out. The police were called. Another gang seemed to be camping out in the gate-lodge. The sergeant who came was phlegmatic. What did my mother expect with the place wide open? The gates were broken. Any Tom, Dick or Harriet could wander in at will. He'd been pleased at his wit, repeating the phrase before admonishing her sternly that security was no longer a luxury. Women living alone in a large house were sitting ducks for the criminal fraternity.

I turned to May. She was only half-listening. All it would take was one lunatic playing with matches for the structural problems of Cedar Hall to become academic.

We sat by the fire drinking tea while May tinkered at the piano – a few bars of Brahms, phrases from Schubert, the opening notes of a Beethoven sonata. She would settle in a moment. She tended to go into a world of her own as if she were talking to herself through music, and then, for no apparent reason, a piece would gather momentum and flow to its conclusion. I loved to listen, to be here by this fire, her music washing over me. It was balm for the soul.

Lillian was nudging my foot. She wiggled her eyes at me, then at the door, and stood up casually.

"I think I'll go for a walk. Are you coming, Eleanor?"

There was a brief skirmish in the corridor as she struggled into coat, scarf and gloves, planted a woolly hat on the blood-red hair and galoshes on her feet. She looked like a line drawing from *Winnie-the-Pooh*.

"I wanted to talk to you," she said as we stepped into the winter sunshine. "In private."

I waited. Lillian had her own pace. We ambled along the pathway, her arm on mine. She paused to adjust her scarf.

"It's about your mother. Frankly, darling, I'm worried."

Lillian had always been fizzy. Lately she was also pugnacious. But she could be shrewd when the mood was on her.

"I think she may be ill."

May, she told me, had been very quiet since her few days away. She refused to be drawn on the details of where she had been or what she'd been doing. With hindsight Lillian realised that she had never actually specified which old friend she was visiting. Then, during the week, Lillian had walked into the hall while May was on the phone.

"She stopped speaking, waited for me to pass. As I closed the sitting room door she said something like, 'I just can't tell them. Not yet. It would only worry them.' And then it came to me," she clicked her fingers. "She was having tests, you see, and they weren't good."

We turned away from the sea, circling the side of the

house and up towards the damaged gate-lodge, where the gradient was less steep. I made to sit on the low granite wall that faced the lodge.

"Don't, dear. Piles."

"Do you think she's unwell?"

Lillian shrugged, elbows by her sides, palms skywards.

"Have you spoken to Dorothy?"

She snorted.

"With the mood she's in? Anyway, darling, it may have escaped your notice, but Dorothy doesn't listen to a single word I say. One of these days she'll stab me with her wretched crochet hook. Mark my words."

The tiny house had certainly been used. The floor was littered with cans, papers, cigarette butts and empty cider flagons. Candles stuck into plastic bottles were dotted around the main room. Plastic sheeting had been laid on the bedroom floor and glass from the shattered window crunched underfoot.

"Eleanor?" shouted Lillian.

"You're safe. There's no one here."

She stepped inside and looked around in dismay.

I sat on the hearth and threw a can at the wall.

"This is hopeless. What's more, it's dangerous."

She squeezed my shoulder.

"Nothing is ever beyond hope."

I thought about that as we made our way back. Right now it seemed to me that quite a few things were beyond hope. Cedar Hall, for one. Missing roof tiles and rising damp were one matter. Vandalism was something else again. What if next time they broke into the house? What if someone were hurt? How could I live with that? I glanced at my aunt's powdered profile and felt love and rage and despair. Why did they have to be so vulnerable?

So much came down to money. I wished my father alive so I could kill him. Up, Edward. Down, Edward. You had your chance and you blew it. Charm and decency and a gift for life are all very well, but look at the mess you left behind.

I wanted to lash out, to kick or scream or inflict physical violence on something. Lillian was shooing away a small dog which had wandered in to use the facilities. It squatted peaceably on the grass.

"Go on, why don't you?" I shouted. "Make yourself at home. Everyone else does."

That was when it hit me. I left Lillian flapping at the unconcerned mongrel and ran in to my mother.

They were silent as I told them about Tom. I was fairly straight with them, saying only that Miss Tuohy thought him a decent man and I respected her judgement. I left out the business of Tom's having been attacked, not wanting to cloud the issue.

"He's gentle, very quiet. We've certainly never seen him drunk. All he has is his dog. Supposing he were to move into the gate-lodge and fix it up a bit. He might even help around the garden."

May was the first to speak.

"I couldn't pay him much."

"That's the point. He gets his meals and a place to live. It's more than he has now."

My heart was pounding. It was crucial they should agree. So long as Tom did not turn out to be a psychopath everyone would win. I could see that Lillian liked the idea. Dorothy was less sure.

"If he's a wanderer he may not want to settle."

"Maybe he wanders because he has nowhere to go."

I left them to think it over. I went to the kitchen to make fresh tea. While the kettle was boiling I closed my eyes to pray: please, please, pleeaasse.

By the time I came back they had made their decision.

"What have we to lose?" said my mother.

It was agreed that she and I would run this past Miss Tuohy who was, after all, the nearest thing Tom had to a guardian. I had her number but had telephoned only rarely on library business. I was so wound up it barely occurred to me that she might not relish being disturbed on a Sunday. In the cycle of awfulness this seemed like a truly inspired proposition.

The first thing that struck me was how young she looked. I'd only ever seen Miss Tuohy with her hair dragged into a bun, her person encased in tweed. Here she stood, hair loosely gathered with a velvet ribbon, smartly clad in linen trousers and a long cotton tunic. She was softer, less angular. She had, in fact, a lovely figure.

The Mini was parked beside her Ford Fiesta, its rear end resting against a boulder in the rockery. No lumps of granite needed here. May had wanted to drive her old Rover, but I put my foot down. It was a car that needed a chauffeur, not to show it off so much as to make it go. I'd walked to my cottage, collected the Mini and picked May up.

Despite the dying light we could see that the garden was gorgeous. It must have taken a huge amount of work, and this was only the front. It had everything: winter-flowering shrubs, a stately monkey-puzzle tree, primula, viburnum, polyanthus and Christmas roses. The house was like something from Shakespeare country, gabled and raftered and very pretty.

Miss Tuohy greeted us with real pleasure. From somewhere deep in the house we could hear barking. She led us to a small sitting-room – chintzy and feminine but not twee. It was warm and welcoming and smelled faintly of dog.

"You'll take a sherry, Mrs St John."

She was already pouring from a crystal decanter into three cut-glass schooners which caught and refracted the firelight. Every inch of wall space was jammed with books. I was touched to see she had a fair collection of romantic fiction.

"So, how can I help?" she asked, drawing a tiny lacquered table to the side of May's armchair and placing the glass on a coaster.

I told her, explaining that we didn't want to put her on the spot, but would value her opinion. As I was talking she drew her feet up and tucked them under her on the couch. Even her body language was different at home. She listened gravely, glancing on occasion at my mother.

"So," she said at last, "you're asking if I think Tom is safe?"

She twisted her glass thoughtfully. I was mesmerised by the flashes of colour. She set it down and folded her hands, then turned to May.

"Over the years I have dealt with a fair number of people – no more than yourself, Mrs St John. And I would have to say that instinct tells me this is a good man. Where he has come from, what he has done – or indeed what has been done to him – I have no idea, and no way of finding out. But he has a quality – integrity, if you like. I feel it in my bones."

Miss Tuohy agreed to broach the subject with Tom when next he came to the Blessed Oliver.

"You'd have to take on the dog as well, of course," she added, a touch anxiously.

May nodded. She seemed suddenly tired. She started to stand up and winced as if in pain.

"Are you all right, Mrs St John? Here, let me help. A person could get lost in that chair."

May was quiet on the way home. I pulled up in front of Cedar Hall and killed the ignition.

"Mum," I said carefully, "is everything okay?"

She looked at me as if I were speaking Swahili.

"I mean, if there was a problem, if you were ill, you would tell me . . .?"

She touched my face.

"You would be the first, my Eleanor. I give you my word."

I sat on, long after she had closed the front door and extinguished the hall light. I felt stupid, as if something were staring me in the face but I was too blind to see. The euphoria of Tom was well and truly ebbing by the time I fired the engine and headed for home.

CHAPTER ELEVEN

I DIDN'T SEE Miss Tuohy on Monday. As luck would have it, she called first thing and told me some bug had felled a number of Billy the Kid's staff and I was needed for relief work.

I set off with sinking heart. So far I had managed to avoid the jewel in the municipal libraries' crown. Now that the Blessed Oliver's days were numbered I felt even more territorial and resented time away.

Billy the Kid's outfit came complete with underground car parking for staff. I nosed the Mini up to the barrier, waiting for the guard to raise it and let me through. He stared at me through the window of his hut, laid down his newspaper and came out, scratching his crotch. He slung an official cap over thinning hair and regarded me with suspicion.

"Yes?"

"Could you let me in, please? I'm doing relief work here today."

"ID?"

"Excuse me?"

"Do you have your identity that was issued by head office?"

I had the vaguest memory of being handed a laminated card with my contract. I hadn't seen it since.

"No. But I'm library staff. You can check."

He pushed back the cap and considered me with a condescending expression.

"Ah well now, they all say that. Anything for free parking."

I kept my tone level. "You only have to lift the phone and check."

He stroked the walkie-talkie hanging from his belt.

"Don't have one."

"Well use your thingummy, then, your . . ."

I pointed at the handset.

He drew himself up, officious again.

"You mean my two-way emergency radio?"

I nodded. He held it lovingly, flicked a speck of dust from the plastic cover. After what seemed like an age he turned and wandered back to his hut. He surveyed me through the glass, shielding his mouth with his hand in case I was lip-reading. He would have gone down a treat at Checkpoint Charlie. I stuck my head out the window.

"The name's Pierce. Ellie Pierce from the Blessed Oliver Plunkett."

He seemed to take no notice. Perhaps he was talking to himself. He went through the motions of speaking, listening, thinking, sizing me up before finally nodding. He came out and lifted the barrier.

"Have to conserve the batteries," he confided as I drove past.

"Eleanor! Good of you to come."

I was greeted by Pam who was, according to the label on her lapel, deputy librarian. She was tall and impeccably groomed, maybe late forties, and wore a cashmere suit in palest blue with a matching silk scarf and a great deal of expensive-looking jewellery. She shook my hand and led me into the staffroom, for all the world as if we were at a cocktail party.

"Ellie," I corrected. "I'm called Ellie."

It was one of those things. Outside of my family the only person who called me Eleanor was Boots. I was planning no long-term, intimate relationship with Billy the Kid's.

"Of course you are," said Pam. She smiled brightly. "Team!" She actually clapped her hands. It was as if a shot had been fired. Everything was arrested in mid-motion. The seven people in the room turned to stare.

"This is Eleanor. She's come to help out in our hour of need."

"Ellie," I repeated doggedly. I waved, feeling foolish.

"Yes, well. Monica here will show you what to do."

I looked around in awe. The staffroom was purpose-built and sported every kitchen appliance known to man. There was a hob, two electric kettles, a proper fridge, microwave, toaster, electric juicer, coffee maker, mineral water dispenser complete with plastic cups, presses for food, others for delft. There were armchairs dotted around the flame-effect gas fire, a wooden table with matching chairs to seat ten, and industrial-strength carpet on the floor. It was, frankly, intimidating. The kind of place where boundaries were strict and you could be lynched for sitting in the wrong chair. There was no sign of an ashtray.

"What's your field?" enquired Monica. Her label categorised her as library assistant. She had shown me where to put my bag (in a locker, with key) and was leading the way into the reading room. It was an enormous circular space surrounded almost entirely by glass. Recessed lighting overhead and individual lamps on the desks struggled to make their impression in all that natural light. Computer terminals hummed menacingly in the background. They were everywhere.

"My field? Ah, you know. General."

She smiled at that.

"We heard you were an information technologist."

This had to be sorted or I might find myself conducting tours of the Information Superhighway before lunch. I wasn't entirely sure what or where the Information Superhighway was. It didn't feature in the Blessed Oliver.

"That was before the invention of the printing press. Let's just say I do my best to match readers with their bibliographic requirements."

"Ah," she nodded. "You know your alphabet."

I liked Monica.

She put me at the enquiries desk with access to an on-line catalogue and promised to stay within striking distance in case I had a problem.

Time passed easily enough. I directed users to back issues of newspapers on microfilm, language tuition on audio cassettes, journals on microfiche – even to the odd book. My chair was high and comfortable. I could swivel through three hundred and sixty degrees without touching the floor. I filled out inter-library loan forms, processed bookstack requests, receipted fines and played with the light pen.

Mid-morning I was assailed by an overwhelming scent of musk. I sneezed. Not once, but three times. My eyes started to stream.

"Can I help you?" I gasped. My vision cleared and focused on the label: William R. Pender, Librarian. He was tall and fit, with a certain boyish charm.

"Oh. Hello." I tried to blow my nose with one hand, leaving the other clean in case he decided to shake it.

He did, a strong, virile grip.

"Eleanor. Welcome aboard. We must get you a label."

I looked at him, horrified. "Ellie," I said, sharpish. "I'm just doing relief for today."

He winked at me, gave me the thumbs-up and sauntered off to his office.

My blood ran cold. Suppose this was a trial run. Suppose that, having seen the writing on the wall, he knew he would have to take someone from the Blessed Oliver and was seeing whether I would fit in. Oh no, I thought. Please, no.

I looked around. This was the future. There was no place in the automated world for geriatric facilities like the Blessed Oliver. Our readers would barely recognise this as a library. Books, bar reference material, did not clutter the shelves but were held in stacks below the reading room. Mr Mulhern would have to select his thriller from a catalogue and have it brought to him. Mrs Clark couldn't terrorise Paul into hauling down entire sections of the local history collection. There would be no shouting and definitely no soup in winter.

And where would they go, our readers? What would become of them? They would retreat to the Valley and live behind locked doors and barred windows, afraid, eventually unable, to go out. The Blessed Oliver was what held the social fabric of their lives in place.

"Mrs Pierce?"

Detective Sergeant Pinchon, smart in a sports jacket. I wiped my eyes and snuffled.

"Are you all right?"

"Fine. Just aftershave."

I slid off my chair and stood at the counter. The picture, I hoped, of efficiency.

"Can I help you at all?"

His visit was noted. Pam fished discreetly over lunch. Such a terrible thing to have happened, and so upsetting for the staff. Was it true there had been an S & M orgy?

Monica, myself and two young library assistants, both called Mary (Mary B. and Mary S. read the labels), sat at the table while Pam reclined in a fireside chair with coffee and *The Irish Times*. Billy the Kid played squash at lunchtime.

I told her that, so far as I knew, there were no indications of anything. The fingerprinting exercise had yielded nothing: all the prints were made by staff or police before the office was sealed.

"The investigating officer came by to tell you that?"

"He came to see Mr Pender. He did mention that the police may want to interview our readers."

"That should be interesting," said Pam. "I gather they're mostly feeble-minded."

"No. Just elderly."

"Either way, I don't imagine they'll be your problem for long."

"Actually," I improvised, "I'll be needed at the Blessed Oliver tomorrow to give Miss Tuohy a hand. Our regulars get upset at any break in their routine."

CHAPTER TWELVE

I WENT FROM Billy the Kid's to Cedar Hall and found Charlie bright-eyed with excitement. School had broken up early and he'd spent the afternoon helping Beattie clear out the gate-lodge. He was dressed in wellingtons and an old pinafore and looked like an apprentice butcher.

"Come on, Mum." He took my hand and pulled me up the drive, anxious to show off his work. He was happy and enthusiastic – almost unrecognisable from the subdued child of the previous week. Neither of us had raised the subject of his going to live with Matt again, but we were being careful with one another and he'd given me a hug and a furtive kiss when Matt left him home after the week-end. Now, seeing him so fired up over all he had done to make the lodge habitable, I was reminded how young he actually was.

The place was transformed. Gone were the plastic sheeting and debris from the floor. Charlie had swept and

Beattie had scrubbed. She had even got Iggie to replace the broken pane and wash the windows. The door would require a locksmith, but Iggie had fixed a temporary lock to keep the kids out. The air smelled of Flash.

"This is amazing. You must have been at it for hours."

"That's not all." Again he took my hand and we went round the back, to the small wooden shed that housed the lavatory. He opened the door with a flourish.

"I did it all myself. Beattie wouldn't even go in."

The wooden seat was missing, but the bowl had been scoured and doused in several litres of Parazone.

"Do you think he'll come, Mum?"

"I hope so."

"Will he bring his dog?"

I looked into his eager face. It had been a running battle between us: I had so wanted to let him have a puppy, but the memory of Matt's German shepherd won through. A dog needed company or at least a lot of space. With me working and Charlie at school, we could offer neither at the cottage.

"Let's call Miss Tuohy."

Tom hadn't been in all day. There had been no word from Personnel or the Library Committee; just an ordinary, uneventful Monday at the Blessed Oliver – apart from a visit from the fidgety detective.

I confessed to having told Pam a fib. "I couldn't bear to go back, Miss Tuohy. And they're not that understaffed."

In the silence we were both thinking that soon I might not have a choice.

"Well," she said eventually, "you weren't far off. The police did speak to a few of our elders this morning, and I know they'd like to talk to Tom."

Next morning I was first in to work. I had the heaters on and the kettle boiling by the time the others appeared. I planted a kiss on top of Martina's head.

"Hey. Mind me hairdo." She checked her reflection in the glass, eyeing me nervously.

"It's good to be back."

"Jesus," she said, pulling on her cotton gloves.

I stayed close to the counter, watching for Tom.

"Steps!"

I was out the door before Mrs Clark could rattle the railings. I took hold of her elbows and hoisted her into the building in record time.

"You're very chipper this morning," she remarked.

"Mrs Clark," I said, as Paul helped me lift her on to her chair, "today is going to be special."

She clucked and put her bony hand on mine. Her smile revealed dentures eerily white and even in the wizened face.

"You're young and in your health, God bless you. Why wouldn't it be?"

Mr Carolan called me over.

"I don't wish to be indelicate, but I was wondering whether you'd had any word on the Council's plans for the library, given, ah, what has happened?"

I shook my head. We looked around at the regulars, each in his allotted place.

"It would be sad to see it go," he remarked. "You do a fine job here."

Detective Sergeant Pinchon arrived just before our mid-morning break, young Garda Murphy trailing after him. He spoke briefly to Miss Tuohy before asking me to follow them in to the office.

He sat on the desk. Garda Murphy pulled out two plastic chairs and parked himself on one. He fished a notebook from his breast pocket. None of us looked at the ceiling.

"I wonder, Mrs Pierce, whether you knew the deceased outside of work."

I shook my head. Pinchon popped a pill and chewed.

"We need to get a sense of the man, how he spent his time, who he associated with – that kind of thing."

I could feel his eyes on me. Garda Murphy seemed to have stopped breathing.

"I can't help you there."

"Hmm."

He pushed himself off the desk and stared out the window. As the view consisted of a blank wall surrounding a dump, I could only assume he was deep in thought.

"What are your politics?"

"Excuse me?"

He turned to face me.

"It's a straightforward question, Mrs Pierce. How would you describe yourself politically?"

I glanced at Garda Murphy who assiduously avoided my eye, studying his biro as if his life depended on it.

"I wouldn't. I'm not. Political, I mean."

"Wouldn't it be fair to say you hold strong views on certain issues?"

I was utterly confused. In the ensuing silence Detective Sergeant Pinchon resumed his contemplation of the back alley. I turned to Garda Murphy.

He was staring at a crucifix on the wall. He looked from it to me and back again.

Some months earlier, Liz had dragged me off to a protest in support of the ordination of women priests. There had been a counter-protest by religious groups – all candles and crosses and plastic Virgins with screwed-on halos containing holy water from Lourdes. A press photographer had been jostled by a couple of youths. In the confusion he had clicked his shutter and snapped Liz and myself clutching one another, our eyes on sticks. On a slow news day the picture had made its way into one of the tabloids.

"What on earth are you implying?"

"I'm implying nothing, Mrs Pierce. I'm asking a question."

"Well, it's a bloody stupid question." Even as my bile rose I struggled to grasp his train of thought. He continued to watch me, his gaze level.

I responded quietly and, I hoped, with dignity.

"I pay my dues to Amnesty. I contribute to the local hospice. I have, on occasion, taken to the streets when the state, in its wisdom, has seen fit to trample the rights of individual citizens, especially women and children. But if you think that Proinsias Ó hUiginn was done in by radical feminists on a religious crusade, I'd imagine you are sadly mistaken. If you think he and I indulged in political foreplay across the barricades you are seriously misguided. He ran the library. I worked for him. That's it. Was there anything else?"

After a moment's silence, he shrugged.

I marched out of the office.

"The man," I informed Miss Tuohy, "is deranged."

Moments later I went in to the staff kitchen to find Martina leaning into the wall, her ear pressed to a glass.

"Miss Tuohy," she mouthed at me, frowning in concentration.

"They're asking about his diary," she whispered. "Here, you take it. I've a fecking crick in me neck. You didn't do too badly," she added, with something like respect.

I took the glass from her. Sounds from the office were distorted but audible. Detective Sergeant Pinchon was speaking.

"And you don't know of any after-hours appointment he might have made, any person he might have chosen to see here?"

There was a pause. I imagined Miss Tuohy shaking her head.

"Surely you should ask his wife?"

"We have, Miss Tuohy, believe me. The persons I have in mind might not have been welcome on the home front."

There was another pause, followed by some shuffling, then Pinchon's voice again.

"Only, if you did happen to recall an individual with red hair it could be useful."

I was filling out order slips – detective novels for Mr Mulhern – when Martina walked into the staff kitchen. Now that the office was available to us, we could none of us bear to work there.

"A fella," she announced, "asking for you outside."

Boots! For all that I'd been telling myself not to expect him to call, I felt a bit hurt when he didn't. It couldn't be long now before he had to go back. I dragged a comb through my hair and went out to the counter. There, leaning against the desk in desultory conversation with Martina, stood my estranged husband.

"Ellie," said Matt, "could you spare half an hour?"

The fizz went out of me. I felt as if I'd been stuck with a pin and reduced to a blob on the floor. Why couldn't I simply say no?

I sought out Miss Tuohy and asked if I could take an early lunch.

"Of course," she said, looking at me curiously.

"Great."

Matt took my arm when we went outside. I shook him off. We walked in silence to the dingy pub at the end of the road.

I had lived with this man for thirteen years. We had a child together. Now, watching as he placed an order at the bar, I felt empty, but anger was never far away. He was working on the barman. After one encounter they would be on first-name terms. It was important to Matt to be known, essential that he be liked. He was incapable of turning off the charm. I wondered idly whether he ever got sick of it.

Coming from a wealthy family that was high in the pecking order of Dublin's social circuit, Matt was drawn to, and slightly intimidated by, the classlessness of life at Cedar Hall. Adept as he was at classifying people, May and the aunts eluded him. Lillian, of course, responded to his charm, but Dorothy and May were wary. They must have seemed like a challenge. I think he came to value their sense of family, so different to his own. Maybe that was what he'd wanted from me: a quiet space where he could be himself, where he wasn't always on show.

We were happy at first. Beneath the charm I saw a decent, vulnerable man. And he was generous to my family. He loved the idea of having a home, messing in the garden, shopping for groceries at weekends.

"You've earthed me," he used say. "You've given me roots."

Only he dug himself up. It was a gradual process. Increasingly, I found his friends a strain, and felt happier staying home with Charlie. Matt became restless. The peaceful life he had wanted became oppressive. He needed to be out there, at the heart of whatever was going on. Bit by bit he reverted to his old ways and in my heart I knew, though I never confronted him or acknowledged it to myself. I was, after all, more than a little to blame. It might have gone on for ever if Bethany had not got pregnant.

"It's Charlie," he said, putting soup and sandwiches on the table. "I don't think he's happy."

I took a deep breath. When all was said and done he was my son's father and they loved one another. I prayed he would not suggest that Charlie might be better off with himself and Bethany. One inkling of that and there'd be bits of him all over the bar.

"He seemed very withdrawn at the weekend. Do you think he should see someone?"

"I think he's trying to work things out for himself."

"What things?" I stared at him. He flushed and went on quickly: "Well, of course I know it's been rough, but he seemed to be handling it well up to now. That's all I meant."

"Maybe it's only now that it's hitting him."

"The baby and that?"

And that indeed. I looked away.

"Only," Matt went on, oblivious, "I've tried to draw him out, do stuff with him, but I think I'm making things worse. I don't know how to handle him."

I nodded. This much, at least, I could relate to.

"So," he said carefully, "do you think he should talk to someone? I'd be happy to pay."

If only it were that simple, I thought: throw money at your problems and watch them disintegrate to order. But I knew Matt was trying, and maybe he had a point.

We agreed to leave Charlie to his own devices until after Christmas. If he still seemed troubled then, we would find a mutually agreed counsellor and try the therapy route.

He walked me back to the Blessed Oliver.

"Awful tragedy for you all," he remarked, nodding towards the building.

I was getting heartily sick of having to listen to people's commiserations. I felt that something insightful was expected of me and I had nothing at all to say.

"Goodbye, then." I turned away as he made to kiss my cheek. "Thanks for lunch."

I went into the library without looking back.

"Oh God," wailed Martina. She held up a stiff brown envelope of the sort used for photographs. It was addressed to Mr Ó hUiginn and marked "Personal and Confidential". The go-slow was over. A full sack of mail stood behind the counter, waiting to be sorted. "What am I meant to do?"

We stared at the envelope. It was similar to any number of others that had come for him at regular intervals. He had insisted on opening his own post. It seemed indecent to be handling it in his place.

"Into the office," said Miss Tuohy briskly. "We'll put his letters aside. The police can take it from there."

I helped Miss Tuohy go through the rest. There were fly-ers, publishers' catalogues, some weekly magazines and a couple of journals, including the quarterly review of the local historical society which I stamped and brought out to Mrs Clark.

When I returned Miss Tuohy was weighing a letter in her hand. It was franked with the Council logo and addressed to the librarian.

"Library Committee," she remarked. Without looking at me she slit open the flap and pulled out two typed sheets. She glanced at them and handed them over.

"It's only the agenda." She was relieved and disap-pointed at once.

"Item 5," I read, "Report on the Blessed Oliver Plunkett branch of the municipal libraries, Proinsias Ó hUiginn, librarian."

He had been in the city morgue at the hour of the scheduled meeting. I wondered had that been noted in the minutes.

Tom appeared as Miss Tuohy was leaving for her halfday. She brought him to the staff kitchen and closed the door firmly. I chewed my nails while Mr Mulhern complained that the last chapter of his book had been removed with a blade.

"But you know how it ends. You've read it twice."

"That's not the point," he shouted. "A person doesn't

make his way through three hundred and forty pages only to be met by vandalism. Sheer unadulterated savagery, that is. And what are you going to do about it?"

I took the book from his hand and dropped it in the waste bin.

"Get you a new one," I offered, "even if I have to buy it myself."

I was entering periodicals on the Kardex when Miss Tuohy emerged. She was smiling. Tom stood awkwardly at her side.

"Mr Tom is happy to accept your proposal. We thought a trial period – say a month – would be helpful. That way no one feels tied to a situation that might not suit."

I could have kissed her. I wanted to shake Tom's hand but he edged away. He would wait for me after work, and I could bring him straight to Cedar Hall.

"You don't think he'd like me to collect him in the car?"

"That won't be necessary," said Miss Tuohy. "He travels light."

The afternoon passed quickly. Garda Murphy dropped in to pick up Mr Ó hUiginn's post. I called May and told her the good news about Tom. She had Iggie standing by to move some basic furniture from the main house to the lodge. It seemed best that on this, his first evening, Tom should not be crowded. May would introduce herself but the aunts would have to wait.

Martina was reading aloud from an article on the new generation of vegetable hair dyes when I felt my pulse quicken. What was it Detective Sergeant Pinchon had said to Miss Tuohy about an individual with red hair?

"Oh my God, Sylvie."

"What do you mean, 'Oh my God, Sylvie?'" said Martina crossly. "That one doesn't have dyed hair. I'd know."

I'd last spoken to her the day before the librarian's

body was found, when she mentioned that some character wanted to photograph her. A woman with long curly hair had been at the funeral, but I couldn't be certain it was Sylvie. And if indeed it was, she would surely have been seated with members of the Ó hUiginn family. I couldn't quite put my finger on it, but something felt wrong. It suddenly seemed important to see for myself that she was all right.

I called Michael on the office phone. He had heard of the Blue Bistro but had never been there.

"You have to come, Michael. I can't go to a night-club on my own."

"What about my hot and heavy date?"

"Bring him too. Please, Michael. It's important."

He was less than thrilled, but he would do it. He would pick me up at eleven.

CHAPTER THIRTEEN

TOM WAITED WITH his dog while I locked up. He carried a small, battered suitcase, presumably loaned by the hostel. The night air was freezing. We set off, Tom lagging a couple of paces behind. I stopped to let him catch up, but after a few steps he fell back again. I felt nervous having got this far and had to stop myself from chattering.

We moved quietly through the streets, the only sound the tapping of the dog's nails on concrete. There were few cars and fewer pedestrians. The sky was black and clear – it was too cold for rain. We went via the cottage to check whether Charlie was home and found the place in darkness. I turned on some lights and collected the car keys. Tom eyed the Mini, a touch unsure, but the dog leaped into the back, tail wagging. Gingerly, Tom lowered the passenger seat and folded himself in. He stared ahead, his case between his knees. With his long hair and bushy beard he looked like a giant from a children's fairy tale.

Charlie was waiting at the gate-lodge. I glared at him but he ignored me, standing back to let Tom pass. A lamp had been lit in the alcove, ceiling bulbs had been replaced and fitted with shades. Curtains had been washed and rehung and a fire burned in the grate. Charlie petted the dog and I stood at the door as Tom moved to the centre of the room. He put his bag down by the armchair and looked around, his movements slow and deliberate. After what seemed like an age he turned to me, gesturing towards the bedroom. I nodded and he went through.

Charlie was hopping with excitement.

"Do you think he likes it, Mum? Do you?"

I shushed him. He tiptoed across the room, clicking his fingers for the dog to follow.

"Charlie," I hissed, "get back here."

With a defiant glance over his shoulder he disappeared after Tom.

I leaned against the doorjamb and lit a cigarette. I'd give them three minutes, then I was going in. Overhead the sky was dotted with stars, the moon almost full. A good omen, I thought.

Something brushed the back of my leg as I ground out my cigarette. I turned, startled, and found myself looking into the mongrel's knowing eyes.

"Where's your master, then?"

Behind the dog stood Tom, still and watchful, Charlie jiggling at his side. We stared at one another in silence until Charlie bounded over.

"It's okay, Mum. He likes it. He's going to stay."

May was as good as her word. She came alone, bringing a wicker basket of hot food wrapped in tinfoil.

"You're welcome, Tom. I hope you'll be comfortable."

He bowed his thanks.

"We'll talk in the morning," she concluded, shepherding Charlie out the door.

We made our way back to the house, Charlie holding May's arm and swinging the basket. At the hall door we turned. The lodge looked snug against the brilliant sky, with smoke rising from the chimney and the windows leaking yellow light. It was a home again.

"Well?" demanded Lillian from the bottom stair. "Well?"

"You'll catch your death out here." I pulled her to her feet and walked her into the sitting room.

"He's nice," supplied Charlie, settling on the arm of her chair, "and he has a dog called Boy."

"Who told you that?" I swung around, a sod of turf forgotten in my hand.

"Tom did. I asked him."

I glanced at May.

"I thought he might be mute. I've never heard him speak."

I had intended to ask if Charlie could spend the night, but he'd beaten me to it. He wanted to miss nothing of the new tenants. I spoke to him severely, warning him that Tom was a private person and not used to company. We had to give him space. He nodded impatiently.

"I know, Mum. I'll just be here if he needs something. Or if he's lonely."

I kissed him goodnight. He was so happy and animated I didn't dare think about what might happen if Tom decided not to stay.

By eleven-fifteen the three of us were squashed into the MG, heading for the city. Michael's friend Anto was very young. Every visible orifice was pierced and adorned with silver jewellery, and the heavy chains at his neck and wrists clanked when he moved. He chatted happily enough, his hand resting on Michael's shoulder, occasionally straying to his hair. His own hair was sleek and blond – like

Charlie's. His eyes were blue and alert, his mouth slightly petulant. Michael drove even faster than usual, his attention veering from the road to Anto while I clenched my fists under the seat and tried to act calm.

A flight of uneven stone steps led down to the basement that housed the Blue Bistro. It was early for clubland and there was no sign of a bouncer outside. Michael pressed the buzzer. He was about to press it again when the door was opened by a heavy-set, bullet-headed individual who sized him up aggressively.

"Yeah?"

In a tone that implied we were doing the club a favour, Michael informed him we would like to enter. Bullet-head, doubtful, leaned out for a better look at Anto. I slipped my arm through Michael's. He made us wait a full minute before stepping aside with a martyred air.

"Righ'."

"Such eloquence," remarked Michael as we made our way into a small, dingy room dotted with tables edging a silver dance floor no more than six foot square. The tables were made from bases of old Singer sewing machines and covered in red and white checked plastic. Each held a candle stuck into a wicker bottle. The look was cheap seventies retro. A young woman in leggings was lighting the candles as we came in. She smiled pleasantly.

"You're early. What can I get you?"

Michael asked for a wine list. I asked for the manager.

"He won't be in till midnight. Is there a problem?"

"We're looking for a friend who works here, a French girl called Sylvie."

She shook her head.

"Sorry. I only started on Saturday. I'm sure Roger will know, though."

People started to drift in from the pubs – mostly men, mostly middle-aged and, at a guess, mostly married. Three women clattered in, in short skirts and tall shoes. From the heavy make-up I reckoned they were older than they looked. They huddled in a corner, giggling and playing with their hair, conscious of being watched.

Anto was getting bored. He wanted to dance. Michael demurred, glancing uneasily at the silver square. Anto sulked and flounced off to the loo and Michael sat back with a sigh. I prayed the manager would come soon.

The Bistro was filling up. Every seat was occupied and people stood three deep at the wine bar. The waitress had given up trying to reach the tables. Music blasted off the walls. It was hard to think, never mind talk. Still no one was dancing. The women in the corner had been joined by three men who laughed and gesticulated, their faces shiny with sweat. Anto, his humour restored, was downing the wine and pounding his leg to the music. From time to time he nibbled Michael's ear, covertly watching a tall, slender African who stood alone in the mass surrounding the bar.

A man in a linen suit materialised at the waitress's side. She spoke to him briefly and pointed in our direction. He served up some wine before elbowing his way through the crowd.

I caught Michael's eye.

"Roger," he mouthed around the side of Anto's head.

"You wanted to see me." I sensed rather than heard the words.

"Are you the manager?" I roared.

He nodded.

"We're looking for a friend, Sylvie Toulon?"

He shrugged. It was hard to know whether he had heard and couldn't help, or had not heard and didn't care.

Michael tapped his arm.

"Is there somewhere we can talk?"

He led us without enthusiasm to a stockroom behind the bar. Anto stayed at the table.

I repeated my question. Roger straightened his cufflinks, resolutely indifferent.

"Lots of girls work here. They come, stay a few nights and disappear. Bloody unreliable."

"This one was French, about eighteen. Very beautiful."

"They're all beautiful," he commented sourly.

Michael spun some saga about a medical emergency. Roger was unmoved. Michael was on the point of making Sylvie a transplant recipient when Roger lost interest.

"Look, it's casual labour. We don't keep records."

"Or pay social insurance?" asked Michael smoothly. "I'm sure if you think hard you'll remember noting down an address or a contact number."

"*If* you will wait," said Roger with exaggerated courtesy, "I'll see what I can do."

Michael went back to Anto and I headed for the Ladies'. The cubicles were cramped and dirty, the waste bin already overflowing with paper towels. I patted my face and neck with cold water. As I came out to the corridor two men were going through a curtained-off door opposite, leading to a stairwell. They turned. One was Roger. The other, though I glimpsed him for only a second before he vanished in the dim light, looked very like Will, Liz's neighbour. Roger stepped back into the corridor, drawing the curtain behind him.

"Sorry," he said, "no joy."

"Come again?"

"As I said, we don't keep records."

"So, you're telling me you take on staff without any way of contacting them? Give me a break."

He shrugged. "Maybe you're mistaken. No one remembers a Sylvie here. You could try the other clubs."

Five minutes later we were out on the street, fuming. Michael had had another go at Roger – to no avail. We had to drag Anto away from the dance floor where the African writhed and pulsed in a world of his own. The night air was a welcome shock. Anto was raring to party.

"Come on," Michael put his arm around my shoulders. "I'll drop you home."

I looked at Anto and shook my head.

"You go on. There's a taxi rank just around the corner."

"Don't be daft – it's late."

"Honestly, Michael, I mean it." And remembering the drive in, I did.

He glanced at Anto who had hunkered down to check his reflection in the wing-view mirror of a nearby car. I could see he was wavering.

"Scout's honour?"

I kissed his cheek. "Call you in the morning."

I set off for the rank. Something was niggling at me. I turned quickly. The street was empty of pedestrians except for Michael and Anto heading the opposite direction. I walked on.

A hundred yards ahead I noticed a man sitting in a parked car. I wrapped my fingers round the hairbrush in my bag, just in case. As I drew level I glared at him and he looked away. I had walked past when recognition dawned. For the second time that night, I'd apparently become invisible. I went back and banged on the passenger window.

"Are you following me?" I demanded of Detective Sergeant Pinchon.

I saw him sigh as he rolled down the window.

"Mrs Pierce," he said without enthusiasm.

"Well. Are you?"

"Is there any reason why I should be?"

With what I hoped was a suitably affronted air, I turned and continued on my way, feeling more than a little uneasy.

CHAPTER FOURTEEN

I SPENT A restless night. Sylvie flitted through my dreams, always moving away, her auburn hair swinging in slow motion as she looked over her shoulder and smiled. I called out, begging her to come back. Then she was gone. In her place a body dangled from a rope. It had no face. I wanted to hide, but there was nowhere to go. The corpse was reeling me in. Somewhere, someone was laughing. Garda Murphy sipped a cup of tea. The body swayed, gathering momentum. In a moment it would touch me and I could never go back. The laughter gave way to barking. I sat up, drenched in sweat. A dog barked furiously in the street.

It was after five. I changed my pyjamas and made tea which I carried back to bed. Irrational it may have been, but I was becoming seriously concerned about Sylvie. Why was Roger being evasive? What could he have to hide?

I thought about Pinchon's parting comment to Miss Tuohy. Could auburn hair be confused with red? The police must have found something, it wasn't the kind of statement to be bandied about as social chit-chat: 'If you did recall someone with red hair it could be useful . . .' Then again, he would surely have made the connection from our description of her. The idea that Sylvie might be in trouble bothered me. She was so young, so artless. But a man was dead and she seemed to have disappeared. That was trouble enough to be going on with.

I was dressed and in the kitchen over at Cedar Hall before anyone was up. Tom's house was in darkness, the curtains shut. I made coffee for myself and tea for Charlie and brought them to his room. He was asleep with one hand tucked under his cheek. I sat on the bed, watching him. When I brushed the hair from his eyes he stirred, grumbling.

He struggled awake, rubbed his eyes and squinted at me.

"Mum." Suddenly alert, he frowned. "What are you doing here? Have they gone?"

I ruffled his hair.

"It's okay. They're here."

School ended early on Wednesdays. Charlie normally stayed for orchestra, but he begged to be let come to Cedar Hall instead. He was tense with longing, alive in a way he hadn't been for months. He swore that he would practise at home for an hour in the evening.

"All right, but I'll hold you to that."

He gave me a bear-hug that nearly knocked me off the bed.

All morning I agonised over Sylvie: she was a grown woman who could look after herself, and it was none of my business. On the other hand she was young and in a foreign country. Someone – either she or Roger – had been lying about the Blue Bistro. It didn't take genius to figure it was more likely Roger.

Michael rang. "Have you told the guards?"

"Not exactly."

"Not exactly what? Ellie, this is a very weird situation. That dickhead was hiding something."

"Michael," I glanced across at Martina who was, as always, riveted. She blew an enormous bubble with her gum and popped it. I turned my back on her, lowering my voice. "Suppose she's involved . . ."

"So? All the more reason for you to talk to the police."

I hung up and retrieved Detective Sergeant Pinchon's card. Nothing sinister, just a couple of numbers for the station and his mobile. I put it down carefully, reached for the handset and dialled. Pinchon was on his way out but would see me at two o'clock at the station, if that was convenient.

The atmosphere in the public office of Divisional Garda Headquarters was laddish, despite the presence of a female garda at reception. Behind her stretched a large, untidy space. A glass press and a tall noticeboard were laden down with keys. A couple of officers huddled against a desk, laughing quietly.

"Mrs Pierce," said the garda, "you're expected. Second from the end on your left."

She buzzed me through a frosted glass door and into the inner sanctum. A long corridor stretched ahead. A couple of doors stood ajar, but mostly the rooms were closed and, from the clicking of keyboards and the whir of faxes, busy.

At the second last door I stopped. The room was empty. I checked for a name but there was nothing. Two desks stood at right angles, the one facing me piled high with papers and folders. There was the usual office paraphernalia with the inevitable computer monitor humming in a corner. I was disappointed. My first time alone inside a detective unit and it was all so ordinary. I sat facing the desk. Perhaps I would hear a confession being beaten out of someone. Several moments passed.

I was becoming impatient. I would wait for one more minute then go back to reception. I wandered around the desk, glancing at various papers. It took a few seconds for the photo to register. It was a ten-by-eight black and white, sheathed in plastic, portraying a dominatrix in full leather regalia leading a naked man on a dog leash. The man was on all fours, his head raised to show the studded leather collar around his neck. The look in those anxious eyes was unbearable. I moved the photo aside. The next one, similarly sheeted, showed the man being whipped on his buttocks, leash trailing on the floor. Saliva drooled from his mouth. The woman brandishing the whip looked bored and disdainful.

I had been staring for some time when I became aware of another presence. Detective Sergeant Pinchon leaned against the wall, watching. I sank into his chair, unable to look away.

"We think that's how it happened," he said eventually.

"But . . ." I wanted to say the man in the pictures was not Mr Ó hUiginn. I gave up.

He pushed himself off the wall and walked to my side.

"We think he was a subscriber. Pics in the post, plain brown wrapper, and then maybe, if you know the right people, you get to act it out."

I stared at him.

"You're saying that these . . . these were being sent to the library? And we thought they were local history."

I started to laugh. It was too absurd. In my mind's eye I saw Mrs Clark being allowed to open the coveted photographs. That sobered me up. My brain clicked into gear.

"You wanted me to see these. Why didn't you just show them to me? Why the charade of leaving me here . . .?"

"I needed to see your reaction. I needed to see if you knew."

He drove me home. I was too whacked to protest. I couldn't face Miss Tuohy and Martina knowing what I now knew.

The post-mortem, he told me, had revealed a second transverse mark beneath the one made by the rope. It was consistent with the shape and size of a heavy choke chain.

"A mark like that can take several hours to show up clearly, which explains why it wasn't picked up at the scene. The autopsy found indications in the deep muscles of the neck and elements of active bleeding under the tissue. It was the chain, and not the ligature, that killed your boss."

He looked across to see how I was taking this. I gazed out the windscreen without a thought in my head.

"He died from vagal inhibition resulting from constriction."

"Thanks a lot," I said.

"I doubt that anyone set out to kill him. Chances are he was playing out his fantasy when something went wrong. The woman, or whoever was with him, panicked. He wasn't a small man – she would have needed help to move him, never mind hoist him to the light fixture. At least one other person was involved, if not more."

We drove in silence after that. It was so sad, so pointless. In a strange way the knowledge of his weakness made my boss more human. Under all that certainty and rectitude he must have been terrified. The stakes for this family man, this pillar of the community, had been so high, his compulsion so base.

I was a million miles away when Pinchon's voice cut in on me. "Is this it?"

I stared at the cottage – my haven in a world that was twisted, sick and evil.

"So you're no longer looking at murder?"

"It's unlikely, though we can't rule it out until we

establish exactly what did happen. And we certainly can't rule out manslaughter. Either way, we need to talk to the people who were with him that night."

"And the stuff you hit me with yesterday, my 'politics' and all that garbage?"

He regarded me calmly.

"No man is an island. Somewhere, somehow, the strands of his life crossed over. Somebody out there knows about the fun and games. We need that information."

We sat on in silence. I glanced across and saw something unguarded in his eyes. He was seeing things invisible to me, but that was his job. I wondered if he was lonely.

"Why did you want to see me?"

Sylvie. The pictures had driven her right out of my head.

"What you were saying about hair," I began. "Where does red hair come into it?"

Too late, I remembered that particular detail had come to me via a glass held to the wall. My face burned with embarrassment. He was watching me, weighing his response.

"It was retrieved from the genital area."

My face was now puce. Mr Ó hUiginn's genital area existed beyond my imagination. I ploughed on.

"Red is red, right? It couldn't have been auburn?"

"Look, if there's something you want to tell me . . ."

"You'd better come inside," I said.

I called the Blessed Oliver and spun Miss Tuohy a yarn about a migraine. She was sympathetic and concerned and told me to lie in a darkened room. I offered to work through my half-day but she was having none of it. "Your health, dear, is paramount. Take all the time you need."

I hung up, less than proud of myself.

"Will you tell her? Miss Tuohy, that is?"

"Not for the moment. The fewer who know, the better."

"Why me, then?"

He shrugged.

"A hunch. You seem the most . . . ah . . . worldly of the library staff. I hoped it might jog your memory."

I made coffee and told him about my concern over Sylvie. He listened attentively.

"I mean, it's probably nothing, but why would she tell me she'd got a job at the Blue Bistro if she hadn't? It doesn't add up."

"Hmm," he said after a while.

"And there's another thing. The day she first came to the library, I heard Mr Ó hUiginn shouting at someone on the phone. I'd forgotten all about it until now. There's a fair bit of shouting in the Blessed Oliver, but not usually from the office."

That seemed to interest him. He made a note in his book. "We'll look into it."

A thought struck me as he was leaving.

"Last night – you weren't following me at all, were you? You were watching the club."

"Goodbye, Mrs Pierce."

He shook my hand. I felt a sudden urge to touch his face. I slammed the door behind him and leaned against it. I really would have to pull myself together.

CHAPTER FIFTEEN

THURSDAY WAS OUR last rehearsal before the concert on Saturday. It was a disaster. Philip Preston roared and ranted, the altos came in late, the sopranos missed their high notes, the cellist played out of time. Everyone was tired and apprehensive and some dark looks passed between the Porch Plotters. It was after ten when Philip finally let us go.

"Jesus," said Michael. He looked exhausted, with dark circles under his eyes. He had probably come to choir for a rest.

"How's Anto?"

"Oh, you know. Lively."

I left him at his car and walked on home. The night was unseasonably warm under racing moonlit clouds. I decided to walk along the shore. It wasn't always safe at night, but I needed to be close to the sea. The beach was deserted, the water calm. A faint sucking sound and a polite ripple were the only signs of the ebbing tide.

Earlier that evening I had called in to Cedar Hall. Tom seemed to be settling and May was pleased, though she had to stop Lillian chasing him round the garden with cups of tea. Lillian herself was ecstatic. She felt safe with a man about the house. She floated around in a chiffon garment that had seen better days. It had a tear at the hem and the side-fastening zipper gaped like a wound, showing her pink satin slip underneath. Her hair, still the colour of violence, was piled on top of her head and stabbed into place with a variety of plastic pins. She kept up a running commentary on Tom's progress outside. Dorothy ground her teeth and kept her counsel, knitting needles flying over what looked like the back of a man's sweater in soft grey wool.

Tom had cleared the garden shed, cleaning and stacking May's tools. He spent all morning in the woods, dealing with trees that had blown over in the fierce October winds. He was chopping one for logs, ferrying the wood in a wheelbarrow to the fuel shed where it would dry over the spring months.

He spoke to May through Charlie. He wanted money for sand and cement to rebuild the boundary wall, parts of which had been lying on the ground since I was a child. He collected his food from Beattie and ate in the lodge or the garden. To Lillian's chagrin he would go no further than the back door of the main house.

Beattie had reservations.

"You don't know the first thing about him. As for that policeman turning up to talk to him . . . who knows what that was about?"

"What policeman?"

Pinchon, from her description. He had interviewed Tom for an hour on Wednesday morning.

"About what?"

Beattie slammed down her pastry board and wielded a rolling pin.

127

"Now how would I know?"

"But did he seem angry or sympathetic or . . ."

"I don't listen in on other people's business." She dropped a blob of dough on the board and started to knead it into shape.

Poor Tom, I thought, pursued by the police on his first day at Cedar Hall, confirming every prejudice Beattie might hold.

"I'd have thought you'd have more sense, Eleanor. Your Mam and the aunties, they wouldn't say no to a stray dog."

"Sometimes you have to have faith."

"And false gods are two a penny. My Iggie will be keeping an eye. I'll tell you that for nothing."

Late Friday morning Mr Condor from Personnel descended on the Blessed Oliver. He brought with him a small man afflicted with a nervous tic. Mr Condor swept into the office while his companion paced the reading room, pausing to make notes. The elders watched him suspiciously. He winked uncontrollably at them. He threw his head back at an alarming angle and Paul rushed him from behind with a chair, decking him in the knees. His face was a study in shock and outrage.

"Hey man," said an apologetic Paul, "I thought you were losing it."

Mrs Clark cackled happily on her throne. Mr Mulhern glared. When the man limped in his direction, examining the ceiling, Mr Carolan tapped him on the arm and had a quiet word.

The pensioners kept us busy. Mrs Phelan called in, flush with the children's allowance. Bobby trailed behind her carrying supermarket bags. He sat by the door, flicking imaginary darts while she made her returns and asked for Miss Tuohy.

"I'm afraid she's busy, Mrs Phelan. A visit from the Council."

"Well, you tell her. Just you tell her from me, that she's a lady and no mistake."

I issued the books that Miss Tuohy had set aside. I wanted to enquire after her daughter, but felt it was not my place. We would hear, eventually, from Bobby.

Mr Condor emerged from the office and eyed the counter queue as if it had been staged for his benefit. Miss Tuohy followed, looking bleak. She fingered her pearls while they waited for his companion to join them and went back inside, leaving the door open. Their voices carried through to the reading room, but not clearly enough to make out the words.

The old folk shushed them to a man, then smirked at one another.

"Jesus," Martina rolled her eyes, "youse are worse than infants."

The man was a Council surveyor, Miss Tuohy informed us. This had been a preliminary visit, he would return on Monday to do a proper assessment of the building.

"What for?" asked Martina.

"I hope his leg's okay," said Paul.

Martina grinned. "Even a lowlife like you can have its moments," she said.

From what Miss Tuohy had gathered, no final decision had been taken on the library's future. The Planning Department and Library Committee had jointly requested the survey.

"It's pointless to speculate," she said. "We'll just have to wait and see."

Matt conceded that Charlie could spend Saturday with me on account of the concert.

"And Sunday?" Charlie was kneeling on the floor beside me, his hands clasped in prayer. "Only it could be a late night, and May would love him to come to lunch."

"So would we," said Matt sharply, then he sighed. "Well, all right, but don't make a habit of it."

Charlie whooped around the room. I hoped this was down to the novelty of Tom and not reluctance to be with his father. It had to be a strain living between two house-holds. I knew that Matt and Bethany gave him things that were beyond my reach. He dealt with it by keeping their gifts in their house. There was little crossover. He had his own clothes, sports gear, and now even a computer in Matt's. As an arrangement it was wasteful but it worked.

"I want your homework done tonight," I warned him, "and your exercises for Mr Wallace."

The evening passed quietly. I read while Charlie studied at the kitchen table. When he went to the sitting room to practise I put my feet up and closed my eyes. The Bach was soulful and calming, and I was nearly asleep by the time he came to say goodnight. He laid his head on my shoulder.

"I love you, Mum."

I stroked his hair, barely trusting my voice.

"I love you too."

CHAPTER SIXTEEN

THE CHURCH WAS packed. People lined the walls and stood five deep at the back. The Cedar Hall contingent had come early and was comfortably ensconced in the middle pews. Charlie sat by the aisle, Lillian beside him in a bird-of-paradise hat. She hopped up and down, craning her neck for a better look at the audience. When she spotted a familiar face she would wave and report back to May.

The choristers were jammed into the vestry. Everyone was smart in black and white, the men in bow ties. There was a good deal of coughing and clearing of throats.

Philip Preston was calmer than we'd ever seen him.

"You've put in the work, now go for it."

He shook hands with the soloists and nodded to the rest of us. We filed out self-consciously and took our place on the stands. The musicians were already seated. The audience clapped when Philip stepped up to the podium. He waited for the applause to die away before raising his baton. The opening notes of the *Requiem* sounded in the silence. We were on our way.

The high point of the evening was the "Benedictus" – the same piece that had caused such ructions at rehearsal. The punters loved it. Some were crying and there was a lot of head-shaking when it ended. I saw Charlie watching me, proud and happy. He gave Lillian a dig and she shook her clasped hands in triumph. We finished with the glorious solemnity of the "Agnus Dei".

Philip bowed to the choir, the musicians, the soloists, the audience and to the choir again. The clapping went on and on. People got to their feet, tentatively at first, the odd cry for "More" becoming a roar. Philip gave them what they wanted and repeated the "Benedictus". It almost brought the house down.

In the vestry we were torn between laughter and tears. The Porch Plotters slapped one another on the back and shook hands with everyone in sight. It had been an extraordinary, adrenalin-pumping experience and now it was over.

"I'm proud of you all," shouted Philip. "Enjoy your break and come back rested in the New Year." He raised his fist in salute. "Until next time!"

There was a scuffle for coats and bags and then we were out in the damp night air.

Anto was waiting for Michael and kissed him on the mouth. "Fucking magic," he declared. People within earshot pretended not to hear. It was that kind of evening.

May had tears in her eyes.

"It was quite, quite beautiful," she said, holding out her arms. There were hugs and handshakes and I was feeling totally wired when a hand grasped my shoulder.

"Eleanor," said Boots, "you were amazing."

We stood there, Charlie leaning into me. May and the aunts were watching. Even Lillian was still. We were like some tableau from a nativity play. Then we all started talking at once. Lillian took hold of Boots's arm and squeezed it in delight. He stood on Dorothy's foot as May shook his hand. He smiled at me over Lillian's head.

"But Robin must come to lunch," cried Lillian. "Don't you think, Eleanor, wouldn't that be lovely?"

"I'm sure he has plans for tomorrow, Lillian."

"Not at all," said Boots. "I'd love to come, if I'm invited." He glanced at May. She nodded.

"Of course, Robin, you'd be most welcome."

Young Dr Saul was waiting by his estate car. He would drive May and the aunts home. It took forever to pile them into the Mini, then they would complain about their clothes getting wrinkled and whoever was in the back would have difficulty getting out. This way they were driven in style and comfort.

We settled them in and waved them off.

"I've been in Cork," said Boots, "with my sister Eileen."

"I thought you'd have gone back by now."

"Tuesday." He held out his hand to Charlie. "I'm Boots. I used to know your Mum."

Well, I thought, doesn't that just sum it up. I looked at the dispersing crowd and noticed a familiar figure.

"Detective Sergeant Pinchon," I called. He was standing beside a blonde woman who was almost as tall as him and beautiful even at this distance. He came over, a shade embarrassed, saying that his father was involved with the hospice and had press-ganged family and friends into coming.

"Not that I'm sorry," he added quickly. "It was very, um, moving."

He glanced at Boots and Charlie.

"Well, goodnight then. Congratulations."

"Goodnight." I felt oddly touched as he sloped away.

Sunday dawned, dry and cold. I woke early and went for a walk, feeling elated and let down at once. A few church-goers and the occasional individual walking a dog were the only signs of life. I headed for an all-night petrol station by the harbour where I picked up milk, newspapers and cigarettes and took the long way back.

It had been a strange night. So much emotion – first from the music and then on seeing Boots with my family. I couldn't help thinking about how things might have been had he stayed, had we ended up together. Charlie would not exist for a start, I told myself firmly. But that crucial consideration aside, there was no harm in wondering . . .

We loaded the Mini with food, wine and Charlie's cello and set off for Cedar Hall at eleven as promised. Dorothy was putting the finishing touches to the table when we came in. She had polished the silver and starched the napkins. A centrepiece of winter flowers from the garden made an oasis of colour on the white linen cloth.

"That's me done," she said. She hated a crowd in the kitchen and would cook alone or not at all. "I'll see to the fire," she called out to May, heading for the sitting room with the Sunday papers.

I set to preparing vegetables and Charlie went off to find Tom. Lillian hummed as she beat egg whites with a whisk, a bowl of puréed fruit at her elbow. She was soberly dressed in a navy wool suit and wore little make-up, sure signs that she was in maiden aunt mode, intent on the third degree.

May seasoned the joint and stood back from the oven.

"Would you, darling?"

She looked tired. Her forehead was damp with perspiration. I dealt with the roast and seated her at the kitchen table.

"Don't you move," I told her. "Time for your preprandial."

In the sitting room I poured sherry for them both.

"Do you think that's wise, Eleanor?" said Dorothy when I offered her some. "You don't think it's a small bit early?"

"No, I do not. What harm can it do?"

She threw me a look and shook out the newspaper. Her silence was eloquent.

Back in the kitchen Lillian was upending the bowl of egg whites. She gave it a little shake and the contents stayed put.

"There," she said with satisfaction. "Perfect."

Lillian sipped at her sherry, May swirled hers around the glass.

"How are things with Tom?" I asked.

"He's a terrifically hard worker," said May. "I wouldn't want him to feel we were taking advantage."

"A man has his dignity," observed Lillian.

Boots arrived just after one, with handmade chocolates and champagne. He looked dashing in a light grey suit, silk shirt and red tie. He fingered the tie with the nervousness of a man unaccustomed to wearing one.

"Don't you look well! Come in, come in." Lillian propelled him to the sitting room and sat him by the fire. She surveyed him fondly, then clasped a hand to her mouth.

"Oh crikey," she said and disappeared. Within seconds she was back with a bottle of Jameson's.

"Men like their whiskey," she whispered, placing it by the sherry decanter. "I've been saving it for a special occasion."

Boots had already accepted sherry. I had his glass in my hand.

"You wouldn't prefer whiskey?" I asked, remembering he never used to drink spirits. Lillian held her breath.

"Absolutely," said Boots without turning a hair.

I poured a tincture and fetched a jug of water. I stood at his side, shielding him from Lillian while he drowned the whiskey.

"Cheers and welcome," said Lillian, raising her glass.

The dining room was some distance from the kitchen and was designed to catch the morning light. A tall bay window overlooked the terraces and beyond them, the sea. A large boulle cabinet ran along one wall. The mahogany table could be extended by adding a centre section parked upright in the corner. Three gloomy portraits of the ancestors hung over the marble fireplace. Something formal in the room's proportions put people on their best behaviour.

The challenge lay in serving food, if not hot, at least lukewarm after its voyage along the draughty corridor. Convention demanded that a person start to eat the moment he was served. As the guest was served first this could lead to a situation where he would have almost finished by the time Dorothy, who saw to the carving, sat down. It was in its way a test of character, an indication of manners. To refuse to eat until Dorothy was seated was to upset May, who would watch her hard work turn unpleasantly cold on the plate. To tuck in with relish, as did Father O'Dea, the parish priest, was to invite the fuss of second helpings before Dorothy had tasted her first.

Boots handled it beautifully. He tasted enough to be credible in his compliments, then turned to help Lillian with the vegetables, chewing vigorously all the while. He held each dish with both hands, steering a channel through the wineglasses. Charlie ran in, bright-eyed and healthy from the fresh air, and was shooed to the bathroom to wash his hands. He came back and took his place by Lillian, who sat directly across from Boots.

"Well, cheers again," she said as Dorothy sat down.

"So, Robin," began Lillian when the wine had been poured, the gravy passed, the food praised and the table admired, "are you married?"

Even for her it was bald. Dorothy coughed and May's shoulders drooped slightly. I stared at my plate.

Boots wiped his mouth with a napkin. "I was," he said carefully.

"And your wife is . . .?"

"Charlie, pass the butter to Robin," put in May. "Would you care for salt?"

He declined both.

"Your wife . . .?"

"She died." It was said gently, but with finality.

Lillian sat back, considering him. "How sad for you."

The clink of glass and cutlery was loud in the silence.

"How is your mother, Robin?"

Relieved, he turned to May. "She's very well, Mrs St John. She still has the house but she spends a lot of time with my sisters."

"And has she been out to visit you?"

He smiled. "I can't tell you how often she's promised, but she hasn't made it yet. It's a long journey."

"How did she die?"

Everyone froze.

"That's enough, Lillian." May was grim. Lillian turned to her, all innocence. "You are being cruel and rude."

"No," said Boots, "it's all right." He glanced at Charlie before going on. "She killed herself."

Lillian was chastened. Charlie looked at each of us in turn. May made small talk about people we had known when young.

Then Dorothy spoke. She had been watching Boots intently.

"Eleanor tells us you work with the elderly?"

He nodded.

"What kind of place would that be?"

It was a residential facility, he told her, with day care attached. Residents lived in bungalows with twenty-four-hour access to nursing and medical care. Meals were served in a communal building which also housed a clinic, a recreation area, a library and, at night, a bar.

"And can they avail of these facilities, your . . . residents?"

"Some can. Others, whether for physical or mental reasons, are less capable."

"So what happens them?"

"They live in an annexe off the community area. They have constant care but are still close to whatever's going on."

Dorothy was clearly upset.

"It's not perfect," he conceded, "but we do try to make it as much like home as we can."

"Excuse me," she said, and left the room.

The mousse was perfect – tart and light. Charlie and Boots had three helpings, restoring Lillian's good humour.

She clapped her hands. "Robin's champagne! It's in the fridge."

I offered to get it. I went upstairs and knocked on the bathroom door.

"Dorothy? Are you all right?"

After a moment she emerged. She seemed composed.

"What was that about?"

"Not now, Eleanor."

She was chatting to Charlie by the time I returned. May had taken fluted goblets from the glass-fronted cabinet and was wiping them with a clean napkin.

"I don't know when these were last out."

"Yes you do," supplied Charlie. "Dr Saul found a sil-verfish in his last Christmas."

"Thank you, Charlie," said May.

The cork was popped, to giggles from Lillian. Boots poured a first glass of froth and looked enquiringly at me.

"Why not?"

He placed it with ceremony in front of Charlie. The fizz settled to barely an inch of wine.

"So," said May. "What shall we drink to?"

Boots got to his feet.

"To friendship," he said.

We sat by the fire while May and Charlie improvised a medley of old tunes. We sang along where we could, then they were off on something new. Even Dorothy was laughing, making up words when the lyrics eluded her.

After a time May got up and patted Charlie's shoulder.

"I'd like to hear your Bach," she said, heading for her fireside chair.

He played. The mournful beauty of the music settled on the air. Each of us was still, lost in thought. The peace was almost tangible. Some instinct made me turn. Outside the window nearest Charlie stood Tom, tears streaming down his face.

The music died away. Charlie pulled back from his absorption and grinned at us. Then he saw Tom. He stood up slowly and laid his cello against the piano.

"Gran," he hissed. "Play something quiet."

She looked at us, surprised, but got up to do as he asked.

"They don't come much quieter than this." She started on Beethoven's *Moonlight Sonata*.

She was nearing the end of the first movement when the door inched open. Charlie crept in, pulling Tom gently by the hand. They stood by the wall, Tom no longer crying but his eyes full of longing. May played on – the slow movement of the *Pathétique*. Nobody moved. On the final chord she turned to Tom.

He looked at her and bowed gravely.

"Thank you," he said, and left the room.

Boots and I walked through the garden. Charlie ran on ahead, looking for Tom and Boy.

"I'm sorry about Lillian."

"Don't be. She wants something, she goes for it. At least she's honest."

"You don't find her a bit . . . relentless?"

He shrugged.

"She repeats herself, you know. Sometimes several times within a few minutes."

"Listen, Eleanor," he said, facing me, "the day may come when she wanders off with no clothes on, or forgets her name and where she lives. You're nowhere near that, and you have a good GP. Lillian will be fine."

Charlie veered off into the woods as we headed for the shore. I sat on the jetty, hugging my knees. Boots nodded towards the boathouse.

"That brings back memories."

"How ungallant of you." But it made me smile.

We looked out to sea, to the enormous car ferries puttering along the horizon like toy boats in a child's bath.

"What was she like, your wife?"

"Anna. Her name was Anna."

He picked up a handful of stones and skimmed them along the water. "She was gentle, kind." He dusted his hands on his trousers and came to sit by me. "She had the lowest self-esteem of anyone I ever met."

He told me how, shortly after arriving in Canberra, he had met Anna through friends. She worked for the government, researching social policy. She helped him with everything: work permit, contacts, even finding him a place to live.

"It was a gradual thing. More friendship than passion in the beginning, but I loved her. Eventually, we moved in together. She supported me – financially and every other way – through college and later my MBA. I'd never have done it without her."

He paused, lost in thought.

"She was older than me, and very conscious of that. When I first asked her to marry me, she thought I was messing. Then, when I finally persuaded her, she said: 'Some people aren't meant to be happy.'"

He walked to the end of the jetty and stared out to the horizon.

"Do you believe that, Eleanor? Do you think it's that simple?"

I shrugged, not knowing what to say, but he was really talking to himself. I watched him watching the sky.

After a while, he went on: "I thought she was happy. I know I was. I knew she wanted a child, I just didn't realise how badly. Jesus! I must have been stupid or blind or both. She took an overdose the day she discovered she was sterile. I was travelling at the time, for work. I truly didn't know how far things had gone. It was only later, when she was invoiced, that I found out about the tests. And I have to live with it for the rest of my life. Such a waste. Such a stupid, pointless waste."

We went back to the house. There was nothing to say. I wanted to reach out to him but his guard was up, just as it used be when we were kids.

He kissed Lillian and Dorothy and shook hands with May. She drew him to her and touched his face.

"Take care of yourself, Robin."

They stood watching as I walked him to the gates.

"Say goodbye to Charlie for me."

I nodded.

"He's a fine kid. You've done a good job."

"I wish there was something . . ."

He shook his head and kissed my forehead.

"Stay well, Eleanor."

I continued to stare down the road long after he had disappeared from sight. I felt old and weary and very lonely.

CHAPTER SEVENTEEN

T HE SURVEYOR FROM the Council, Mr Perkins, came back to the library on Monday. He measured and gauged, fiddled with a spirit level, stuck a damp meter in the walls, squinted and winked and generally made a nuisance of himself. Paul offered to hold the tape measure.

"Scab," hissed Mr Mulhern as they went past.

The library was quiet. Martina took Monday mornings as her half-day to make the weekend longer. The place was calm for want of her karma.

Miss Tuohy received written notification that no further acquisitions for the Blessed Oliver would be sanctioned by the Council's finance department. A separate letter informed her that members of the Library Committee might call in at any time to assess our situation.

"It's the beginning of the end," she remarked.

"They've shafted us. A few quid for the odd thriller – it's not exactly Library of Congress expenditure."

"You know," she said slowly, "you're absolutely right."

She spent the next half-hour on the phone in the office. No one had been there alone for more than five minutes since It happened. She was smiling when she came out.

"That was most satisfactory."

"What have you been up to, Miss Tuohy?"

"I just called in a few favours, dear. Barbarians at the gates, and so on," she added darkly.

Mr Carolan watched the surveyor's antics with amused detachment. I wandered over to his table.

"Do you know what he's at, Mr Carolan?"

"I did ask. He's not, apparently, at liberty to say."

"What would the smart money be on?"

He leaned back, hands behind his head, and considered the reading room.

"Hard to say. Architecturally, it's an important building. But there's the problem of location. Not to mention the cost of refurbishment should they decide to continue using it. I'd say their cheapest option would be to leave it to the vandals. Then, when things reach a certain stage, the Council can claim justification in knocking it down."

Mr Perkins chose that moment to stab the wall at Romantic Fiction. A large lump of plaster thudded to the floor. I was on to him in a flash.

"Kindly refrain from interfering with library stock," I said coldly. "You're disturbing our readers."

He winked at me, gathered his gadgets and notebook and headed down to the bookstacks.

"Steps!"

Paul, who had been sheepishly following, hesitated as the rattling grew louder.

"Duty before pleasure, Paul. Mrs Clark awaits you."

She was accompanied by her friend, Mr Dixon. Though more able-bodied than she, he was quite deaf and his sight was bad. His left eye was milky, both were inflamed and sore-looking. He was inclined to whinge and became animated only when mouthing abuse at figures of authority. Mr Mulhern couldn't stand him.

"Mr Dixon! Good morning," I called as I helped Paul with Mrs Clark. "We haven't seen you in a while."

"Well I've nothing overdue. Celia here saw to that."

Mrs Clark flashed her dentures. "Men," she crowed happily.

Mr Mulhern gathered his newspaper and moved to the far side of the room. He coughed loudly and pointed to a notice on the wall: "CIÚNAS/SILENCE", it read. I gave him the thumbs up and went to put on the kettle.

I was on the soup run when Paul tapped my shoulder. Miss Tuohy had gone down to the post office.

"You'd better check this out," he said.

I handed him the tray and went to the counter. The back of a tall, immaculately clad male presented itself. I sneezed.

"Can I help you?"

"Eleanor. We meet again." The virile grip of Billy the Kid. I could see he was amused. "So this is the famous repository of knowledge."

He dusted his sleeve absently, as if afraid he might have contracted something from the counter. His eye lingered on Mrs Clark, slurping soup on her throne.

"My, my, my, my, my."

"If you'd care to wait in the office, Miss Tuohy shouldn't be long."

He followed me, the Library Committee's Golden Boy, King of the Information Age, portent of things to come. Compared to his outfit, the Blessed Oliver would seem like the Black Hole of Calcutta. Inside the office he looked straight at the ceiling.

"Goodness me."

Whatever else, he did not impress as being highly articulate.

"Would you like some tea while you wait?"

"Oh no. No, thanks. Is that Meals on Wheels you have out there?"

"Sort of."

"I've never been in this room, you know." He wandered round, his fingers trailing over the furniture. He paused by the fireplace to admire the rare book collection. "Your Mr Ó hUiginn wasn't keen." He was like a man in a dream. Suddenly, he snapped out of it. "So. I presume you have user statistics and data I can be reading while I'm here."

"I'll do ya. I fucking will, I'll do ya."

The words had been uttered with some force and carried clearly through the closed door. Billy the Kid looked up, alarmed.

I checked my watch. Martina wasn't due in for a good half-hour.

"Excuse me," I backed out of the room. "I'll just see if Miss Tuohy is back."

Out in the reading room a girl of about sixteen was chasing a sturdy toddler round the tables. A large, placid baby sucked on his foot in a buggy. Mr Mulhern's jaw dropped in astonishment. Mr Dixon was mercifully asleep, his hearing aid turned off. Mrs Clark, determined to miss nothing, leaned forward at a precarious angle. Paul was nowhere to be seen.

Whenever the girl tried to head the child off, he ducked under the nearest table and scuttled to the far side, shrieking with delight. She was close to tears of rage and frustration. She looked vaguely familiar. The toddler holed up close to where Mr Mulhern was sitting. I signalled to her that I would take one side, she the other. After a good deal of pulling and shoving she managed to haul him out. He started to howl.

"Glory be, whatever is going on?"

The girl turned to Miss Tuohy, her anger spent. She clutched the crying infant and started to sob.

"It's Patricia, isn't it? Mrs Phelan's girl?"

"Patty," she sniffed. "My Mam told me to come."

Miss Tuohy considered her, realisation dawning. "Oh my dear," she said gently, "I'm so very, very sorry."

She guided them towards the office. I shook my head frantically and they made for the staff kitchen instead. I followed with the buggy.

"When you have a moment, Miss Tuohy, Mr Pender is waiting inside."

The eldest girl, Julie, had died in hospital in the early hours of Saturday. Mrs Phelan was too distraught to go out, but she wanted Miss Tuohy to know since she had always been kind enough to ask after her. The end had been peaceful, with the family at her bedside. The babies had been cared for by neighbours. There was to be a removal at six in the evening.

Miss Tuohy thanked Patty and summoned Paul to carry the buggy down the steps.

"White flowers, I think, would be best." Shaking her head sadly, she went in to confront William R. Pender.

As Billy was leaving Mrs Clark thrust her stick at him.

"Facilities!" He looked at her, mystified. "I need to go," she elaborated.

His face was a study in dismay. Miss Tuohy swung around him and stood by the throne.

"It's all right, Mrs Clark. We'll see to you in a moment."

"What's wrong with you, woman? Isn't that a grand strong man you have there. He can lift me down. You can do the rest."

"Mr Pender is a visitor," she began.

"He's staff, isn't he? It's not every day I get handled by a fine thing."

Miss Tuohy continued to protest. Taking a deep breath, Billy the Kid lifted Mrs Clark by the armpits and placed her gingerly on the floor.

"Stick!"

Miss Tuohy passed it to her and called me over. Mrs Clark twisted her bent neck at an awful angle to look up at him.

"You're a grand lad, God bless you."

He shook Miss Tuohy's hand with some warmth on his way out.

I got home to find our boiler had finally given up the ghost. I tried to call Mr Flynn but his mobile was powered off. I was wrapped in an eiderdown, reading in bed, when the doorbell rang. It was nearly midnight. I grabbed a dressing gown and ran to the hall, afraid another ring might wake Charlie. I looked out, safety chain in place. It was Boots.

"I had to say goodbye."

I slid the chain off and opened the door. We stood like that for a long time. I held out my hand and he took it, moving slowly towards me. I kicked the door shut. In his eyes I saw it all: pain, sadness, hope, regret and a kind of love.

"I'm seeing someone . . ." he began.

"I don't want to know."

I knew for sure that this time we'd get it right.

CHAPTER EIGHTEEN

O VER THE NEXT few days I went back to the memory of
that night like a child with a comforter. It was tender
and warming, and something had been resolved. I had
watched Boots leave at dawn with sadness but no regret.
He was going back to his life. Mine, imperfect as it might
be, was here.

Lillian had taken to watching me. Occasionally she
would pounce.

"You're in good form, darling. Have you seen Robin?"

And again I'd remind her that he had left first thing on
Tuesday.

"Hmm," she would say.

She had relinquished both the navy suit and the chiffon
creation, reverting to pleated skirts and warm jumpers
which could be dressed up with lots of jewellery for following Tom around.

Tom spent long periods in the garden with Dorothy as

she surveyed her plants, deciding what to cut back and what to move once the frost set in. They could work together for hours without speaking.

When May sat down at the piano all bets were off. Tom would gravitate to the window and listen, utterly still. She played to herself but also for him.

"He *feels* music," she observed. "It's in him somewhere."

I heard through Charlie that Dorothy was doing trial runs up and down the drive on her ancient Vespa.

"Whatever for? That thing hasn't been out in years."

"She's planning a trip," he said. "She's a bit wobbly though."

I decided to call her. She was not forthcoming.

"But the Vespa, Dorothy. Is it taxed?"

"Doesn't need to be. Too few ccs or something."

"I'll check, but I think that may have changed. What about your licence?"

She was silent. I pressed my advantage, offering to drive her on my half-day.

"We could have afternoon tea when you finish whatever it is."

Again, there was a pause.

"I'll think about it," she said quietly, hanging up.

I spent a great deal of time chasing Mr Flynn. When I finally ran him to ground he was sanguine.

"The thing of it is, you don't want to be too impatient."

"Mr Flynn. It's December. Not the best time of year to be without hot water."

"True," he conceded. "Very true."

He still had my house key. He promised to get on to the supplier that afternoon and check the status of my new boiler. There was one thing to be said for dealing with Mr Flynn: by the time anything got done you were so relieved to see him you stopped worrying about the cost.

Detective Sergeant Pinchon called to the cottage on Wednesday evening. We sat in the kitchen drinking coffee while Charlie practised his music.

"Whatever else she may be, the French girl is not Ó hUiginn's niece."

For some reason, I was disappointed. I'd wanted that relationship, at least, to be innocent.

"The widow was very clear on that point."

"So, who is she?"

"We're still checking, but we think he may have met her through his street work."

"Did you have any joy with the Blue Bistro?"

He looked at me sharply, but said nothing.

"Do you think she'll turn up?"

He shrugged. "As I said, we're working on it."

"This may sound daft, but I really don't believe she'd do anything, you know, unlawful. She just wasn't the type."

"Is there a type?"

"You know what I mean."

Charlie's cello filled the silence.

"Music must run in your family."

I told him about May, which got me on to Cedar Hall and the aunts. He was easy to talk to. His eyes tended to wander while he was speaking but fixed intently on mine as he listened. It was a shock when Charlie came to say goodnight. The time had flown.

He stood up to leave.

"Was that your, ah, husband the other evening?"

"That was an old friend. My husband and I are separated." As if you wouldn't know, I thought, given the background checks you must have run on the library staff.

"Ah. Well goodnight. Thanks for the coffee."

"You're welcome, Detective Sergeant Pinchon."

He smiled. "Nick," said he, as if we were agreeing a truce.

"You're welcome, Detective Sergeant Nick."

CHAPTER NINETEEN

By two o'clock on Thursday I was waiting for Dorothy. She'd insisted we meet at the cottage and I still had no idea where we were going.

She was dressed in her good coat and a pork-pie hat. She had a bag of fruit and a box of Dairy Milk chocolates. I sat her into the Mini and fastened her seat belt.

"Where to, Boss?"

"Just head for the city."

We drove in silence for about three miles.

"There's a turn here, on the left."

We travelled inland for maybe another ten miles. The roads were narrow and banked by tall bushes. We could have been anywhere.

"Are you going to tell me?"

She stroked the paper bag on her knee and stared out the window.

"It's Vera," she said finally, in a small voice.

Vera Debney was her lifelong friend. She was big of person, heart and voice. A stronger contrast to my gentle aunt would have been hard to imagine, but they were devoted. From the time her husband died until about three years ago, she had brought Dorothy on a foreign holiday every summer. Then arthritis struck, she had difficulty in getting around, and Dorothy would visit her at home. Now that I thought about it, I hadn't heard her mentioned in a while.

Initially, said Dorothy, Vera had managed with a kind of nurse/companion. "Then her memory began to fail. She started seeing things and hearing voices. One minute she'd be fine, the next she'd be raving about people tormenting her. Eventually, the companion walked out. The GP got on to Vera's niece and said they were now looking at full-time care. The cost of private nursing was prohibitive, so the niece put her in an institution." She took a deep breath before adding, "I came once before, by taxi. There are no buses. And when I saw her she didn't know who I was."

"Oh Dorothy. Why didn't you say?"

"What could you do? What could anyone do?" She was close to tears. "Anyway, I vowed I would try one more time. If she still doesn't know me . . ."

A hoarding at the gate welcomed us to St Philomena's Psychiatric/Geriatric Home under the aegis of the Eastern Health Board. A smaller notice directed us to follow the arrows to reception.

The building was set in agricultural land, monotonously green with not a sheep or a cow in sight. The windows were barred, the granite façade cold and forbidding. An attempt had been made to brighten the place by planting flowers close to reception. That these were now withered only made things worse.

"Shall I come with you?"

Dorothy shook her head. I held the packages while she straightened her hat. She took them from me without a word and made for the entrance. Her steps slowed, and at the door she stopped altogether. After a moment she turned.

"Maybe just as far as the ward."

A further notice informed us that all visitors must register at reception.

"Yes?" said a cross-looking woman as Dorothy coughed discreetly.

"Vera Debney, please. I think she's in St Joseph's."

The woman sighed and rooted in a card file.

"Second floor. On the right." She buzzed us through without looking up.

There was a lift but Dorothy chose the stairs. I sensed she was playing for time.

A cheerful young nurse met us on the landing.

"Vera Debney? I think she's on the commode. Hang on and I'll check."

She bustled into the ward. Dorothy was very pale. She twisted the paper bag once too often and fruit spilled on to the floor.

"I'm sorry. How stupid."

I touched her arm.

"It's okay. Really."

An elderly woman with vacant eyes shuffled towards us. Although fully dressed, she wore teddy bear slippers on her feet. She had a handbag parked on each arm and tightened her grip on them as she drew near.

"Are you my lift?" she asked Dorothy, without hope. "I'm waiting for my lift."

The young nurse returned and threw her eyes to heaven.

"Now Mary," she shouted brightly, "back to the day room. Don't be bothering the visitors." She guided the woman towards a room further down the corridor. A television blared through the open door. "You can go in now," she called back to Dorothy then, seeing the fruit in my hands, she added, "Hold on and I'll get a bowl for that."

I waited while she dealt with Mary, then followed her into a kitchenette where I rinsed the fruit and dried it on a paper towel.

"Are you relatives?"

I shook my head. "They're old friends. How is Vera doing?"

She wiped the bowl and glanced at the door.

"Not great," she conceded. "They can go downhill very quickly from here. It's a mercy, really."

We had afternoon tea, as promised. It was Dorothy's turn to ask where we were going and I looked at her in horror.

"Afternoon tea, and you have to ask where?"

For the first time that day, she smiled.

"The Shelbourne," she said with satisfaction.

Neither of my aunts had ever crossed the threshold of a public house. On special occasions they would go to a restaurant. An extraordinary celebration and they might take a glass of sherry in the Shelbourne Hotel on Dublin's St Stephen's Green. It had a dowdy elegance and the service was tactful and courteous

Dorothy settled into a deep, chintz armchair and surveyed the lounge. A pianist tinkled in the corner.

"Not a patch on May," she whispered.

The waitress brought our tea and pulled up a second table to lay it out.

"I don't think I'll go again," said Dorothy when she had gone. "There's no point." She was silent for a long time. "She knew things, you see. Things I've never spoken of except to her. She made me feel I had *lived*."

Dorothy fished in the zippered compartment of her bag and produced a photograph of three young women on a park bench. She laid it on the table and pointed to each face.

"That's me, and Lillian in the hat, and this . . ." her finger pointed, then gently stroked the features of a dark-haired girl between them, ". . . this is Fanny."

I had seen pictures of Fanny before, but they were formal portraits in which she was little more than a child. The young woman who smiled out from this one was somehow more real, as if she had a life, a history beyond the confines of family.

"She's beautiful, Dorothy."

"Yes," she nodded. "Yes, she is."

"Who took the picture?"

She blushed. "It was a gift."

She put the photo back in her bag. I poured tea for her and coffee for myself and messed around with the milk and sugar. I sensed she was struggling, whether with the decision to tell me something or with what words to use, I couldn't know.

"There was a man," she said eventually. "His name was Geoffrey Deacon. I was in my twenties – long before you were born."

"When you were living in London?"

She nodded again. "You know most of the story already. Lillian and I had found work and lodgings through an old friend of the family – Father Jim." She looked at me questioningly, but the name meant nothing. "He was a curate in London at the time. If it hadn't been for him, Mother would never have let us go. Anyway, things were going well, our landlady was strict enough for Mother's tastes, we had neither of us converted to Protestantism and I imagine the money we sent home was welcome. Father Jim prevailed on Mother to let Fanny join us. She was taken on by a couture house. In those days, the client would sit on a sofa while house staff modelled the latest garments. Fanny wore clothes so well. She was lovely, you see, she really was."

She stopped speaking. I lit a cigarette and waited. She was staring at nothing I could see, her eyes sad. I was so mesmerised by her face that I was startled when she spoke again.

"On Sundays, we used go to nine o'clock mass in the parish church. Geoffrey was usually there before us. When mass was over, he'd wait outside and walk us back to our lodgings. It may sound foolish to you, but there was something about the way he walked beside me and listened when I was talking, the way his hand would brush my back when he held our umbrella open . . . I knew that it was me he liked."

She blushed again, avoiding my eye. When she resumed I had to lean forward to hear her.

"What I told no-one, bar Vera – I even managed to keep it secret from Fanny and Lillian – was that I'd started a bottom drawer."

She looked at me, embarrassed but defiant.

"You can't imagine the tedium of those winter evenings. The landlady chaperoned us as effectively as Mother would have done. Night after night, we used sit there – reading, sewing or writing home. I had always sewn, so nobody paid any heed. I started to embroider small things: napkins, handkerchiefs, pillowslips. And in my mind I gave each item its place in the house I'd share with Geoffrey."

She was quiet for several moments before going on. "And then that letter arrived: Mother was unwell, she wanted us to come home."

"All of you?"

Dorothy was dismissive. "Naturally. We were her unmarried daughters, our duty lay with her."

"So what did you do?"

"What I've always done," her tone was bitter. "Nothing. I went to mass that last Sunday, willing him to say something – anything – that would let me tell Mother that my place was in London, but once my husband and I were settled we'd do everything in our power to help. My husband and I," she snorted, "as if I were the Queen."

"And did he?" Even as the words came out, I knew it was a stupid question. I could have kicked myself.

"Of course not," she said matter-of-factly. "He kissed my hand and said he was sorry for my trouble, he'd miss our Sunday walk, he'd miss us all. Two days later we were packing. Right to the end, I kept hoping he might come to the house and ask me to stay. I was so preoccupied, so caught up in my dream . . . Anyway, on the morning of the day we were to travel, Fanny informed me she wasn't coming. I pleaded and threatened, but Fanny would not budge. I couldn't begin to imagine the repercussions of leaving a nineteen-year-old girl to fend for herself in a place like London. What would Mother say? Who'd look out for Fanny? To every objection I raised, Fanny replied that she had a good job and Mrs Pugh's was hardly a house of ill repute. Her mind was made up. 'Don't make me go, Dottie,' she said. 'I'll suffocate.'"

I lit a fresh cigarette while Dorothy looked into the fire.

"Do you know what I felt? Envy – pure and simple. I asked myself, when had little Fanny become so wise? No, not even wise, brave. Fanny had courage. And I remember thinking: at least one of us has."

And so it was that she and Lillian, who had followed her since childhood, found themselves being seen to the boat-train by their younger sister. The journey home was grim. Lillian was wide-eyed at the prospect of trouble ahead, Dorothy sick at the thought of prospects abandoned.

And in the bottom of her trunk lay a tissue-wrapped package of linens embroidered in bright silk threads.

She touched my face.

"Don't take on so, Eleanor. It's no big deal, as Charlie would say. But it was *mine*, can you understand?"

"Did you ever hear from him again?"

She shook her head. "Though I learned, in a roundabout way, that he had landed a job in the City. A stockbroker or something. And he married, of course."

"And Fanny?"

"There was a tremendous row. Mother raged that no good could come of such crass insubordination. Sadly, she was right." Her tone was flat. "It was barely three years later that Fanny died in a car crash. She was engaged to be married."

CHAPTER TWENTY

I WAS HAUNTED by that image of Dorothy and her admir-
er. I could see them all – Dorothy, Lillian and Fanny –
young women with bright eyes and innocent dreams, tentative in their delight at having finally got away, only to be
manacled by filial duty. It seemed such a small thing to ask,
the freedom to love and be loved. In denying them that,
Edith had stunted their lives. Dorothy and Lillian were still
dealing with the fallout half a century later.

And how did they feel, I wondered, as they went about
the daily task of caring for that bitter woman who had
given them life, but resented them for living it at the
expense of her sons? At last I understood Dorothy's
reserve. Lillian's emotions were plain as a child's: she was
happy or she was sad. She had a gift for living the moment
without introspection. With Dorothy feelings ran deep.
She had nursed her secret, so trivial in the scheme of
things, so devastating for her, and been obliged to find

some way to go on, the dutiful daughter, dependent sister, maiden aunt.

Perhaps it hadn't all been bleak. The aunts had loved my father, and life with my parents had been escape of a kind. They were valued within the family. A childhood without them at its centre was unimaginable. Their love for George and me, and later for Charlie, went to the heart of our sense of security.

I watched Miss Tuohy as she went about her duties. Reserved as she was, she still found a word or a smile for the pensioners at the counter. In her way she made a difference. She earned her own living and answered to no one. Did she regret the years with her invalid mother? Did she have dreams or, like Dorothy, some underlying sadness for what might have been?

My reverie was interrupted by Martina.

"Office at twelve-thirty. Fatso from Personnel is coming."

So this was it: the end of the road. With the mood I was in I felt like crying. I wondered what would become of us. Paul and Martina were young – they would simply move on. Perhaps Martina would finally get to yank the hair out of tender scalps in some upmarket salon. As for Miss Tuohy, try as I might I could not envisage her belabelled and user-friendly in the company of Pam and Billy the Kid. Maybe she would retire. She could walk her dogs and tend to her garden. She would be missed for a while and then forgotten.

For myself, I saw no choice. I had my child to support and this was the work I knew. I would retrieve my laminated identity card and claim my parking space under Billy the Kid's.

The very thought made me feel ill.

Mr Condor's belly undulated as he exuded self-importance.

"Here we all are. You'll have been anxious to learn of the Council's intentions with regard to your place of work."

He droned on. I could hardly bear to listen, much less look at the man. He was seated in the librarian's chair, the rest of us grouped around the desk on plastic seats like schoolchildren. By right, not to mention in courtesy, the leather chair belonged to Miss Tuohy. I felt a surge of anger on her behalf.

He leaned forward, watery eyes alight with sincerity.

"You will of course be accommodated in other branch libraries. Mr Pender, in particular, is in need of extra staff."

He sat back, pleased with himself. To him it must have seemed like the offer from paradise. I glanced at the others. Paul was levelling his spots, Martina pushing back her cuticles with an earring. Only Miss Tuohy sat to attention, her expression unreadable.

"Well then," he began, miffed at the lack of enthusiasm. He was interrupted by a knock at the door. Without waiting for an answer, Mr Mulhern stuck his head in.

"I'll just put the kettle on, shall I? Only it's gone one o'clock."

Miss Tuohy nodded. The head withdrew.

We stared, fascinated, as a lurid red washed over Mr Condor's face.

"He'll just do what?"

Miss Tuohy broke the silence.

"It's for soup. When the weather's cold."

"You encourage your users to trespass on private Council property in order to feed them at public expense?"

"It's paid for through fines," she said wearily. "I myself make up any shortfall."

"This is not a social club . . ."

"With respect," Miss Tuohy got to her feet, "what would you know?"

She was being demoted with every step she took. We

trooped out after her, leaving him fuming at Mr Ó hUiginn's walnut desk.

The afternoon was sombre. Mr Condor had left an official notice to be displayed in the reading room. Miss Tuohy spent ages lettering one of her own in Gothic script. By two o'clock she was done. She slipped both versions into perspex stands and placed them on the counter. Mr Mulhern was first up.

"What does it say?" asked Mrs Clark.

Mr Dixon hovered at his shoulder. Mr Mulhern moved away, taking the notice with him. He looked around to check he had everyone's attention and cleared his throat.

"It says, 'The Blessed Oliver Plunkett branch of the municipal libraries will close with effect from midday on December 23rd. All future business will transfer to the Padre Pio branch at Watkins' Lane. Any inconvenience is regretted.'"

Their faces showed disappointment, but no surprise. Mrs Clark sank even lower on her cushions.

"And the other one?" she said after a moment.

Mr Dixon squinted, enunciating slowly. "'The library staff will, no, wish . . .'"

Mr Mulhern took the notice from him. "'The library staff wish to take this opportunity to thank their readers for many years of loyal support. Be assured of our warmest good wishes for the future.'"

Miss Tuohy and I spent until closing time down in the bookstacks. The stock would need to be boxed and labelled for transfer. It would be hard, dirty work.

"We'll start on Monday," she said. "Remind me to get masks."

By the time we came up the readers had gone. I wandered round, switching off lamps. I sat on a desk and surveyed the room. In this light it looked cosy, secure in its history. The shabby books had been through thousands of hands. In its heyday the library had been at the centre of a community, giving access to knowledge and ideas as the right of any citizen. And now we were abandoning it to dopeheads and cider gangs.

"Can I give you a lift, Ellie?"

"No, thanks. I'll let Mrs Kelly in and walk."

As if I'd conjured them up a gang of teenagers was congregating on the steps when I left. They were rowdy and eager, hyped by being part of a pack. It was hard to differentiate between them. The girls had long hair and dressed alike, in denims and shiny jackets. The boys all wore runners and earrings.

When I was a kid I thought old people all looked the same. Now, to my eyes, a wrinkled face was the map of a life. It was these smooth youngsters who confounded me. I was careering into middle age, no doubt about it.

One of the boys called after me, "Let us in, Missus, we'll mind the place for ya." Some of them snickered. I waved and walked on, unconcerned. A few hours later, their mood turning ugly from booze or dope or plain boredom, it might be a different matter.

Charlie was waiting at the cottage.

"Dad's picking me up at eight. He said they'd be in the area, so he might as well." He didn't look too happy.

"Great. You'll get a lift to music in the morning."

"Mum," he hesitated, "do I have to go every weekend?"

I sat down, facing him.

"Your Dad loves you, Charlie. He'd really miss you if you didn't."

"But it's boring. I mean, Bethany's okay, but he makes such a fuss and it's not like it was . . . It's not like when we were together."

"Listen to me," I said firmly. "Right now you want to

be here because there's so much going on at Gran's. Your Dad can't help that. Tom and Boy will still be here when you get back and Christmas is coming. You can spend all day, every day at Cedar Hall if you want."

"Can I sleep over?"

"If it's all right with Gran, it's fine by me."

The bell rang promptly at eight. Charlie hugged me.

"Tell Tom I'll be back on Sunday."

He walked past Matt to the car. When he opened the door an internal light came on. Bethany and her Bump sat Madonna-like in the back. I looked away.

"I hope you don't mind, only we were out this direction and what with missing last weekend . . ."

"It's fine, Matt. Really."

I shut the door.

Not one of the regulars was in on Saturday morning. A couple of women from the Valley came by with babies, buggies and shopping bags to change their romances. They clucked over the notice.

"That's a crying shame, that is. How are we meant to get to Watkins' Lane? I bet there's not one of them knows what it's like trekking this lot on a bus."

Her friend nodded.

"Maybe they'll lay on a coach, special like. Drive us in style."

"Or one of them limos. Like the film stars."

They laughed uproariously. I issued their books, taken with an image of Mr Condor chauffeuring a limousine while the women quaffed champagne in the back, babies everywhere.

Martina fiddled with my hair. There wasn't much else to do.

"You should wear it up," she said. "You've good bones."

I asked about her plans and she shrugged.

"This here wasn't the worst. You get used to it."

We were reflecting on that when, unusually for a Saturday, Mr Carolan appeared.

"Quiet today," he remarked. "I wonder . . . I wonder if you realise how deeply people feel about this?"

"It's not our doing," said Martina sharply.

"No. Well, just thought I'd mention it. Enjoy your week-end. That suits you, by the way," he added, waving towards my head.

"He's not such a bad old bollocks," she said, pleased.

CHAPTER TWENTY-ONE

MONDAY MORNING PAUL and I donned our masks and set to in the bookstacks. I was wearing my House Attack uniform. Sadly, with Paul around, there was no question of treating this as a special concession to the Seaview management. The dust was incredible. Paul went at it with gusto. I lifted a few volumes at a time and laid them gently in the box provided. I was hoping to set an example, but since he had effectively disappeared in a whirl of dust motes and had his headphones on, it was lost on him. Eventually, I thumped his shoulder.

"Go easy," I yelled.

"What?" We faced each other like a couple of surgeons, his eyes wide behind goggles. He lowered his mask. "Oh. Right, sorry."

Miss Tuohy reported that things were slow in the reading room. Mr Carolan had not shown at his normal hour.

It was early afternoon when the elders drifted in. They

seemed more warmly dressed than usual. I was on counter duty, Martina having replaced me downstairs. No one commented on my holey jeans and filthy sweatshirt. Mr Carolan was right: they would have to be pretty upset to let something like that pass.

Mr Carolan arrived just after three, loaded down with supermarket bags. I took some from him and brought them to his desk.

"Thanks," he gasped. "There's just one more box outside."

Walking back to the counter I became aware of a strange tension. The elders avoided my eye. There was quite a crowd for a Monday – ten or so. They were riveted by Mr Carolan and his groceries.

Miss Tuohy came out to say tea was ready. Mr Mulhern strode to the counter.

"We want you to know," he began, eyeing her nervously, "that it's nothing personal. You've always been a decent woman."

The elders clapped.

"However," he continued, gaining in confidence, "the Council has acted in what we can only describe as a cavalier manner by shutting our library without consultation. Therefore, we have no option but to protest. This building is now occupied."

"Well of course it is," said Miss Tuohy. "We're all in it."

"That's not the point," he hissed, and gestured round the room. "Only we're not leaving."

We retreated to the staff kitchen for a council of war.

"Goodness," said Miss Tuohy, "this is all we need. If I can't persuade them to go we'll have to notify . . ."

"Personnel!" we roared, and fell around laughing.

"It's no joke," she said crossly. She thought for a moment. "I'll speak to Mr Carolan. He'll know what to do."

She was back within minutes, her expression dazed. "Extraordinary. He's their media co-ordinator, if you can credit it."

He had, apparently, worked as press officer to a junior minister in the previous government. He assured her that he had not encouraged the elders, but had simply agreed to arrange media coverage should their protest go ahead. He'd offered to stay with them and keep an eye on things overnight. Miss Tuohy was appalled.

"Surely it won't come to that," she pleaded.

The elders had chipped in for provisions to last several days and Mr Carolan had camping gas canisters to heat tinned foods. He was to contact the press at five o'clock if the old folk were not satisfied with the Council's response. That way, the story would make the morning editions.

"Oh really," said Miss Tuohy, exasperated.

She tried reasoning with Mr Mulhern, who'd sprouted a war medal on his chest. He was immutable.

There was no way out. Mr Condor would have to be told.

He arrived with an acolyte, a keen junior management type. We stood by the office and watched him remonstrate with Mr Mulhern. He was getting nowhere fast.

Mr Condor appealed to Mr Carolan, man to man. Mr Carolan shrugged.

"It's out of my hands, I'm afraid."

Mr Condor hitched up his trousers.

"You leave me no option. Either you vacate the building or I will be forced to call the police."

No one moved. The elders stared at him mutinously. Mr Carolan removed a mobile phone from his jacket and placed it carefully on the desk. The acolyte whispered in Mr Condor's ear. They eyed the phone.

"Look," he pleaded, "we don't want trouble. If you

leave I guarantee your position will be relayed to the Council. It may even agree to meet with you."

"Big bloody deal," shouted Mr Dixon. He stood close to Mr Condor, not wanting to miss anything. "I'm sure we're overcome."

The others nodded.

"Send for the polis," challenged Mrs Clark. "Are you man or mouse or what?"

Garda Murphy was cruising in a squad car when the call came over his radio. Although some miles away, he was asked to respond. It was now five-thirty.

The front door was still open. A couple of dubious-looking pressmen turned up and slouched against the wall, cameras dangling. Mr Condor had retreated to the office. His aide bustled up to the reporters.

"Now lads, this is hardly necessary. Let's just keep things calm."

"And you are?" enquired one, flipping open a notepad. The young man stepped back, uncertain.

Garda Murphy arrived with Sergeant O'Brien. The cameras whirred.

"How's the Mammy, Gerard?" called Mrs Clark.

"What are you up to at all, at all?" he asked, before being whisked into the office.

"Is this what we fought for?" shouted Mr Dixon, brandishing a home-made banner which read "NO SURRENDER". "A police state? The abuse of our civil rights? Let any one of that shower of shites in Leinster House come down here and I'll give him what for."

The reporters scribbled. Garda Murphy, symbol of police brutality, came out and nodded towards the office. "Your man, Mr Contour, wants them moved. I'd have to advise against it. I mean, look at them."

We did. They glared back, ready for martyrdom.

"I'd give them all a nice cup of tea. They'll get bored, or

cold, and leave of their own accord. We'll have a word anyway, but I don't think it'll do much good."

He was right, but they did accept the tea. Martina went to make it while they debated what biscuits to have.

Mrs Clark was scathing.

"If you can't decide between Mikado and Digestives I can't wait to see you come the revolution."

Garda Murphy assured us he was available to negotiate at any time. If we called the station they would radio through to him.

Mr Condor went off, having told Miss Tuohy that he would hold her personally responsible for any damage. As to liability, God alone knew what would happen if some geriatric were to fall and break his neck while illegally encamped on Council property. At the very least, he said, a member of her staff was to be on the premises at all times.

We drew up a rota. Miss Tuohy took the first shift, until midnight. Martina volunteered for midnight to nine, when I would replace her.

I called May and filled her in.

"Goodness," she said, "how assertive. Do they need anything?"

The press had taken their pictures and gone. A Zimmer frame had materialised by Mrs Clark's chair.

Mr Mulhern may have been spokesman, but the war office seemed to centre on Mr Carolan who was enjoying himself hugely.

"For heaven's sake," said Miss Tuohy. "I thought you had more sense."

I sat on his desk. "Tell me, what is it you do here all day?"

"Me?" He laughed. "I write story books for children. I find the atmosphere inspirational."

We discussed practicalities: they were surprisingly organised and had even brought sleeping bags.

Chapter Twenty-One

"But what about Mrs Clark? You can't just sling her on the floor."

"Ta dah!" went Mr Carolan, like a magician, pulling a rubber square from one of his bags. "Inflatable bed. She'll have the sleep of her life."

"You know she needs help with the bathroom?"

"The redoubtable Mrs Murray is on hand." He bowed in the direction of a matronly woman who normally called in on pension day. They must have roped her in on account of Mrs Clark. She waved her knitting in response. "Don't worry, they're not children," he added quietly.

"No," said Miss Tuohy slowly. "I don't suppose they are."

CHAPTER TWENTY-TWO

I RETURNED JUST after seven the following morning, anxious to learn how the night had gone. At Martina's request I brought a couple of Dimplex heaters and a two-bar electric fire.

"Them gas things are giving off fumes," she'd said on the phone. It was pitch-dark and spookily quiet driving through the streets. Not even the milkman was out.

I'd gone to Cedar Hall the previous evening for a bath. Dust from the bookstacks was ingrained in my pores and I felt like a health hazard. After ten minutes Lillian knocked on the bathroom door.

"Careful, Eleanor. Thrush."

She decided to bake for the elders. "Nothing fancy, darling. Just simple things that won't upset the digestion."

We listened to the evening news, but the sit-in wasn't mentioned. My mother and the aunts were whole-hearted in their support.

"There's far too much bureaucracy riding roughshod over people's lives," said May. "Why shouldn't they take a stand?"

Charlie was thrilled. "Will they be arrested? Will you?"

"Will it make any difference?" asked Dorothy.

"I doubt it, but you never know."

"At least they'll have stood up for themselves," she remarked quietly.

Martina shushed me as she took the heaters.

"They're asleep," she whispered.

The air was stale and muggy with gas fumes. There was a gentle chorus of snoring. I looked down at Mrs Clark in her inflatable bed. She was tiny, like a fledgling that had fallen from the nest. Her white hair had been freed from its pins and fanned out on to the floor. Her face, normally so contorted, was peaceful. I eased the blanket over her shoulder and she stirred, but didn't wake.

A row of plastic cups stood on the counter, each labelled with a name.

"Dentures," said Martina. "They kept getting knocked over, so I confiscated them."

The reading room resembled a morgue with bodies on tables and a few on the floor. The night had been quiet except for frequent flushing of the lavatory.

"Do you fancy real coffee?"

I was pouring from my Thermos when Mr Carolan appeared in the staff kitchen.

"I'd murder for some of that." He massaged his neck, bleary-eyed. "I must have been lying in a draught."

Martina drank quickly. "I'm off, I need some kip. See youse later."

"She's very good with them, you know, underneath," he remarked. "Half the time she scares them rigid, but then she'll surprise you with her kindness."

The old folk were troopers, he went on. Not a serious moan all night. There had been some skirmishes over Mr Mulhern's Scrabble, but with so many dictionaries around these had been sorted.

"I should've thought of Bingo. They could all have played at the same time."

A faint rapping sounded in the reading room.

"Facilities!"

We smiled. The day had begun in earnest.

Miss Tuohy arrived with the morning papers. The *Irish Independent* carried a brief paragraph on the home news page, *The Star* gave the story three columns capped by a photograph of Mrs Clark contorting away for the camera, her hand resting on the Zimmer frame. "SENIOR CITIZENS REVOLT" ran the headline.

"A mite ambiguous," remarked Miss Tuohy.

The article dwelt at some length on "recent tragic events" in the Blessed Oliver. A police spokesman would say only that an investigation into the circumstances surrounding the late librarian's death was ongoing. "Informed sources" were again credited with speculation on "sensational aspects" to the tragedy.

Mrs Clark was thrilled. When Paul came in she dispatched him to pick up five extra copies of *The Star* to send to the grandchildren.

Shortly before ten Miss Tuohy got a call from the post office.

"Those will be my books," she said with satisfaction. Mr Carolan offered to help her and they set off together. I opened the front door to let in some air and was surprised to see small knots of sightseers gathering by the steps. Some of them made to come in. Mr Mulhern swooped.

"This is an occupied zone. No admittance except on official business. They might be spies," he added, from the side of his mouth.

The phone rang again. A national radio chat show wanted someone to speak on air.

"I'll do it," offered Mr Dixon.

Mr Mulhern regarded him with contempt. He pointed to the hearing aid and mouthed, "How?"

Mr Dixon was still adjusting his volume control when Mr Mulhern took over, introducing himself as the official spokesman of the occupying force.

"And what exactly is it you want?"

"Justice. Courtesy. Consultation. We're too old to go traipsing around town just to avail of our right to a library service. We'll see this through to the bitter end."

He returned to his chair by the door, ready to repel all comers.

By the time Miss Tuohy got back the numbers outside had swollen. She and Mr Carolan carried a large box between them.

A *Star* reporter followed them in.

"What's in there? Provisions?"

"In a way." She slit the plastic tape with a knife and pulled back the flaps to reveal gleaming dust jackets. There must have been thirty titles. She lifted them out proudly. Hardback thrillers and romance, they all bore the imprint of a London publishing house. The reporter selected two particularly loud covers and brought her out to the steps to be photographed.

"I'm not sure about this," she began.

"You're the senior staff member, aren't you? It's important to show the Council's side of things."

Several determined-looking women alighted from a minibus.

"The Historical Society," said Miss Tuohy, waving. A woman in tweeds grasped her shoulder and demanded to be introduced to the man from *The Star*. A small group of elderly people clustered under a banner identifying them as "OLDIES FOR OLIVER".

"This is more like it," said Mr Mulhern. Mrs Clark swapped her stick for the Zimmer frame and inched her way outside.

"Glory be," said she, waving like royalty.

The atmosphere turned festive, with onlookers shouting encouragement to the protesters inside, Mr Mulhern in his no man's land between. A collection box was passed round.

"Is there anything you need?" shouted the woman in tweeds.

"Bog roll," replied Mr Dixon.

More reporters showed up and drifted through the crowd before speaking to Mr Carolan. Mrs Clark had her picture taken again and again.

Councillor Dooley's office called. The Council chairman had cancelled his morning's appointments and would be available to negotiate in person by midday. He hoped the crisis might be quickly resolved.

"Don't we all?" said Miss Tuohy, but she didn't look optimistic. "Either way," she drew me aside, "I think you and I had better put our heads together this evening, Ellie. Could you manage supper at my house?"

"I'd love to."

I watched the elders. They were happy and animated, having the time of their lives. For once the spotlight was on them. They had a lot to lose and not much to gain by giving in quietly. Mrs Clark, I knew, had married grandchildren who wanted her to live with them. Only her fierce independence kept her here, but who could know how long she had before her deformity forced her into a wheelchair. Mr Mulhern sometimes referred to his late wife, but neither he nor Mr Dixon had mentioned children. For all their sparring they had become family, with the Blessed Oliver as home.

Chapter Twenty-Two

Detective Sergeant Nick had to flash his ID to get past Mr Mulhern.

He looked around, impressed. "Garda Murphy said you were having a spot of bother. Just thought I'd drop by and see for myself."

Mrs Clark shuffled past. "Are you the polis? Only I've seen you here before," she nodded towards the office, "when we had our Tragedy."

He bowed his head. "Detective Sergeant Nick Pinchon at your service."

"Fair enough. Celia Clark at yours. You could oblige me by moving my chair so I can see what's going on outside. The chairman's coming, you know."

He did as she asked and helped me lift her on to her seat.

I glanced at her expectant face and felt an overwhelming need to get out. For all their bluster, the dice were loaded against Messrs Mulhern and Dixon. Councillor Dooley was a political animal who would reap maximum publicity from defusing the situation while conceding as little as possible. His trades union background had made him a skilled negotiator, and he was shrewd enough to make the elders think they held the upper hand. By the time his promises turned to dust he would have moved on, probably to national politics.

"I need some air," I told Detective Sergeant Nick.

He shook Mrs Clark's birdlike hand. "A pleasure," he said gravely.

She pulled me back with surprising force. "He's not as handsome as the other chap, but looks aren't everything."

Miss Tuohy handed me the latest Lavinia Mosse.

"Since you have company," she nodded in Pinchon's direction, "you might just drop this over to Mrs Phelan. I'll get the address."

CHAPTER TWENTY-THREE

I HAD NEVER been in the Valley before. Detective Sergeant Nick glanced at the address. "Mountain Valley Way, that'll be round the back."

"You know it?"

"Unfortunately."

We walked along concrete paths. There were no children playing in the streets. The single phone box we passed had been vandalised. Occasionally the sound of a radio or television filtered through an open window. A dog threw himself frantically at a door as we passed.

"It's like something out of a western," I whispered. The sensation of being watched was so strong I felt we should be walking backwards, guns at the ready.

We found Mountain Valley Crescent, Heights, Lane and Road before coming to Mrs Phelan's house. I rang the bell. Nothing happened, so I knocked. The door was opened by Patty, the placid baby balanced on her hip.

Chapter Twenty-Three

"Yes?" She looked past me to my companion. She could probably smell a cop at a hundred paces. Her eyes narrowed. "What do you want?"

I handed her the book. "Miss Tuohy from the Blessed Oliver sent this for your mother, with her best regards."

We were turning to go when she called out. "Ma! It's for you. Hang on a minute," she added, "she'll want to see you."

Mrs Phelan appeared, the fleet-footed toddler trailing after her.

"Where are your manners, girl," she said to her daughter, ushering us inside. "You'll take a cup of tea."

It was a statement, not a question. We followed her into a small room that was spotlessly clean in spite of the toys that littered the floor. Patty dumped the baby on a rug and went off to make tea.

Mrs Phelan sat on a worn fireside chair, smoothing the cover of her book. The toddler clambered on to her lap. She put the book down as if it were fragile, absently stroking the child's hair instead.

"That was a beautiful thing you did for my Julie. Lovely, lovely flowers. You tell Miss Tuohy I said so."

"I will. We're all so very sorry, Mrs Phelan."

She sighed. A woman with no more tears to shed.

"It's the children," she said softly and started to rock. The little boy's eyes were closing. She looked into his face. "Who will look after all the children?"

We didn't talk much on the way back. As we passed the first tower block Detective Sergeant Nick took my hand. "I want to show you something."

Our footsteps echoed off the walls of the stairwell where the stale smell of urine was overpowering. We went up maybe three flights and turned into a long, dark corridor.

"Now," he said, "listen."

From both sides came the sounds of people living their

lives. Chairs creaked, kettles hissed, TV sets droned. A couple argued about money and we could hear every word. A vacuum cleaner started up, making me jump.

"It's the acoustics," he said. "Every sound is magnified."

It was like a foretaste of hell.

We made our way back down the stairs.

"It's the kids I worry about," he went on. "They're second-, even third-generation unemployed. They have no prospects and people without prospects are dangerous. They have so little to lose."

He walked me to the library steps. I would have to fight my way through.

I shook his hand. "Thanks for the company."

He bowed. "Any time."

"Aaaaaaaaaagh," wailed the voice on my answering machine. "Ellie, it's Liz. I am losing my mind, girl. Christian's away and I need to get out." The voice dropped to its normal pitch. "So, I propose to come round to you tomorrow, Wednesday, after work, when I shall drag you out for something to eat. I do realise . . ." The machine cut her off. There was a series of beeps. "Me again. As I was saying, I do appreciate that you are up to your neck in criminal activity down at the library, but I hope you'll make time to fill me in. If they come for you in the meantime, I'll bring a takeaway to your cell. Tomorrow. Love, Liz."

We had a date. A good, long gossip would be the business. It fascinated me that a woman as lively and capable as Liz should be so bad at being alone. Twenty-four hours on her own and she'd be hearing voices, seeing little men in green marching over the furniture. Normally she would organise things in advance, filling every waking hour with work and friends, but if Christian had to leave at short notice she tended to go into a tailspin.

I went round to Miss Tuohy's at seven with the evening

paper and a bottle of Châteauneuf du Pape. Miss Tuohy was chic in black linen trousers, her hair down and loosely tied.

"Just stand still for a moment, dear, if you would. I could lock them away but it'd be easier if they got your scent."

Two of the biggest dogs I'd ever seen launched themselves at me.

"Now that's very naughty. Manners, manners," cried Miss Tuohy.

I held out my hand, respectfully, and they sniffed it for what seemed like an age. They smelled me all over, down to my shoes, before stepping back, tails wagging.

"There, they like you. We're in the kitchen, Ellie. I hope that's all right."

The dogs bounded ahead and flopped into an enormous basket, chewing on rubber bones. It was a delightful room with windows on three sides giving on to the darkness of the garden. The refectory table, chairs and presses were of stripped oak. Strings of garlic and bunches of herbs hung from the ceiling. A heavy rocking chair faced a grate filled with blazing logs.

She sat me in the rocking chair, a glass of sherry and an ashtray on a footstool at my side.

"You don't mind, Miss Tuohy?"

"Not in the least, I love the smell of smoke. My father used to take a pipe in the evening."

Pottering at the stove, she filled me in on Councillor Dooley's visit. As she had feared, nothing had been resolved. He had set out to charm the elders, which was a big mistake, with Mr Dixon sitting by his side, sniffing all the while as if he could smell corruption. The chairman had tried to explain that there simply were no funds to keep the library open.

"'And how much did that junket to India set you

back?'" Miss Tuohy did a fair imitation of Mr Dixon. "'Not to mention your burning need to get to the Philippines? Were you pricing grass skirts or what?'"

"That would explain it." I handed her the evening paper. "JUNGLE JUNKET JINXES GERIATRICS" ran the headline.

"It's getting out of hand, Ellie. There must be something we can do."

The food was good: steak cooked in butter and garlic with a splash of cognac, a salad of baby spinach leaves with warm goat's cheese and baked potatoes with soured cream. After some initial slobbering the dogs went back to their basket and watched us eat with mournful eyes.

"It's not just a lack of funds," remarked Miss Tuohy. "There's no political will to keep the library going."

"I was wondering, though. Supposing we used some of Mr Carolan's contacts in the civil service, we might be able to make a case for converting the building to some other use – maybe a day care centre, or at least something that's community based."

She reached behind her for a notepad and pen.

"Now we're getting somewhere."

As we tucked into a sinful chocolate soufflé, she asked after Tom. I told her about his reaction to music and May's theory that it was something he knew. Miss Tuohy was thoughtful. Perhaps, she said, that was a clue, our starting point in trying to find out about him.

"You could always ask your detective, see if he's been reported missing."

I was carrying dishes to the sink when a framed photograph caught my eye. A small, fierce-looking woman with a chest like the prow of a ship stood sideways on to an older man who was seated. On the floor by his side sat two lovely young women, skirts flowing behind them.

Miss Tuohy took the dishes from my hands.

Chapter Twenty-Three

"This is you?"

"Me at sixteen," she said cheerfully. She pointed to the other girl. "That's my sister, Mildred."

"I never knew," I began, then stopped. How or why should I know the first thing about her?

"She's in England. Headmistress of a girls' boarding school. I don't see her as often as I'd like."

She offered me more wine. I was on night shift at the Blessed Oliver and felt it wise to decline.

"Have you thought about the future, Miss Tuohy, what you'll do if the library goes?"

"Oh yes. It's all settled."

"It is?"

She laughed. "I thought an observant individual like yourself would have figured it out."

We were interrupted by the telephone. "Paul," said Miss Tuohy. "He sounds upset. I'd better go and see for myself."

We drove separately and arrived to find the Blessed Oliver ablaze with light. It looked majestic against the inky sky. There seemed to be a great deal of activity on the steps. As we drew near we saw a number of middle-aged individuals striking poses for photographers. The men wore togas, the women were draped in yards of white fabric, presumably in figure-flattering imitation of the Muses. At the centre of the highest step stood a metal waste-paper bin stuffed with straw. A centurion sprinkled it with liquid and dropped in a match. The straw erupted into flames.

"Pretty effective, don't you think, Agnes?" said Miss Tuohy's tweedy friend from the Historical Society. "One must be visual. In today's world image is all."

Miss Tuohy was at a loss for words. The sight of Paul trying to smother the flames with his jacket brought her to her senses.

"What on earth is going on?" But she didn't wait for a

reply. She started up the steps as Mrs Tulle-Morris from the Amateur Dramatic Society held a book over the bin. Cameras whirred politely. Her sleeve went up in flames and film was shot like gunfire. The Society's caretaker managed to douse the flames with a bucket of water, leaving Mrs Tulle-Morris looking like a modest entrant in a wet T-shirt contest. The photographers were ecstatic.

"Visual is right," muttered Miss Tuohy grimly.

Paul was at his wits' end. Even before the tableaux on the steps his shift had not been easy. The elders were getting fractious, squabbling over little things and generally driving him mad. Monopoly had nearly ended in blows. He fixed some Ovaltine, hoping to calm them, but it only made them worse. Then he had been hit by the combined forces of the Historical and Amateur Dramatic Societies.

"I've had it up to here. It's tranquillisers they need," he concluded, a youth who spent too much time around Martina.

CHAPTER TWENTY-FOUR

I SENT PAUL home. Miss Tuohy rescued our waste-paper bin and left it in the hall. Then she became nervous it might reignite and put it back outside. "*Julius Caesar*," she intoned as she went to and fro. "*Julius Caesar*." The Dramatic Society's last outing had been a production of Shakespeare's tragedy for the examination classes at the local community school. They particularly enjoyed the play because the costumes were so fetching.

"God alone knows what tomorrow's papers will bring." Unusually stooped, Miss Tuohy headed for her car.

Mr Carolan had gone home. His young son had kicked up the previous evening, refusing to go to bed unless his Dad kissed him goodnight. The elders had agreed to his leaving on condition he returned with the morning papers.

The dentures were again lined up on the counter, their owners worn out from all the excitement. Mrs Clark was fast asleep in her rubber cocoon. Mr Dixon was snoring loudly. I wondered if he could hear himself. The temperature outside had dropped; even with all the electric heaters going full blast it was still chilly.

I thought it unlikely they would make it through another night. The novelty was wearing off and it couldn't be easy, sleeping on hard surfaces in an underheated room. It was vital for their self-esteem that something should come of their protest. At one level it was as simple as liking the elders and despising Mr Condor. At another I knew that Dorothy was right: they were standing up for themselves, refusing to roll over and bow to authority, and for that alone they deserved to win.

Mr Carolan returned just after eight. All the dailies carried some version of Mrs Tulle-Morris aflame over her brazier. *The Star* split its front page, one half depicting a wet Mrs Tulle-Morris, the other Miss Tuohy who had the serious, self-conscious look of a person uneasy at being photographed. The thriller in her hand featured a sleazy individual training a gun on a busty female in fishnet stockings and suspenders. The romance portrayed a doctor in white coat fondling a nurse in a most unprofessional manner. "DOOM OR DELIVERANCE: YOU DECIDE!" read the caption. Inside, a readers' poll claimed 98 per cent support for the protest. There was a passport-sized picture of Mr Condor over a paragraph headed "RESOURCES AT BREAKING POINT, SAYS COUNCIL OFFICIAL". Neither photo nor text was flattering.

The Irish Times ran a feature on the measure of a civilised society being its treatment of the vulnerable. A professor of geriatric medicine was quoted as saying that a positive attitude, such as that displayed by these senior citizens, was more enabling than any medication.

An article in the *Irish Independent* cited Nóra Bean Uí hUiginn on the protest being a fitting tribute to her late husband's memory. That raised a few eyebrows, but the elders let it go.

Chapter Twenty-Four

"You've done well," I remarked to Mr Carolan.

"Not at all. I just made a few calls, the old folk did the rest. I do regret missing the fireworks though."

I made tea and served it at a table in the reading room. Mr Carolan had brought brown bread and jam and there were two kinds of cereal. The elders pored over the pictures as they ate, Mr Mulhern reading the accompanying articles aloud.

I told Mr Carolan about my chat with Miss Tuohy while we had coffee in the kitchen. He reckoned we would need to approach the Departments of Health, Education, Local Government and Social Welfare. He would get on to it as soon as their offices opened.

"Only I don't think time is on our side," I said. "They're starting to flag."

I called Charlie at Cedar Hall. He was pretty well living there now that my schedule was so erratic. His voice shook with excitement. "They said your name on the news. Some old lady thought you were brilliant."

Lillian had done a load of baking and would be down during the morning to lend her support. May wanted to know if we had enough heaters as the forecast was for snow. Charlie informed me brightly that there was no orchestra because of house exams.

"Fair enough, but you need to study."

"Two hours, Mum. I swear."

He was clearly having the time of his life. I only hoped he wouldn't act up when life returned to normal.

"Is everything else okay? Only I feel I've been neglecting you. . ."

He sighed. "Honestly, Mum," said he, in a tone that warmed my soul.

I left before nine, unwilling to face Miss Tuohy's reaction to her media celebrity. I drove home, thinking about Tom and the effect he was having on our lives. I hoped, for

Charlie's sake I prayed, that he would stay. But I knew Miss Tuohy was right: he might have a home and family, people who loved him. We had to at least try to find out.

The telephone woke me. It was Dorothy.

"Can you come to the hospital, Eleanor? May's had a fall."

It didn't look too serious, she said, and yes, she had called young Dr Saul. He was on his way to Casualty.

Lillian was distraught when I got there. "I didn't know what to do, so I called the ambulance. It was all my fault, you see. I spilled some oil last night and forgot to clean it up."

She was very pale, clasping her hands and cracking the joints. I put my hands on hers to still her.

"Oh Eleanor, will she be all right?"

Dr Saul arrived. He waved to us and was directed to the cubicle where May was being examined.

"See, Lillian, Dr Saul will look after her."

Casualty combined the Accident, Emergency and Outpatient Departments of our local hospital. The wooden benches were jammed to capacity. Small children thrashed around, bored. The place was utterly depressing with institutional green gloss on the walls and a ceiling the colour of tobacco. The woman beside Lillian was bleeding copiously from her nose. She threw her head back and tried to stem the flow with paper towels.

"Happens all the time," she said cheerfully. "Lucky for you I haven't got AIDS."

Young Dr Saul emerged, talking to an Asian intern. He patted Lillian's shoulder.

"You did the right thing, Lillian. May's going to be fine."

He motioned to Dorothy to stay with her while we went outside.

"Is that the truth?"

"Absolutely. Nothing's broken. She'll be sore for a few days, mark you. I'd be worried if she'd passed out and then fallen, but that's not the case."

"Look, this may not be the time and I realise you have surgery, but I have to ask . . ."

He waited.

"Is there something seriously wrong? I mean, has May's health deteriorated?"

He shook his head, frowning. "The arthritis has been bothering her lately, but I've increased her medication. Apart from that, she's grand." I must have looked unconvinced. "Why, have you noticed a change?"

"She seems preoccupied, quieter than usual. Even Lillian's concerned."

"Well, whatever's on her mind you need have no worries about her health."

I drove May and the aunts back to Cedar Hall. Tom was waiting outside the kitchen to help May out of the Mini and into the house. She went straight to her room, leaning on him for support. Her wrist and ankle were bandaged, but otherwise she seemed fine. Lillian settled her into bed, clucking like a mother hen. May sent her to fetch a glass of water and gripped my arm.

"There's something we need to discuss. Can you come to dinner tomorrow?"

"Fine, but we'll do it at my place. You're in no state to be cooking."

"A person could get used to this," she said, lying back with a smile.

I walked back to the library after lunch. It was bitterly cold but I needed the exercise. The onlookers had gone and the elders were subdued. There had been three defections, reducing their number to six, and the ones who remained were getting tired. Mrs Clark in particular looked grey with fatigue. Lillian's cakes couldn't have come at a better time.

Mr Carolan was quietly confident. He'd spent a good part of the morning on the phone and had spoken to the secretary of the Department of Health, who was an old friend. He appreciated the urgency of the situation and was trying to set up a meeting for late afternoon.

"It can't be here though. We'll have to go to them."

If we hoped to achieve something, he said, it would need to be done in private. Any hint of a tabloid headline and the civil servants would back off.

I found Miss Tuohy in the staff kitchen. Martina would see to the night shift, if it came to that. Miss Tuohy seemed unfazed by fame. Mr Condor, on the other hand, was livid. He had been quite abusive on the telephone. Support had come from an unexpected quarter: Billy the Kid had offered to mediate with the Council or do anything Miss Tuohy considered helpful.

"That was decent of him."

"It could be crucial," she said, "when the chips are down. He has access to people at all sorts of levels."

"Get over here, Gerard." Mrs Clark's words drifted clearly through the open door.

"Garda Murphy," I mouthed to Miss Tuohy.

"Sit down there a minute, like a good lad." She lowered her voice marginally. "About that other chap, the one who's been sniffing round our Mrs Pierce, what kind of a man is he?"

I felt my face burn. I stared in disbelief at Miss Tuohy who shrugged, eyebrows raised and head nodding like one of those toys you see in cars.

"Who's sniffing round who?" shouted Mr Dixon.

"Whom," supplied Mr Mulhern.

Mrs Clark ignored them.

"I'd say he's a decent fellow," went Garda Murphy.

Chapter Twenty-Four

"Quiet, like. I wouldn't know much about the personal life."

"Is he married? You'd know that at least."

"Oh really," I breathed, appalled.

"Not to my knowledge, Mrs C. I'll find out if you like."

"Good lad. We need to know what she's letting herself in for. There are some right dogs out there."

Garda Murphy put his head around the door. I reached for the kettle, unable to meet his eye. He sighed happily.

"Any chance you'd stick my name in the pot?" He sat by Miss Tuohy and placed his hat on the table. "It's brutal outside. That was a terrific picture of your good self in the morning paper."

Miss Tuohy inclined her head.

"You'll be needing agents soon to handle the publicity."

"I devoutly hope not."

Mrs Clark's grandson was visiting when the summons came shortly after three. A delegation from the Blessed Oliver was invited to the Department of Health for "informal discussions". Garda Murphy offered to organise a car, but it was felt this might draw too much attention to the meeting.

"I've never been in a squad car," remarked Mrs Clark wistfully.

It was agreed that her grandson would drive. Mr Carolan checked for pressmen outside, then he, Miss Tuohy and Mr Mulhern got into the back of the car while Mrs Clark was strapped in front.

"The ladies must be represented," Mr Mulhern told Mr Dixon firmly.

I put the cushions from her throne in the boot and waved them off.

Mr Dixon switched off his hearing aid and lay on a sleeping bag. Five minutes later he was up and prowling, upset at being left behind. My heart went out to him, but the meeting would be calmer for want of his rhetoric. I brought him to the staff kitchen for tea and a smoke and gave him the evening paper. The lead story reported the conviction of a number of priests for sexual abuse of boys in an industrial school over a twenty-year period.

"May they rot in hell," he spat, milky eye streaming. "When I think of those bastards laying it down when I was a nipper: 'Mother Church says this', 'God's law ordains', 'Blessed are the meek', it would make you sick. And the women! What the women—my own mother among them, Lord rest her—what they had to put up with while Mother Church turned a blind eye and told them to offer it up . . ."

He dragged on his cigarette and cupped the burning end in his palm. Smoke flared from his nostrils.

"And then they'd get clattered if they said a word. A new child every year and all the priest could say was: 'Your duty is to your husband. Offer it up.' They wore themselves out with the work. You'd have been hard put to guess the age of a young wan over twenty from the look of her. The good old days, my arse. Dublin was a bitch whore of a city to be poor in."

"How old were you when you went away?"

"Old enough to see sense, though it broke the mother's heart, but there was no work here. I joined the merchant navy. Then I did some time on the buildings, but the sea pulled me back." He grinned and spat delicately into a handkerchief. "She's a fierce bloody mistress, that wan. I'll tell you something else: the day I clean up on the Lotto, I'm off to get myself a small house on a big cliff sticking out over the water. It'll be herself and myself and the sunset, and nothing else in sight. It'll be grand entirely."

CHAPTER TWENTY-FIVE

Martina offered to hold the fort and I went home gratefully. The morning's lack of sleep was catching up on me. A catnap before Liz arrived would put me to rights. When I saw the large car parked across my gate I assumed Liz had come early. I was nearly level with the bonnet when I realised it was Matt. He was leaning against the headrest, his eyes closed. He looked exhausted. For a moment I considered sneaking away but dismissed the idea as childish. Anyway, I thought, this is my house. Why should I be the one to leave?

I stood by the gate, waiting for him to look up. When he did, the eagerness in his eyes made my heart ache. I turned away, wishing him anywhere in the world but here.

"Ellie, wait." He was out of the car and shadowing me up the path. "Please. I need to talk to you."

Tiredness washed over me. I did not want to listen, I did not want emotion. All I wanted was my bed.

"What is it, Matt? I'm dead on my feet."

"Bethany's in hospital. I didn't know where to go."

Not to me, I wanted to shout; to anyone but me.

Looking at his drawn face, I was visited by an image of the night Charlie was born. Matt had been tired then, too, and worried, and impatient for the whole messy business to be over. Badly as he wanted a son, the reality of pregnancy and childbirth defeated him. From the end of my sixth month I was enormous, waddling around with a pain in my back and a tendency to burst into tears over nothing. I felt bloated and uncomfortable and deeply unattractive, a view Matt was not inclined to dispel. He came, under protest, to one antenatal class. He laughed so raucously when the instructor produced a knitted doll to demonstrate the journey along the birth canal that it was suggested it might be better for morale if he stayed away in future.

I was angry with him, thinking he had done it deliberately, knowing he wanted no part in the birth. I didn't realise until later just how scared he was.

When I went into labour he had my bag in the car before the first contraction had passed. I tried to reason with him, telling him that nothing would happen for hours yet, but the panic in his eyes persuaded me I'd be better off in hospital. My limited reserves of courage would not survive his naked terror. Already I was thinking that maybe this wasn't such a good idea, maybe I could tell them I had changed my mind, I didn't really want a baby after all. With Matt as my moral support God alone knew what could happen. I got into the car, resigning myself to an extra night in hospital. At least I might sleep.

The nurse who admitted me was kind and reassuring. She took one look at Matt and said I might as well stay, now that we had come this far. Matt almost fainted with relief. She asked if he wanted to wait, but it was me she was watching. I shook my head. He kissed me then, and in his eyes I saw fear and longing and shame. He backed away from me and I thought I might never again know him so completely, or love him as much as I did at that moment.

The nurse brought me tea. We chatted in whispers as it was late and the other patients were asleep. There were eighteen beds in the ward, and a robust degree of snoring.

"Try to rest," she said. "I don't think it'll be tonight. We can always send for your husband if anything starts."

She was still on duty when, three hours later, the mother and father of all pain told me that Charlie was ready to embark on his journey into the world.

"Will I call your husband?"

I shook my head again. "Maybe later. He needs his sleep."

We smiled at that, this stranger and I. She was still smiling when she transferred me to the labour ward.

"You'll do great," she said, gripping my hand. I vowed I would write and tell her how much her kindness had meant. But, like so many things, I never got round to it. I never even learned her name.

Matt arrived just as the baby's head was crowning. He held my hand and stared into my eyes with a kind of wonder. "You're so brave," he said.

I wanted to tell him that it was not a question of courage, that some things, once begun, carried their own momentum and there was no turning back. But there was no time. Our son, this brand new member of the human race, was mewling and clasping his fists, demanding recognition. I held the tiny naked body and thought: We did this, we created life. Nothing will ever be the same.

The baby was wiped, weighed and wrapped in his shawl. The midwife handed him to Matt. He stood there, my tall man, awkward and proud and devastated, holding

Charlie as if he were a tray of eggs. I watched them both, thinking that after this there was nothing we could not do, nothing we couldn't overcome because together we made a family.

"Bethany's blood pressure is up." Matt's voice cut through my memories, and just as well. "They're keeping her in."

He followed me into the house, restless and agitated, his concern now focused on another woman, another birth. I felt anger, pity and intense dislike. I would give him tea and send him on his way. He could find himself a new confidante.

"I'm sorry to put this on you. I'm sorry . . ." He sat down and passed a hand over his face. He looked like a hunted animal. And then I understood: this was it, the momentum, the no going back. It was the final, irrevocable break. In days, maybe even hours, he would have a new family. To face that reality he needed approbation from the one he had abandoned.

"I'm sorry too, Matt. I truly hope they make it through safely. There's nothing else I can say to you."

"No. You're right. I shouldn't have come." He stood up and pulled himself together. "It wasn't fair."

"No," I said, "it wasn't."

I fell into bed the moment he left, but could not sleep. I prayed for the baby's safe delivery as a kind of counter-balance to my dislike of Bethany. I'd never before wished her well, but something had changed. I realised she had no relevance to me any more. Regardless of what happened between herself and Matt, he and I had no future. Whatever hope of comfort or sympathy had brought him here today was false. We might paper over the cracks, we might even manage affection in our twilight years, but we could never go back. I felt empowered by the absolute conviction that I no longer wanted to. I could do better, alone or with the right Someone Else, and that would be my choice.

My marriage was over.

Liz arrived, laden as ever with packages which she dumped on the kitchen table.

"What, in the name of all that's holy, have you got in these?"

"Oh, you know," she said vaguely, "things."

A goat's cheese log, Brie, Cambazola, some serious-looking red wine and a bottle of Hennessy.

"You shouldn't do this, Liz. Really. You're the end."

"It was only going off in the fridge," she lied with aplomb. I picked up a bag with the Helena Rubenstein logo. "That's for Lillian. Just a few samples."

Liz adored Lillian. Whenever she shopped for cosmetics she would look out for the bright make-up so loved by my aunt. She would spend a fortune, then assure Lillian the products were freebies. Lillian would shut herself in her room trying everything out, tripping downstairs from time to time to ask whether this eyeshadow went with this frock or whether it was better with her silk shirt. It gave her as much joy as her birthday and Christmas rolled into one.

A second bag contained moisturiser, toner and cleansing lotion.

"Samples?"

She waved it off. "Samples," she repeated firmly. "So, tell. What's going on down the road?"

I gave her a big hug from Lillian and filled her in on the Blessed Oliver. Miss Tuohy had phoned to say the meeting had gone well. The civil servants had been courteous and encouraging, promising to explore every possibility of keeping the building open to the local community in what-ever way that might be achieved. To a man they had been captivated by Mrs Clark. Mr Mulhern had wisely let her argue their case. The result, while falling short of a definite commitment, was positive enough for him to call off the protest without losing face. He couldn't resist warning the officials that if their fine words were not backed by action, he would reoccupy the library, and next time a hunger strike might not be out of the question. Mrs Clark's grandson had driven them home in relays and Miss Tuohy had locked up.

"It was the best we could do," she said, "and they really need a proper meal and a decent night's sleep."

Mr Dixon accused them of selling out and refused a lift home. We would have to be extra nice to him over the coming days. "Balm to his wounded soul, and so on," said Miss Tuohy. She wanted everyone in for nine o'clock as there was a fair amount of clearing up to be done.

"I'll get Mrs Kelly to come in. Do you think Tom might lend a hand? Those desks are heavy for Paul to shift on his own."

I promised to ask. The Blessed Oliver was back in business.

Liz and I decided to celebrate at a new Italian restaurant in town. I called Michael and told him to meet us there. We giggled and gossiped and drank too much wine. Then we had several Sambucas on the house. We toasted the elders, Michael's parents, Christian and Charlie. We toasted everyone we had ever known, arguing over where we'd met them and where they were now. It was silly and fun and we knew we would pay dearly in the morning.

Liz started on about my manless state and Michael stood up for me while I swayed between them, smug in my newly found self-knowledge, and relived my night with Boots.

"I don't need a man," I began, but they ignored me.

"Not at the moment anyway," I concluded for my own benefit.

Perhaps someday it would be nice. The time might come when I would hurry home to someone other than Charlie, someone I could share things with, care about, have great sex with, worry over, cuddle up to and love. Out of left field came a vision of Detective Sergeant Nick reclining on my couch in smoking jacket and tartan slippers, his ulcer a distant memory. Or maybe not. Perhaps I was destined to become a high achiever in the library world and find fulfilment in work and friendship. "Nothing wrong with that."

"What are you on about?" said Liz crossly. "See! She's talking to herself. What you need," she went on, poking me for emphasis, "is sex. Lots of sex. You're clearly frustrated."

"No, I'm not."

"No, she's not," put in Michael. "She's doing fine. And it was sex got her into this mess in the first place."

"Oh for heaven's sake. It was Dogbreath, not sex, that fucked her up – if you catch my drift. And I don't see why you're getting so premenstrual," she added, "you with your teenage boyfriends. There's clearly a fair amount of fornication in your life."

Michael slapped her wrist. "Nasty, nasty. Some of us just have what it takes, dear."

The bill was placed on our table with polite finality. We left an enormous tip and lurched out to the street.

"There's a taxi rank up here somewhere," began Liz.

"We know something else around here," said Michael, winking at me and taking us each by the arm. "Come on, girls. Let's party."

Bullet-head at the Blue Bistro looked us over without recognition. In fact, he barely looked at us at all.

We found a table and ordered criminally overpriced wine and mineral water that wasn't a lot cheaper.

"Do you come here often?" asked Liz in some disbelief.

"Oh, you know," said Michael, "we thought you might like it."

"Why?" Her eyes raked the room. "Am I missing something?"

Just then the music pumped up to the ear-splitting volume of our previous visit. I sat back and looked around. A different girl was serving at the wine bar. Punters were trickling in but there was still room to move. There was no sign of Roger.

Michael persuaded Liz on to the dance floor where she did a soft shuffle, arms wrapped around herself, while he strutted and leaped like some mad Russian.

I headed for the Ladies', glad of any respite from the pounding music. I paused at the curtained door opposite. The corridor was deserted. Edging the curtain aside, I put my ear to the door. There was no sound over the muffled hum from the club. Gently, I pushed it open.

I have no idea what I was thinking, or if I was thinking at all. The booze had given me Dutch courage. I wanted to know what lay beyond the stairwell; it seemed reasonable to go and look.

The wooden stairs were uncarpeted, and dark after the lit corridor. I held tightly to the handrail and crept up. At the top, three doors faced on to a landing. All were shut, but a shaft of light was visible under the one nearest me. I hesitated. Hearing nothing, I tiptoed past and eased open the middle door. This was clearly an office, with a serious-looking telephone system, papers piled on a desk and cardboard boxes labelled "Fragile" stacked by the wall—wineglasses, from the look of them. A metal filing cabinet stood in the corner.

I moved to the third room, wiping my clammy hands on my skirt. I turned the knob and found myself facing yet another door. Judging by the cornice, the original room had been subdivided. The space I was in was little more than a glorified hallway. The internal door was locked.

I almost tripped over some cardboard boxes that had been flattened and neatly tied together. A roll of industrial-strength rubbish bags had been tucked under the string. I hunkered down and scrutinised the boxes; in the gloom, the words "Ilford Hypam" were just legible.

I was about to step out to the landing when I heard foot-steps on the stairs. I leaned into the wall, praying I wouldn't have a heart attack.

A voice called from below. "I'll send him up, then. Around two?"

There was a grunt of agreement from somewhere close by. In the seconds that followed I bargained furiously with God. I would amend my ways. I would become a Good Person. I would work my guts out in Billy the Kid's if only He, in His divine omnipotence, would get me safely down those stairs.

I heard a door close and heaved myself out of the room. I took the steps two at a time and was almost at the bot-tom when I was dazzled by bright light. I missed my foot-ing, grabbed at the banister, did a half-turn and found myself looking up into the lizard eyes of Will.

"Well," his tone was neutral. "What have we here?"

I continued to back down the stairs.

"Sorry. Wrong door. Nice to see you again. Actually, I'm here with Liz." My mouth was going at much the same pace as my knees. It was a miracle I was still upright.

"With Liz. Is that so?"

He was assessing me as a cat might a mouse. With those eyes there was no way of knowing if there was anyone home.

I squeaked, tried again. "Do join us for a glass of wine."

I had my hand on the knob when the door was pushed in, almost knocking me over. Roger looked from me to

Will. I was gaping at him, certain I would faint, when there was a shout from across the corridor.

"There you are! I was getting worried."

I rushed at Liz, grabbing her arm for support.

"Your nice neighbour is upstairs. Isn't that great?" I babbled. "You know, Will."

She looked at me, perplexed, then leaned around Roger.

"Hiya, Will. Are you coming down for a drink?"

"In a while."

I backed into the Ladies' and threw up.

CHAPTER TWENTY-SIX

I WOKE UP wishing I were dead. Then I remembered my stairwell encounter and felt grateful I was not. Making my way to the kitchen, I drank several pints of water and stared at my reflection in the window, my brain scrambled. Had I imagined the sense of threat that emanated from Will? Perhaps it was no more than my own guilt at snooping where I had no right to be. He hadn't joined us in the end, but had sent his apologies and a bottle of champagne via Roger. I had not felt safe till we hit the pavement and the cold, blessed night air.

It was nearly nine by the kitchen clock. I was going to be late for work and had missed my chance to call Charlie before he left for school. I forced myself to eat some cheese and walked to the library as briskly as I was able, vowing never, ever to be so stupid again. I would stick virtuously to mineral water when May and the aunts came round for supper.

Miss Tuohy had already set to with relish. Every window in the building was wide open. Papers fluttered in the freezing draught. Mrs Kelly was hoovering with an industrial vacuum cleaner. Paul was plugged into his headphones, stacking chairs out of Mrs Kelly's way. The din was appalling. I staggered past Martina, who was wielding a feather duster without conviction. Miss Tuohy followed me into the kitchen.

"Do I still get my half-day?"

"You look as if you shouldn't be here at all." She suggested I keep the door shut and deal with the washing-up. I went into Seaview mode, various guests commiserating on my terrible illness and the fortitude I had shown in coming to work.

"No, no. It's nothing. I couldn't let you down."

"Couldn't let who down?" asked Martina. I hadn't heard her come in over Mrs Kelly's racket.

I shook my head. It was too complicated. She fished in her bag and handed me two tablets which I swallowed gratefully.

"Go on," she said gruffly. "You make tea and I'll finish up here. Heavy night, was it?"

I groaned in response.

"Was that your fella called in the other day?"

I shook my head again. "My ex. The only male in my life is twelve years old and my son."

"That's all right then. Only I thought your man was a bit smarmy."

Paul backed into the kitchen. "Yo. Get a load of this."

We followed him to the reading room. In my delicate state it took more than a moment to recognise the clean-shaven, newly coiffed, gorgeous creature as Tom. Dressed head to toe in denim he had shed twenty years. He glanced at us but had eyes only for Miss Tuohy. Mrs Kelly, oblivious, continued to vacuum.

"Well, Mr Tom," Miss Tuohy was saying, "if you could give Paul a hand with the tables . . ."

I returned to the washing-up. Martina had retrieved her feather duster, anxious to keep an eye on developments. She swished it over desks as they were being moved. Paul was not much better, staring open-mouthed at Tom while his headphones emitted electronic gabble.

"Goodness," said Miss Tuohy, carrying in the last of the cups, "I barely knew him."

Lillian, I thought to myself. All her life she had been passionate about appearance. The challenge of Tom would have been irresistible.

"Do you approve?" I asked.

"I'm not entirely sure."

Mid-morning Liz rang.

"Isn't that a blast? I'd never have seen Will running a nightclub."

"Liz," I probed, "what do you think of him?"

"I don't, really," she said slowly. "As neighbours they're fine – which is to say we hardly ever see them. Why do you ask?"

"He gives me the creeps."

"Hmm. I can see how he might. I'd say he's harmless enough."

I shopped for supper on my way home, grateful that it was a family meal and not some lavish production. My friend of our-special-on-a-bedside-table was on the checkout. I was fascinated by her hair. It had been bleached, probably at home, either using too much or leaving it on for too long. The result was a greenish tinge not unlike something Lillian might have aimed for. She slit her eyes at me and I smiled back in what I hoped was an enigmatic manner. She did not offer me coupons.

Back home I made a beef casserole with red wine and

put it in the oven to simmer. I could cook the rice, wash the salad and heat some garlic bread just before going to Cedar Hall to collect my guests. Then I climbed into bed and slept for two hours. I woke thinking I would give my right arm for a long, luxurious bath.

As if he could read my mind, Mr Flynn chose that moment to phone.

"The thing of it is," he said without preamble, "we could fix you up in the morning. But there's a small snag."

"How small?"

I could hear his pipe tapping away.

"Let me put it this way. The boiler would have a greater capacity than you actually require . . ."

"Mr Flynn. Let's cut to the chase. You could install a water heating mechanism tomorrow. It would function. It would be covered by a guarantee. And it would cost more than you quoted before. How am I doing?"

I could imagine him nodding.

"That's about the size of it."

"And the alternative?"

"We could be looking at the far side of Christmas."

"Do it."

I glared at the phone, then looked up a number for the maternity hospital.

"Are you family?" asked the girl on the switchboard. I toyed with the idea of debating this, as in: "This individual is my husband's mistress. Her child will be my son's half-sibling. Does that make me family?" but said only, "Not exactly."

She put me on hold. The jingle that cut in was, incredibly, "Thank Heaven for Little Girls". The operator cut through it to say that Bethany was being kept in for observation, but both she and her unborn baby were fine. "Would you like me to put you through?"

I hung up quickly.

They were waiting for me at Cedar Hall, grouped formally just inside the hall door. They had, each in her way, gone to some trouble over dressing. Lillian's hair was fading to cerise. A purple bow perched at the side of her head. Her matching velvet frock was tailored and chic. She was brightly made up and raring to go. Dorothy was wearing her good coat and May's bandages were just visible under a smart trouser suit. Charlie and Boy came running from the side of the house, followed more slowly by Tom.

"Oh Lord. I forgot Tom."

"Beattie's left a tray in the kitchen," said Dorothy.

Charlie and Tom helped the aunts into the back of the Mini, then Charlie jumped in between them causing squeals of distress over the state of their good clothes. Tom handed May into the front and strapped her in, taking care not to touch her injuries. Miss Tuohy was right: there was an extraordinary gentleness to him.

We set off, waving and beeping at Tom. The atmosphere became tense with anticipation. I was utterly at a loss. May's expression was inscrutable.

Charlie poured their sherry while I put the finishing touches to the food. Knowing May, she would probably say nothing until the meal was over. They chatted in the sitting room, out of my way, as I wondered what she could have to tell us. Could she have met someone? She was a handsome woman, barely into her seventies, it wasn't inconceivable. Could she be ill but attending a doctor other than young Dr Saul? I was mixing dressing for the salad when I froze. She had decided to sell. That must be it. She had fought the good fight but it was over. Structural damage, the lack of cash and the sheer size of Cedar Hall had finally defeated her. I gave myself a mental shake. This would be hard enough for her without me emoting all over the dinner table. I would be calm, congratulate her on a sensible decision, and look as if I meant it. I went to the door and called them in.

We concentrated on eating. The casserole was good, and hot. Apart from Charlie's chatter, conversation was desultory until we got to Liz's cheese. May laid her napkin on the table and looked at each of us in turn.

"A situation has arisen which affects us all. I want you to hear me out, then tell me how you feel."

Dorothy and I looked down at our plates, some premonition making us unwilling to face one another. Only Lillian watched May expectantly.

"Should I stay?" asked Charlie.

"If you like, darling. You can leave if you get bored."

George, she told us, wanted to come home. There was a stunned silence. He had been gone for almost thirty-five years.

"Brilliant," said Charlie.

"Why?" said I, the one who was going to make things easy.

"He is, as you know, married. His wife is from Boston and is independently wealthy . . ."

"I thought his wife was from Houston," put in Dorothy.

"His former wife was from Houston," conceded May. "This one, however, is from Boston where her family run a number of hotels. She is second-generation Irish on her mother's side and has always dreamed of living here."

Anyway, May went on, George had waxed lyrical to his bride about his childhood at Cedar Hall. She was looking for a property that could be developed as an intimate family hotel, on the lines of a country house open to guests. She had seen photos of Cedar Hall and thought it might well be the place she wanted.

"And where would we live?" asked Dorothy. "Has he thought of that?" I could almost see Vera's institution looming before her eyes.

May, unusually, took her hand. "He has."

If the proposition was accepted, George's wife was ready

and able to spend a great deal of money upgrading the house. There was some mention of a tennis court in the garden, but we could ignore that. When the work was done, May and the aunts would continue to live at Cedar Hall, each having her own room as before. The difference would be that strangers would sleep and eat there as paying guests of the family.

"One would be expected to socialise before dinner, that sort of thing. It's a form of hospitality for hire."

"How wonderful," breathed Lillian.

Dorothy frowned. "And who exactly will cook these dinners if we're busy 'socialising'?"

There would be a proper staff, May assured her. The whole operation would be run as a business. The aunts would have room and board and a retainer for their "hostess" duties. May enunciated the word as if it belonged to another language. Lillian and Dorothy repeated it, the one with awe, the other with disdain.

"What about me?" asked Charlie.

"I'm sure you could earn pocket money serving drinks or something," said May. "Anyway, that's the gist of the thing. If you agree, they would like to come as soon as possible to view the house."

"And if we don't?"

"If you don't, we shall carry on as before, though none of us has any illusion about the condition of the house. My own view, for what it's worth, is that eventually we'll be forced to sell. It boils down to deciding whether we do so now, to family, or later, to a developer."

Lillian could barely contain her excitement. Dorothy looked impressed in spite of herself.

"You're very quiet, Eleanor."

"It sounds like an answer to prayer . . ."

"But?"

I hesitated. The last thing I wanted was to rain on their

parade, but this brother I hardly remembered sounded like a man who got around.

"I think you'd need to be careful. Where would you stand if his marriage broke up, or if the business wasn't a success?"

"I would do nothing without independent legal advice. I have been absolutely clear on that point."

Everyone started to talk at once. When had this come about? When had she heard from George? Why had she said nothing?

"It's a big decision," said May. "I didn't want to put it to you until I had sorted out my own thoughts. And George insisted on secrecy. I gather he's rather shy about coming home. His wife, however, seems determined."

I made coffee on the simmering plate while May described his wife, Merry Lou.

"Mary Lou?" echoed Dorothy.

"Merry, as in joyful," amended May, producing a photo. "It's a corruption of Marie Louise."

We crowded round, anxious to see the woman who held the future of Cedar Hall in her bank balance. She was big, not in the first flush of youth and had a wide, happy smile.

"Hmm," said Dorothy. "Comely."

I pointed to the balding, middle-aged man at her side.

"That's never George?"

May nodded. I took the picture from her and held it up to the light. Nothing in his expression or attitude gave any sense of the person he had become. He had put on weight, though not in the explosive way I considered peculiarly American. He appeared to be shorter than his wife, but that might have been down to the camera angle. I was still studying his face when the doorbell rang.

"Mum. It's for you."

I looked past Charlie to where Detective Sergeant Nick was standing awkwardly at the kitchen door.

Chapter Twenty-Six

"Forgive me. I'm disturbing you."

"No. Please, come in. You haven't met my family."

Lillian was appraising him as I made the introductions. Please God, I thought, don't let her start. She turned to May. "Doesn't he have a great look of that boy in the tennis club when we were young, the one who was doing medicine? He was Pinchon too. Douglas, Duncan, something like that."

"Dominic," supplied Dorothy. "All the girls were after him until he married that French beauty."

Detective Sergeant Nick was mortified and trying hard not to show it. He looked at me in an agony of apology. "My, um, father," he conceded.

"No. Your father! Isn't that extraordinary." They were off. Lillian manhandled him into the chair beside hers and poured wine into my unused glass. Dorothy cut some cheese for him and May demanded news of his father.

"I just wanted a word with Mrs Pierce. I'd never have come if I realised you had company."

"Why not?" enquired Lillian. "Would you rather be alone with Eleanor?"

"That wasn't my meaning," he began. I smiled at him. When he smiled back, I felt warm all over. He gave in graciously, eating his cheese, drinking his wine, and fielding their questions as best he could. I sat and watched him, unreasonably happy.

They grilled him on his work. Lillian sorted his marital status: single, but with a grown-up son who lived abroad. There was a slight pause as we digested this. Deciding to postpone judgement, Lillian moved on. Was he involved at present? He hesitated, embarrassed.

"Pay no attention, Nicholas," said May. "We were just discussing some plans for the house. I'm sure we'd welcome another perspective."

He listened gravely, glancing at me from time to time, as

they vied for his attention. I couldn't take my eyes off his face.

"It sounds like a winner if, as you say," he nodded in May's direction, "you get sound legal advice. My own parents sold off land for housing and have always regretted it. They didn't take account of how drastically the lack of a decent garden can alter an old house. Eventually, they sold up altogether and moved to an apartment. My mother loves the convenience, but it broke my father's heart."

He finished his wine and stood up to leave, to a chorus of protests.

"Really, I have to go. But I'd be happy to drive you home if that suited?"

We were left facing one another across the table while Charlie organised coats, bags, scarves and a bathroom rota.

"I should have called. I didn't mean to barge in."

"You're welcome, whenever."

Had the house not been full of my elderly relatives I might have kissed him. But it was.

He pushed himself off the chair and started to pace.

"About last night . . ." he began.

"Last night?"

"You were seen – at the club." He looked away.

I could feel my temper rising.

"Seen by whom? If there's something I should know, spit it out. If not, don't spy on me."

"I'm just asking you to be careful."

I moved across to where he was staring out at the garden.

"What's Ilford Hypam?"

He looked at me then, his expression cold.

"At the Bistro," I ploughed on, "there were boxes, as if they buy a lot of it."

"Mrs Pierce, Eleanor. This isn't a game, and it's not

healthy to draw attention to yourself. Stay away from the club."

I was wondering which element of this to take issue with first when Lillian made a great show of knocking on the kitchen door. "We're ready, Nick dear, whenever you want to go."

He extended his hand – the truce again.

"Goodnight, Eleanor."

Annoyed as I was, I found myself wishing Lillian had persisted. He hadn't answered her question about the current state of his heart.

CHAPTER TWENTY-SEVEN

"ELEANOR." THE SOUND of that voice echoed in my brain. "Eleanor, Eleanor, Eleanor." I was paying now for having slept in the afternoon. I was tired, it was late and sleep was nowhere close. When I shut my eyes it was Nick's face, serious and thoughtful, that I saw.

"This," I admonished myself, "is infantile."

I took my hot-water bottle into Charlie's room and curled up on his bed. It always soothed me to watch him sleep. I stroked his hair and wondered what he thought about the baby. His diffidence made it hard to know what he was feeling. We had done that to him, Matt and I. When he was small he had no defences. Every emotion went straight to his face. Partly it was a simple matter of grow-ing up, of not wearing his heart on his sleeve. But in some other, deeper way, we had made him careful. He was so anxious not to offend, not to make things worse, that he deemed it safer to keep his feelings to himself, at least where our family situation was concerned. In a real way Tom and Boy had given him back his sense of joy, had allowed him to be a child again. But I knew it would be dangerous to rely on them too heavily. Somewhere, Tom had a life before Cedar Hall. He might well choose to move on to another.

How to strike a balance, to make Charlie feel safe while giving him the freedom to grow away, this was the crucial issue. I thought back to the summer he was nine and off to Scouts for a week-long jamboree. He was sick with excitement and his bag had been packed for a month. It was his first big break from home. I drove him to the pick-up point, confirmed for the umpteenth time that he had money and a phonecard, that he had left nothing behind. The coach was waiting. Charlie jumped out of the car, wriggled into his haversack and staggered on to the bus. It had become terribly important not to be in any way demonstrative in front of his pals. I waited, charting his progress down to the back, ready to wave and leave. His face, when he appeared at the window, crumpled with distress. He hadn't said goodbye. I grabbed hold of a passing scout leader and told him there was something I'd forgotten to give Charlie. He came to the steps, his eyes bright, his lower lip trembling and we went behind the coach. I knelt down, put my arms around him and held him tight for a full minute. Then he kissed me, flashed his cheeky smile and was gone without a backward glance. I was left shaking with relief. It had been a salutary lesson: in trying to get it right I had so nearly got it horribly wrong.

Perhaps the baby would be good for him. It would help to anchor his life with Matt. In that sense, I knew I held the winning hand. Home for Charlie had always been where I was. Nowadays it might be based in a smaller house, without other kids on the street, but our proximity to Cedar Hall and his involvement with my family had more than compensated. And that was before the arrival of Tom. But with Matt there was not much by way of familiarity to build on. Matt knew his routine, but not how or why it had evolved. And he had the added pressure of needing Charlie and Bethany to get on. If either one were to resent the other life would become fraught. I hoped the baby would create a focus for all of them, a new person with no emotional baggage. My last conscious thought was to wish the unknown child a safe journey into life.

I tripped into work with a clear head and a light heart. A constant stream of pensioners kept us going all morning. It was heart-warming to see their determination to back the stand taken by the elders. The date stamp for issuing loans had been set at December 23rd, the day the Blessed Oliver was due to close. Mrs Murray informed Martina in a loud voice that this did not give her the full two weeks to which she was entitled, never mind the extra time traditionally allowed over Christmas. Miss Tuohy abandoned the cataloguing of her new thrillers and romances to investigate the rumpus. With a flourish she set the date to January 10th. Mrs Murray bowed to the queue.

Mr Mulhern appeared, the war medal still on his lapel, and kept up a running commentary from his desk by the heater. He accepted the pensioners' gratitude and admiration as a feudal lord might the homage of his vassals. There was no sign of Mrs Clark. I hoped her grandson had persuaded her to rest at his home for a while.

In the early afternoon Paul and I were working in the office when a worried Miss Tuohy appeared and called me out.

"Your aunt's inside," she said, indicating the kitchen. "She's rather upset."

Lillian was seated at the table, utterly forlorn. Her mascara was streaked and smudged. Her white face, red lips and black eyes gave her the look of a tragic clown. I took her hand.

"What is it, Lillian? What's happened?"

"Oh Eleanor. I've really done it this time." Tears leaked from the sides of her eyes, forming black streams along her cheekbones. I dabbed at her face with a tissue, crooning nonsense all the while. She made a great effort to compose herself.

"Tom has gone. And it's my fault."

She handed me a note, which read: *There are things I must do. Thank you for your kindness. The dog is for the boy. Tom.* The ice of fear washed over me. It was too soon. He couldn't do this now when there had been no time to prepare, when everything was in a state of flux. Oh Charlie, I thought, hoping he'd cope, knowing it would break his heart.

"Try to be calm, darling. Tell me what happened."

Lillian became incoherent in her effort to get the story straight. She repeated herself, contradicted what she had said moments earlier, countered her contradictions. I could get no sense from her. She was inconsolable.

After a while I gave up, made her tea and went for Miss Tuohy, whose presence seemed to calm her.

"Drink your tea, Miss Lord. Don't try to talk. Everything's under control." It was like watching an anaesthetic take hold. Lillian's breathing slowed, an occasional shaky hiccup the only sign of her distress. Miss Tuohy held her hands and coaxed the story from her. She listened, nodding her encouragement from time to time. I stood apart, knowing my anxiety would only make things worse.

Lillian had been spending a lot of time around Tom. Mostly she just chattered away, unconcerned as to whether or not he was listening. She told him about Edith, about having to leave her job in London, about Edward's death and family life at Cedar Hall. It wasn't ordered or sequential, but one way and another she had pretty well told him her life story. She became aware that he paid more attention when she talked about the past, particularly when she spoke of love or loss or missed opportunities.

"I was striking a chord, you see," she told Miss Tuohy. "There was great sadness in the man."

Gradually she was emboldened to ask about him, whether he had family, where he had come from. Initially he ignored her, but as the days went on she could see that while he didn't speak, he was turning things over in his mind. Then, when after many requests he agreed to let her at him with scissors and shaving foam, he told her there was something bad in his life that he needed to put right. More than that he would not say and, to her shame, she forgot about it.

All morning the dog had been howling. When she finally went to investigate she found Boy tied up in the gate-lodge and Tom's note on the table. May and Dorothy were out. Unable to face them, she'd called a taxi and come here. Everyone would be cross and she had nowhere to go.

"Nonsense," said Miss Tuohy firmly. "No one will blame you. Isn't that right, Ellie? Tom is a grown man, Miss Lord. You can't be responsible for his actions."

"But you don't understand. It was my chatter that put it into his head. Mother always said my babbling would land me in trouble one day."

"Sod Mother."

"Language," said Miss Tuohy, but without conviction. "Now, to practicalities. Your sisters will be worried about you. I think Ellie should take you home and you should rest. Then we can alert Ellie's detective and ask him to keep an eye out, make sure Tom's all right."

"Would he do that?" The hope in her eyes was painful to see.

"Of course he will. I'll speak to him myself, but you

really must go home. Perhaps Ellie could call first, let the family know you're safe."

Miss Tuohy was right again, May was frantic. "Thank God," she said, when I told her Lillian was with me. She had come home to no sign of Tom, a frenzied dog and Beattie who informed her that Lillian had gone off in a taxi, clearly upset. Beattie hadn't been quick enough to prevent Lillian's leaving, but she had called Iggie and sent him out on his bicycle to look for her.

"We'll be there in ten minutes," I told her.

A taxi was waiting outside. I kept my arm around Lillian on the way home. Feeling in her handbag for more tissues, I pulled out a bottle of Leotone. She looked at it dully.

"Dr Saul's pick-me-up," she said. "It won't be much use now."

For the first time I noticed how thin and frail she was becoming. I understood the force of May's reaction. She too was watching Lillian. She too had realised that the day might come when she could start to wander. I was devoutly grateful it was not yet here.

We tried to persuade her to lie down, but like the good Catholic she was Lillian insisted on confession. May sat across from her as Miss Tuohy had done. The whole garbled story came out again. May nodded wisely as if she understood. Dorothy sat by her side on the couch, not touching exactly, that wasn't their way, but close enough for Lillian to feel her support. Beattie busied herself pouring tea no one wanted.

"That's fine, Lillian," said May eventually. "It was clever of you to get Eleanor. You should rest now, dear, you look exhausted."

We sat in silence while Beattie took her to her room. We had known from the start that this might happen; we just hadn't known how much we would come to depend on Tom's presence.

"I want you to do something for me," I told them. "I want you to lie. Well, maybe not lie, but be economical with the truth." Charlie was due to go to Matt's in the evening. Assuming the baby did not choose that particular time to be born, Charlie need know nothing of this before Sunday. I could bring Boy to meet him from the train and feed him some line about Tom being busy. It would buy a little time. And apart from anything else, Matt was in no condition to deal with Charlie's grief.

"Yes. I think that would be best," said May. "Though we'd better keep him away from Lillian."

In the event no deceit was necessary. Matt called to say he would collect Charlie directly from school as it was on his way to the hospital.

With the immediate crisis averted, I needed some time alone. I collected Boy and headed for the shore. We walked for miles, scrambling over rocks from beach to beach. It was cold and wet and we had the coast to ourselves. Once the tide turned the rocks would be cut off, but we could go home by road. Daylight faded to grey and on to darkness. With the dog for company I felt no unease. He would run ahead or go off to investigate some rat-hole, but he always came back. When I stopped for a smoke he lay at my feet, ears cocked.

"I don't know, Boy. I don't know where your master is. I just hope he's safe."

We walked on to the mouth of the river. It was early evening and pitch-dark. Some of the dock cranes were already bedecked with fairy lights for Christmas. They looked ludicrously wonderful against the night sky. I went into a dockers' pub and ordered a hot whiskey. It was not the kind of place that welcomed strangers, and fifteen pairs of eyes (one of them the barman's) watched, more or less openly, as we moved to a corner table. Boy rested on his haunches and growled quietly. This seemed to reassure the drinkers, who turned their backs on us and resumed their conversation.

The anonymity of it was glorious. Nobody knew or cared about me, Charlie, Matt, Tom, Cedar Hall or even the Blessed Oliver. We might none of us exist as far as these men were concerned. I leaned back in the seat, sipping my whiskey, and glanced at the old photographs on the wall. Black and white and sepia, they were of Dublin street and dock scenes, some dating from the turn of the century. The one nearest me featured a woman wearing an ankle-length skirt in dark fabric, nipped at the waist and flared at the end, topped by a light-coloured jacket with high collar and wide puffed sleeves. She was walking casually into the path of an oncoming tram, one hand steadying a boater hat trimmed with an extravagant bow. Her face was in shadow, turning away from the tram at an angle to the camera. I wondered who she was and what she was thinking. Was she meeting a lover, going to the dentist or off for a bit of shopping? I looked again at the street, so wide in the absence of traffic, and at the open-topped tram trundling along its metal track. I had been contemplating the scene for several seconds before the advertisement running across the front of the tram sank in: Ilford processing. I knew the name was familiar! Ilford manufactured the paper and chemicals used in photographic darkrooms I had seen it on old photos in Cedar Hall. I lit a cigarette, trying to figure the connection.

Too many things led back to the Blue Bistro. Sylvie had worked there, but the club had disclaimed knowledge of her. She had said something about a man wanting to take her picture, and I'd seen packaging that suggested they bought photographic chemicals in bulk. The police were watching the club and Nick clammed up whenever it was mentioned. There was a locked room upstairs that might conceivably be a darkroom or a studio. And, I thought slowly, there were the subscription specials Mr Ó hUiginn was getting by post.

I whistled under my breath. It was conjecture, but it added up to one hell of a coincidence. If I was right, Will would have good reason to be displeased that I was wandering round his premises uninvited. The man was evil. I had felt it the first time we met.

I would go home and ring Nick. The garda attitude to Sylvie seemed altogether too casual. Auntie Ellie would stir things up.

Although I was no longer aware of being watched, all went quiet when we got up to leave.

"Goodnight," I ventured, more from curiosity than in expectation.

"Goodnight now. Mind how you go." Almost to a man they responded.

I set off to find a taxi with a big, stupid grin on my face, the dog trotting at my heels.

My answering machine was blinking, but I ignored it. I dialled Nick's mobile.

"I think I've figured it out. I think the club is connected to the subscription service you told me about. I also think you've been extremely cavalier about the fact that you haven't traced Sylvie, and what are you going to do about it?"

"Hang on, Eleanor . . ."

"No. Not this time. I wish you'd stop telling me what to do and listen. She's only a kid and she may have wandered into something without realising. It's been weeks, for Christ's sake. She could be dead."

I was steaming myself up to a rage of epic proportions. As I worked on catching my breath I could hear only silence from Nick.

Chapter Twenty-Seven

"Are you calm?" he asked eventually.

"Don't patronise me. No, I am not calm, and a good thing too. It'd be no harm for one of you shower to wake up and worry."

He was silent again. I hoped his conscience was killing him.

"She's safe," he said quietly.

"Who?"

"Sylvie. We found her."

I slumped to the floor.

"Is she all right? Why didn't you tell me?"

"I'm telling you now."

Boy set about hoovering up smells around the cottage. Perhaps I could fool him into thinking he was on holiday. It might be no harm to see how we got on in a confined space.

I went to the bathroom to wash my hands and scalded myself. I looked at the clouds of steam and ran to the back hallway. An enormous, spanking new boiler throbbed in the corner.

Mr Flynn, I thought, I love you. For a day that had been going so badly, things were definitely on the up. I decided against calling him. The sound of my voice might conjure up other catastrophic things-of-it-being.

There was no news at Cedar Hall, other than that Lillian was very subdued and the hapless Iggie had now been dispatched on his bicycle to look for Tom.

"I think Beattie feels bad about mistrusting him," said May. "It's her way of compensating."

When I finally accessed my messages, there was one from Miss Tuohy, saying she had spoken to the police and would be in touch in the morning.

The other was from Nick, telling me that Sylvie was safe. I could stop worrying.

I banged my forehead against the wall.

Ellie

I was in bed by ten o'clock, mentally and physically drained. Boy curled up at my back, his warmth oddly comforting. I'd learned from Miss Tuohy's experience and had not even suggested he sleep anywhere but with me. If only, I thought, I could be this wise about my life . . .

There was something of great significance here but I sank under its weight and slept.

CHAPTER TWENTY-EIGHT

SATURDAY MORNING WAS gloriously sunny and cold. I opened the windows to air the kitchen while I waited for my coffee to percolate. Boy sniffed around the garden, marking his territory.

I turned on the local radio news. ". . . in connection with the death of Proinsias Ó hUiginn, well-known political activist and librarian of the Blessed Oliver Plunkett municipal library. Further arrests are expected." I zipped through the other stations but heard nothing more. I tried calling Miss Tuohy but there was no answer; she had probably left for work. I would take a shot of caffeine then run down to the newsagent's for the papers.

I found Nick on my doorstep with the milk. For a split second I saw myself through his eyes – hair like cobwebs, outsized striped pyjamas and boat-like Mickey Mouse slippers missing an ear.

"Ah, no."

"Good morning to you too, Eleanor."

He picked up the bottles and followed me to the kitchen where he laid the Irish papers on the table.

"I thought you'd want to see these."

The story was front-page news in *The Star*: "LIBRARIANS' LURID LOVE LIFE" went the caption over a photo of Mr Ó hUiginn shaking his fist during a demonstration. The *Times* and *Independent* announced soberly that two men had been charged at a special court sitting the previous evening and that further arrests were expected over the coming days. *The Star* showed no such restraint. "RANDY ROMP GOES WRONG" went the headline on the inside page over a story speculating on my boss's secret sex life.

"Is Will from the Bistro involved?"

"You were right about the darkroom, but there's nothing illegal in processing pornographic pictures. We can't touch him on that unless we find evidence that the photos involved children or bestiality, and so far there's nothing. Still," he added, looking pleased with himself, "he's left us plenty of scope for putting him away."

"And Sylvie?"

"We were reasonably sure she had nothing to do with your boss's death. Will runs a tight ship. He's clever and he's careful. It was unlikely that any of his girls would risk wandering into the librarian's place of work in broad daylight. There are strict rules about fraternising with clients outside of paying sessions. In truth, they weren't related, but I imagine Ó hUiginn was like an uncle to her."

I poured the coffee and brought it to the table, almost tripping over Boy who had curled up on Nick's foot.

"Her boyfriend is a junkie," he went on. "They met when he was working in France. I don't think she knew how bad his habit was until he lost his job. He came back here and she followed. His parents did what they could, but there was no reaching him. Eventually, they were advised to throw him out – he'd been at all the classic stuff, stealing, lying, threatening the mother. The lad took to the streets, and that's where your boss came across him and, in time, Sylvie – through his work with kids living rough. Sylvie was trying to get the boyfriend into rehab, but every time she caught up with him he moved on."

He eased his foot out from under the dog and massaged his ankle. Boy fixed him with a reproachful eye, stood up, turned, and settled on his other foot, facing away.

"I think you've hurt his feelings."

"I think he's cut off my circulation. Anyway, do you remember the phone call you told me about – when you heard shouting from the office? That made me think. From what she said to you, Sylvie had already mentioned that she was in line for a job at the Blue Bistro. Ó hUiginn would have been freaked by that. I think he was probably fond of her, he was genuinely trying to help, and the last thing he'd have wanted would have been any association between Sylvie and Will. Waitressing is one thing, but your boss was well aware of the club's other activities, and Sylvie is – as you said – something of an innocent, extremely beautiful, and would have been desperate for extra cash to fund the boyfriend's treatment. Ó hUiginn wasn't about to stand by while Will offered her a 'modelling' break."

"Are you saying Will had him killed so Sylvie would work for him?"

Nick smiled. "No, that's not what I'm saying at all. His death was an accident, all pretty much as we suspected. Will's woman pulled too hard on the dog leash, panicked and rang for back-up. The business with Sylvie was just weird coincidence."

"Why did she disappear then?"

"She was still trying to cope with the boyfriend. And she was scared. When she saw you and his family at the funeral, she realised her mistake in claiming he was her uncle. She also knew that, given the circumstances of his death, it was a fair bet we'd want to talk to her. Her instinct was to hide – it was that simple."

"Poor kid."

"As you say. Anyway, she's gone home to France, and I don't think she'll be back."

"And the boyfriend?"

He shrugged. "I think she's finally understood that you can't help people who don't want to be helped."

"I still don't see how Will is involved if he wasn't physically present in the library that night."

"Will runs a stable of men and women who offer 'specialised' services that link in with the subscription photos. Appointments are arranged by mobile phone, so neither punters nor hookers need to come to the club – one of Will's men collects his cut and brings it to the Blue Bistro where it gets slipped in with the club's takings. All of this has been known for some time. The problem, from our point of view, was finding a way to catch him out. As I say, he's meticulous and clever."

"I'm with you so far."

"Right, well given the degree of efficiency in covering up your librarian's death, we were pretty confident it had to be down to one of two big operators, who between them have organised-prostitution sewn up in the city. A unit involving detectives from the National Bureau of Criminal Investigation as well as the Bridewell and Harcourt Terrace had been working on them for months. Through its contacts we managed to establish that Ó hUiginn had been with a woman called Rosie on the night of his death. She didn't set out to kill him, but the unintentional taking of a life is a crime, and anyone who assists in the preparation or aftermath of that crime is also answerable in law. It was Will who sent her to Ó hUiginn and Will who took her call and organised some lads to cover up what had happened. Either way, we'll get him."

As soon as Nick left, I called Miss Tuohy at the library.

"Have you seen *The Star*?"

Martina took the phone from her.

"I always said he was a slimeball. On your knees for a quick decade of the rosary and whatever else comes to mind."

In the background I could hear Miss Tuohy say, "That will do, thank you." She retrieved the phone and sighed. "It's a sad business. His poor family." She was quiet for a moment, then asked after Lillian. "I spoke to Garda Murphy about Tom. He promised to look into it and let us know if anything turned up."

I was trying to psyche myself up to doing a Seaview on the house when May called.

"He's on his way."

"Who, Tom?" I looked at Boy. We could never be that lucky.

"George. He's just called from Heathrow. They're getting the next flight over."

It must have been ten years since I'd seen him. Oddly, it had never occurred to me that he might involve himself in Cedar Hall. I felt no connection to him at all—my brother.

"Would you like me to meet them?"

"Would you, Eleanor? It'd give me time to organise food and sheets and so on." She sounded nervous and excited. "You'd need to leave now."

I set off in the Mini, Boy in the passenger seat by my side. I wondered what George was like. He would be in his early fifties now, had been barely eighteen when he left home.

I'd never known the exact circumstances of his departure. I had assumed he was fleeing Edith's curse, unwilling to take his male chances in this family of women. But perhaps there had been more to it than that.

He was gentle as a boy, patient and protective. It was he who taught me to swim, giving me a love and respect for the sea that I carried to this day. He had a tree house in one of the old cedars. More than anything, I longed to be allowed up but it was considered too dangerous. For my fifth birthday he helped Edward build a smaller version on the low-lying branches of another tree. They managed to keep it a secret, and I remember being led out, blindfolded, to my very own tree house with its rope ladder. I knew I should be thrilled. I was, instead, obscurely disappointed: in making it safe they had defeated my purpose. I spent many hours playing there, but with an eye to George's domain magnificently beyond my reach. To scale that height became my first conscious aspiration. By the time I did, death and desertion had rendered my achievement meaningless. The tree houses were left to disintegrate until May, worried that they might collapse, had Iggie dismantle them altogether.

One part of his life from which I was excluded was his Hornby train set, built up for him over the years by Edward. They would spend hours closeted in George's room, buffing the tracks, oiling the locomotives, burnishing the carriages and constructing outbuildings and scenery from cardboard. The track was fixed on an enormous plywood sheet and sported bridges, signals, level crossings, even an aqueduct, everything to minute scale. Occasionally they would let me watch as they set their trains in motion from various stations, but I was never allowed operate the controls. It was many years after they had gone that I understood the importance of this bonding, of their need to have something exclusively male in their lives. I set it up again as soon as Charlie was old enough to appreciate it, and ran my own train as a form of revenge.

Chapter Twenty-Eight

I parked in the chaos of the airport and left Boy to mind the car. A TV monitor recorded the arrival of a Heathrow flight moments earlier. I thought about paging George and decided against it. I wanted a chance to study him before he saw me. Twenty minutes later, with the last London passengers straggling out, I wondered whether this had been wise. I was about to check on the next flight when I saw what could only be Them.

A tallish, heavy-set man with thinning hair was scanning the faces at the barrier, walking slightly ahead of a statuesque woman a good head taller than he. Her every limb and lobe was laden with gold jewellery as if she were trying to reduce her height by force, weighting her body groundwards. Her clothes were beautifully tailored and designed to flatter the fuller figure. I groaned inwardly. Her size and ornamentation confirmed my worst fears of a Loud American. George looked past me, then back again in wondering recognition.

"Eleanor? Is it you?" He hurried over, followed more slowly by his wife. When he reached me he pulled up short, like a horse refusing a fence, unsure of what was appropriate.

"Hello, George." I stepped towards him and shook his hand, feeling suddenly shy. Merry Lou moved to his side. In a moment she would yell "Hiya, honey" and clasp me to her bosom. George ran his fingers through his hair and introduced us.

"It's lovely to meet you at last," she said, in a voice so low I had to strain to hear her. She smiled the smile of the photograph and it was I who felt an impulse to throw my arms around her.

George wanted us to drive through the city centre as this was Merry Lou's first visit.

"But I thought you met May . . ."

"She came to London, to a hotel the family is thinking

231

of buying into," said George. "It was a real treat to be able to look after her for a few days."

Hmm, I thought. Our eyes met in the rear-view mirror and he turned quickly to point out Trinity College to his wife, who sat enraptured in the front seat. She wound down her window to let the dog get some air. Boy parked his muzzle on her shoulder and sniffed greedily. I made to swipe him away but she stayed my hand. "It's fine, really." She had hardly said two words and already I liked her.

Dublin sparkled in the sunshine like an elderly ingénue. The newly restored government buildings on Merrion Street held smug, elegant watch over vistas of Georgian architecture. The still waters of the canal reflected in sedate, painterly fashion the trees that lined their banks. Traffic was moving and even pedestrians seemed cheerful. A traffic warden touched his cap politely to women laden down with shopping or children. Merry Lou drank it all in.

"What do you think, Hon?" George looked anxiously at his wife, who shook her head slowly. "Was it worth the wait?"

She smiled as if he had given her a gift.

"I never imagined it so beautiful. You're lucky, Eleanor, to live with this."

"It's not all beautiful, believe me."

"Even so," she replied quietly, resuming her contemplation of the streetscape. "Even so."

The sea, when we came to it, was a shade of blue it had no business being in December. A tanker and two ferries puttered whitely along the horizon. A lone rider galloped along the water's edge, spray flying from her horse's hooves. Merry Lou and Boy kept their faces at the window, breathing in the salt air. She reached back and took hold of George's hand. His eyes again glanced off mine in the mirror, proud and proprietorial.

Chapter Twenty-Eight

When we turned in at the gates of Cedar Hall, Merry Lou, up to now placid of gesture, clutched her chest. I braked, worried she might be having a heart attack. She had turned very pale.

"Are you all right?"

She nodded mutely.

"We'll walk from here if that's okay," said George.

Merry Lou hauled herself out of the Mini and held the seat up for him. Boy jumped out and hopped back in beside me. I drove on, leaving them to their moment. If Cedar Hall's destiny had to be relinquished, it might as well be to someone whose heart lurched at her first sight of the house.

Lillian ran out on hearing the car. She looked like a nun in her grey wool frock buttoned at neck and wrists and reaching almost to her ankles. It was her penitential gear, worn only when something lay heavily on her conscience. That she had on neither make-up nor jewellery was an equally damning pointer to her state of mind. She looked tired and pale. I went to kiss her and saw she was trying to contain her excitement, as if she had no right to it. She glanced at me, uncertain.

"Did they not come?"

I took her arm. "Let's meet them halfway."

It was, as I told Michael later on the phone, a surprisingly painless reunion. Merry Lou had deflected attention to George, quietly letting us know that she was happy just to be here. She was especially nice to Lillian and I wondered whether this was down to her skill at reading people or whether George had briefed her. Either way, Lillian responded to her warmth, and by the time lunch was over she was almost back to herself. May brought Merry Lou on a tour of the house, Lillian glued to her side as she had formerly been to Tom's. It took a while to sort out which keys belonged to which rooms, but they made it eventually. Merry Lou was knowledgeable about old buildings and obviously enchanted by this one. May basked in her approval. Merry Lou then asked Dorothy to bring herself and George around the gardens.

"She's rather likeable, don't you think?" said May.

Definitely the woman had something. Neither May nor Dorothy succumbed easily to charm. It was a kind of charisma that emanated from her quietness, from the size and solidity of her. She was nothing like what any of us had imagined. I felt a bit ashamed of the way I'd prejudged her.

I was calling Michael in the hope that he would let me hijack his VCR for an hour in the evening. Garda Murphy was sending a video round to Miss Tuohy's, but neither she nor I had a machine to play the thing on. I was banking on the fact that Michael was rarely home on Saturday nights and we could view the tape without disturbing him.

"Come to supper," was his response.

"You're having people in?"

"You. I'm having you to supper."

"You're not going out?"

"Ellie, let me put this simply, then you can stop fishing. Anto and I are no longer an item. I'm fed up, I'm bored. I do not feel up to launching myself into a club and I'd enjoy the company. Now, are you coming or not?"

I wanted to say that Miss Tuohy was a bit . . . What was the word anyway: innocent? other-worldly? old-fashioned? It wasn't Michael's being gay that I thought might bother her, it was the fact that she might not be casual about accepting the hospitality of strangers. And I knew from experience that Michael could be camp, caustic and hurtful when he himself was hurt. Then I thought: the hell with it. I was becoming seriously adept at underestimating people.

"Okay, thanks. I'm sure Miss Tuohy would love to. And Michael?"

"Uh-huh."

"I'm sorry about Anto."

"So am I," he sounded grim as he hung up.

Miss Tuohy collected me from Cedar Hall just after seven. May was annoyed that I should consider going out, thus forfeiting precious time with my brother. I thought it wise to pace myself – all this togetherness could wear thin. I had spent the afternoon with them and had agreed to meet for Sunday lunch at a restaurant in town (George's treat). Enough was sufficient.

I wasn't sure how I felt about George. There was something missing, some quality in him that was unfinished. Perhaps he was shy. Perhaps he felt guilty. Even allowing for the circumstances there was a nervousness to him that was unsettling. He tended not to look you in the eye. The ambivalence of my feelings towards him seemed all the more treacherous in view of my admiration for his wife, whom I knew not at all. Either she was very clever or she had a real gift with people. Nothing specific had been said about the plans for Cedar Hall, but it was clear that May and Dorothy had taken to Merry Lou.

The videotape lay on the Fiesta's back seat. Miss Tuohy checked on it every time we turned a corner. She caught my eye and smiled.

"I've never used one before."

"This could be the start of your brave new world, Miss Tuohy. After this evening, your life may be consumed by nightly movies, pop promos, serials from the BBC. The possibilities are limitless."

"Perhaps," but she didn't sound convinced.

"One of these days," I told her, "I'm going to have to stop gallivanting, stay in and cook like a normal person. I seem to have been out every night for a month."

"Unusual times," she observed mildly.

We drew up at Michael's building, an old granite granary on the docks. Michael occupied half the top floor, the other half being leased to various companies requiring a home from home for visiting executives, film stars on location and the like. There was always the chance that you would meet some famous individual on the stairs, there being no lift. To date I had passed nothing more memorable than men in expensive suits, but I lived in hope. I preceded Miss Tuohy up the flights of stone steps with their carved oak handrail. Fortunately she was fit from walking the hounds. The first time I brought Liz to visit Michael she had stopped every few seconds to ask how much further she had to go – this from an estate agent who knew better than most the location of a penthouse.

Michael was waiting at the top. He wore a floor-length lavender kaftan bought on holiday in Egypt, and his feet were bare. He brushed my cheeks like a French person or someone involved with theatre: mwa, mwa, mwa. I found this irritating, never knowing how many feathery kisses were in store. It made me feel like a turkey, sticking my neck out to left and right, invariably caught at an angle when Michael decided he'd had enough. Moving on at last, he raised Miss Tuohy's hand to his lips.

"A great honour," he said.

If Miss Tuohy was taken aback she gave no sign.

"It's kind of you to accommodate us."

The apartment was at the opposite end of the spectrum to Miss Tuohy's snug home. Other than offering shelter it couldn't be considered at all in relation to my cottage. The drawing room was spacious, high-ceilinged and walled on three sides. The fourth, the side overlooking the river, consisted almost entirely of glass. Large abstract canvases provided colour in a room that was designed to be neutral. Low, flattering light emanated from recessed spots in the ceiling and lamps with delicate shades. The floors were of polished wood, the furniture mostly glass and chrome with the odd antique cabinet thrown in for good measure. Off-white upholstery on the sofa and chairs blended with the decor of the walls. It was tasteful, expensive and curiously impersonal. I envied Michael the views, which were particularly stunning at night, but beyond that his penthouse left me cold. Even the lilies in their sleek Finnish vases were somehow too perfect.

Miss Tuohy and I looked down on the river while Michael made drinks. I thought about Mr Dixon and his love of life on the water – there must be immense freedom in gliding past buildings like these, seeing them merge into the anonymity of the city you were leaving behind.

Miss Tuohy had placed her tape on the glass table. Michael glanced at it as he handed her a schooner of sherry.

"Do you need to see that straight away or can we eat first?"

She assured him that would be fine and complimented him on his apartment. Michael beamed and offered to show her around. He couldn't resist giving the Grand Tour, as he called it. They would be gone for ages. He'd take her inch by inch through every room with its concomitant design/building challenges and details of the wars he had waged over eighteen months with three sets of builders. He never tired of telling the story, never doubted it was as fascinating to every dog in the street as it was to him.

The windows framed the river like an enormous animated painting. The black water was calm, a slight ripple causing reflected street lights to shimmer. There was no activity at this time of night. On the far bank cargo containers stood empty, waiting to be loaded and hitched up to cabs for their short journey to Dublin Port. Beyond them a semicircle of lights ran out to the far side of the bay. The lights of the city itself and the mountains could be seen only by hanging out of the window at a ninety-degree angle.

Miss Tuohy returned from her tour, slightly dazed, and sipped sherry while Michael saw to our supper.

We sat down to Michael's incomparable cheese soufflé and salad. The video, Miss Tuohy told us, was of a British television documentary on missing persons. It had been recorded by "a friend in the gardaí" who took a personal interest in such matters and had built up quite a library of material over the years. He had suggested we view the tape and call him if anything struck us as significant.

"And how about that symbol of moral rectitude, the bold Proinsias?" said Michael brightly. "Quite a coup for the police. They had four in custody at the last count."

Miss Tuohy shook her head, distressed.

"But if he wasn't murdered, where's the crime? What are they being charged with?"

"If you go dragging a punter round the room by a dog leash attached to a choke chain, you need to be a small bit careful not to disregard potential dangers like asphyxiation or heart failure. What we have here is serious assault and/or unintentional killing or manslaughter. On top of that we're looking at concealing an offence and failure to report a death. And," he paused for emphasis, "there's the Sexual Offences Act of 1993 under which the organisation of prostitution is a criminal offence. Ó hUiginn committed no crime in paying for sex, the prostitute committed none in providing it – they were, after all, consenting adults and he wasn't importuning women on the street. But the upstanding citizen who provided this lady for our friend's gratification and subsequently helped clean up after her exertions can be made answerable in law for the crimes committed."

"A pimp," remarked Miss Tuohy.

Michael looked at her. "Effectively, yes. And when, within an organised network, one is charged the whole edifice starts to crumble. One girl talks, then another, maybe a rent boy and before you know it the cells are filling up with males of dubious virtue and expensive habits whose Mammies are unaware that they live off the immoral earnings of decent working girls."

He reckoned the fallout would be horrendous and ongoing.

"I'd say a fair few burghers are shaking in their rubber gear tonight," he was saying when the doorbell rang.

"Bollocks! I beg your pardon, Agnes." Agnes! On his way to the intercom he hissed, "If that's You Know Who, up he is most certainly not coming."

Within seconds he was back, his face stricken.

"It's dreadful Aunt Bea. Stall her. Try to keep her out."

He rushed off in the direction of his room. Miss Tuohy peered after him. "Never a dull moment."

"So, do I let her in, this Dreadful Bea, or not?"

"I think it might be best if you did, dear."

We sat there, our food forgotten, until a hammering at the door announced Dreadful Aunt Bea's arrival. I opened up, a smile nailed to my face, but she was past me and ensconced in the drawing room before I had managed hello.

"Who are you? Where's that nephew of mine? Who's that woman in there?"

"These are my friends, Auntie. Say hello to Agnes and Ellie."

Michael sailed in, suave and elegant in navy suit, white shirt, socks and shoes. Miss Tuohy didn't blink. "Ladies, my Aunt Beatrice. Why on earth didn't you let me know you were coming? How did you find me?" he added, a mite sharply.

"Your mother sent things for you. They're in the car. Batty had to come up to the Mater for tests." She turned to stare at me. "So you're the one I've been hearing about."

With her sharp nose and beady eyes she looked for all

the world like a ferret. Batty Bea and Boozy Bat – Michael's father's sister and her husband. Michael's mother wouldn't hear a word against them, but the vibes when either was mentioned were unmistakable. Batty was said not to have been sober in living memory and Bea spent every waking hour plotting for her son Jamie to inherit her other brother's farm.

"I don't suppose you've time for a drink," said Michael hopefully.

"Vodka. Just a splash of tonic. You can help Jamie with the parcels."

He wanted to kill her. It was written all over his face. Instead, he went meekly to fetch her drink, then down to his waiting cousin.

"Fancy, this," she remarked, small eyes darting over everything. "Not cheap, I'd imagine, and all that polishing. Still, each to his own. You're the girlfriend, then?" As she had her back to me, examining one of the paintings, it took a moment for this to register.

"Hmm."

"Have you a long drive ahead, Mrs, Mrs . . .?" enquired Miss Tuohy.

"Brophy. An hour and a half, less if the traffic's good. And you, Agnes, was it?"

"Nothing like that, thank heaven."

We envisaged the long road to the midlands and fervently wished her on it. I could see another approach to the girlfriend question forming in her brain.

"I'll just give Michael a hand."

"Nonsense. He can manage."

"Still . . ." I fled, praying Miss Tuohy would forgive me.

Dreadful Aunt Bea stayed for an hour. Michael was in agony. Jamie sulked when she refused a drink on his behalf.

"You have to drive, pet," she reminded him.

She regarded Michael, nose twitching. She considered me. Short of downright rudeness she could not persist in asking about our relationship. This didn't stop her speculating. Miss Tuohy threw in the odd comment about Michael-and-Ellie this, Ellie-and-Michael the other, and Dreadful Aunt Bea had to concede defeat, though her suspicions continued to lance through the air.

"You," said Michael when he had seen his aunt safely out of the building, "are a good woman, Agnes. May you reap your reward in the next world. I'll *kill* Ma for giving her my address."

He set up the VCR and went to phone his mother.

CHAPTER TWENTY-NINE

THE TAPED PROGRAMME was in three parts. Each section opened with a voiced-over biographical note on the missing person, showing photographs of happier days, family celebrations, an occasional clip from a home movie. Then family and friends were interviewed, each in his or her way begging for news of a loved one. It was emotionally charged and difficult to watch. As part three opened I felt Miss Tuohy stiffen. We stared at the blurred photograph of a large, smiling man in a tuxedo. It was followed by grainy footage of the man rolling down a hill, an Irish setter snapping frantically at his heels. When they reached the bottom the dog sat on his chest, pinning him to the ground. The man was convulsed with eerily silent laughter.

"Michael! Michael, come quick."

He stuck his head around the door, still glued to the phone.

"Can you freeze that image?"

"Hang on, Ma. Domestic crisis."

He showed us how to work the remote control and went back to upbraiding his mother.

We rewound to the start of part three and froze the photo. The blurring was accentuated in the still. We played on to the end of the hill sequence and froze that. Miss Tuohy gasped. Lying on his back, laughing up at the camera was Tom, younger, leaner, happy, but undeniably Tom. It felt obscene to be staring into that face, knowing how it had altered.

I poured another sherry for Miss Tuohy and a stiff gin for myself.

"Right, let's be calm. We need to take this in."

We sat through the presentation on Tom's life, his family, the people he'd left behind and his reasons for going. At some point Michael came back into the room. Sensing the atmosphere he sat on the arm of my chair, saying not a word.

When it ended I looked at Miss Tuohy. Her eyes were very bright but a lifetime of exercising control stood to her now.

"Is anyone going to tell me . . .?" asked Michael.

"It's a person of whom we've grown fond," began Miss Tuohy. She went back to the start, to the days when Tom used come to the Blessed Oliver to get warm. She spoke of finding him battered on the library steps and of all that had happened since. "It seems he was involved in an accident where an elderly cyclist was killed. Tom couldn't live with the guilt and disappeared. The cyclist's daughter made a televised appeal for him to come home. She said her father was an accident waiting to happen. He was careless and his hearing wasn't good. His family blame themselves, not Tom. They should have taken his bike away, should have insisted the father wasn't fit to be out alone, but they knew it would deprive him of his last vestige of independence and they backed down. Poor Tom. Poor, gentle Tom."

I started to sniffle. Michael produced a box of tissues, held one to my nose and told me to blow.

"Are you all right, Agnes?"

"Thank you, Michael, I'm fine. Do we know how long ago this was made?"

He rewound the closing credits.

"Two years, though with transmission delays it might be a bit longer."

"I'd better call our policeman, Ellie. It was clever of him to make the connection." She turned to Michael: "He didn't know Tom all that well. And he'd never seen him clean-shaven."

"Whose policeman?"

"I feel like a whale," I said, getting to my feet. "I'm going to wash my face."

"Tears finished, do we think?"

I kissed the top of his head and went to the bathroom.

I sat in Michael's black en suite feeling bleak and drained. Tom had paid such a dreadful price for an accident that wasn't his fault. Other people set out to maim and murder and slept easy in their beds. Why was the world so evil? Why was life so unfair? I gathered up all the bad things in my own life and wallowed in them. My marriage was over, my son was growing up and away, my home was about to be turned into a tourist attraction for rich Americans, I was going to lose my job, I was a disaster and my husband was having a baby. The baby! I had hardly thought of Bethany all day. Suppose it had been born? Suppose Charlie were trying to find me, or worse, had been left back to an empty cottage by his distracted father?

I ran out to the hall and dialled the maternity hospital. No messing with this are-you-a-relative business. No ditty warbling "Thank Heaven for Little Girls". My call was transferred immediately and Matt answered the phone.

"It's me, Ellie. I just wanted to know how Bethany is."

There was a long pause. Disaster flashed through my brain.

"Matt? Are you there?"

"I'm . . . We're just so touched that you should call. We have a little girl. Seven pounds three ounces. They're both fine."

I know he continued to talk, I got the bit about Charlie being there with them and was that okay, only he was thinking of doing medicine and Matt felt there was no time like the present and thank you for caring . . .

I hung up, fresh tears starting up even as Michael opened the door to Detective Sergeant Nick.

Michael settled me on the sofa, the tissues by my side, a waste-paper basket thoughtfully positioned at my feet.

"Early menopause," he mouthed to the others. I kicked his ankle and was gratified at the shock and pain on his face.

"Fuck off, Michael."

Miss Tuohy inhaled but said nothing.

Nick sat with the calm gaze of one to whom all will become clear. Eventually.

I got up and moved out of his eyeline. I had assumed the tape belonged to Garda Murphy. It seemed appropriate that my day should end as it had begun, with Nick finding me a complete mess. Only now I had the added distinction of red eyes in a bloated, snuffling face.

Miss Tuohy told Nick what we had seen. Michael crept back to my side, rubbing his ankle and my neck simultaneously. He went to blow my nose again, but I took the tissue with as much dignity as I could muster and did it myself.

"Good girl," said he, as if I were a toddler.

I sat back in my chair, defeated. I had behaved badly, I was behaving badly, I would probably continue to behave badly as long as I lived. I sensed that Michael was barely listening to Miss Tuohy. He was scrutinising Nick, assessing him.

No, I thought. No. No. No. That would be too much.

With a great effort I managed not to start bawling again. I went back to the bathroom and this time I stripped and took a shower. I stayed there for quite a while, hoping that Nick at least would have left by the time I came out.

I found Michael alone in the drawing room.

"Feeling better?"

I nodded. "The others have gone, then? Did he say anything?"

"The detective? No. Just that he had to go, he'd someone waiting in his car. I promised Agnes I'd get you home safely. She was exhausted."

"Poor Miss Tuohy."

"Poor Ellie," he stroked my hair. "Been through the wars a bit, what with one thing and another."

CHAPTER THIRTY

THE VICE STORY was front-page news in all the Sunday papers. The assistant commissioner in charge of the Dublin region was jubilant. Arrests to date, he was quoted as saying, were down to painstaking police work over a twelve-month period, and a tribute to all officers involved. Criminals who lived off immoral earnings could expect the full rigour of the law to be applied. The city would be a better, safer place with this network disbanded.

Matt phoned to say Charlie had spent most of the previous day at the hospital and he felt a second day would be too much. Could he drop him off on his way to see Bethany?

I went back to the papers, but couldn't concentrate. I was going to have to tell Charlie about Tom. At least now there was something to say. I made fresh coffee and practised on Boy who was lying at my feet. Keep it simple, I told myself. Be truthful. Don't speculate and don't elaborate. I wandered round the kitchen, gathering up papers and exercise books, putting bills to one side. The place was filthy. I tried to remember when I had last cleaned properly and could not. There wasn't much point in starting now, with George's lunch looming.

I called Cedar Hall. May said she would expect myself and Charlie around midday. The table was booked for one-thirty. If I would take George and Merry Lou in the Mini, she'd order a taxi for herself and the aunts.

I was putting Liz's wine into the press when I found the cosmetics she had bought for Lillian. Thoughtful, generous Liz: if ever Lillian could do with a lift this was the time. I left the bag out in the hall where I'd be less likely to forget it again.

I was in the bathroom dealing with my face when the bell rang. My eyes looked a bit strange from the previous night's trauma, but otherwise I would pass.

Matt stood on the doorstep, his arm around Charlie.

"Hi, Mum." Charlie moved across and leaned into me, facing his father, in a gesture of solidarity.

"Congratulations, Matt. You must be relieved."

"It was nice of you to call. It meant a lot."

We were awkward, not knowing what to say.

"I wish you well. You know that."

He nodded and touched Charlie's hand in mine. We stood there, my son and I, as his father walked away to spend his first full day with his new family.

Charlie knew something was wrong the moment he saw Boy.

"Where's Tom? What's happened?"

I made him sit and hear me out. His eyes were worried, his face pinched, but he didn't cry. He stroked the dog's ears obsessively.

"What about Boy? Will you send him to the dogs' home?"

"Tom wanted you to mind him."

"But we can't keep a dog. You're always saying so."

"I don't think we could manage a puppy, but Boy has more sense. As long as he doesn't get too lonely."

"You mean I can keep him?" His eyes widened with hope and disbelief.

I nodded.

"Really?"

"Really."

He got down on his knees and put his arms around the mongrel's neck. "It's you and me now, Boy, till Tom gets back."

On the way to Cedar Hall I told him about Lillian and how badly she felt.

"The thing is, Charlie, you're probably the only person who can get through to her. She knows you're Tom's friend. Will you talk to her?"

He nodded, feeling important. It struck me that Tom was both wise and kind. In leaving the dog he had given Charlie a lifeline. Charlie sat very straight, his head high, empowered by the responsibility of ownership.

Dorothy and Lillian were in the sitting room when we arrived. George and Merry Lou were still upstairs, May outside somewhere. Lillian was wearing the navy suit she had on the day Boots came to lunch. She clasped her hands nervously when Charlie came in.

"I've something for you, Lillian," he said, waving the Brown Thomas bag. "Can we go upstairs?"

"What about me?" said Dorothy, looking up from *The Sunday Times*. "Don't I get anything?"

He came back and kissed her forehead, then followed Lillian from the room. Dorothy raised her eyebrows. I crossed my fingers.

"Ah," she said.

"So, how did you get on last night?"

They'd had a wonderful time, apparently. Merry Lou had a fine singing voice and played a mean hand at poker.

"I like her," said Dorothy. "I'd be inclined to trust her to do things properly."

I told her about Matt's baby. I wanted her to brief May and Lillian so there'd be no awkwardness if Charlie brought it up. "He needs to know that we can all deal with this as part of his life."

"Yes." She took my hand. "I think that's the right thing, Eleanor."

I wandered into the garden and down to the shore. I stood on the jetty and thought about Boots and new beginnings. I hoped he was happy. I hoped the woman he was seeing was good for him and would bring laughter back to his life.

I hadn't been this free for years. I had resolved my first love into something warm and positive that I could cherish without regret. There was relief too in facing up to the end of my marriage. I had my child. I loved him more than life itself. With that as my anchor it was time to move on.

"Eleanor?"

I turned to find May at my side. I hadn't realised she could still manage the path, the gradient was so steep. Sheepishly, she produced a walking stick and pointed to her strapped ankle.

"Just until the swelling goes down."

She leaned on my shoulder. We watched the car ferry churn its way towards Holyhead. On the rocks a single heron perched on skinny legs. Rain clouds were massing, gulls screaming landwards.

"We are lucky, darling, to have had the use of all this."

"Oh yes. So lucky. In so many ways." We stared out to sea, peaceful together. "If I can give Charlie a quarter of what you've given me I'll be happy." May looked at me, questioning. "Love, beauty, space. Especially space. And I don't just mean this."

Gently, she touched my face.

"I know about Matt's child. Are you all right?"

"No. But I will be. I'm going to be fine."

The restaurant was French, pretentious, expensive and served "high" food. We spent ages reading the menu. Each dish was described in loving detail, down to the vegetables and garnish that would accompany it. The food on the plate bore little resemblance to its eulogy on the menu. Lillian prodded at her circular tower of beef in search of the baby spinach she'd been promised.

"I see it! Look, Lillian. There's a green thing sticking out underneath," cried Charlie, thrilled at his discovery.

With careful poking Lillian managed to extract a single leaf from the bottom of her foodpile. "It's more like a foetus," she said. There was a moment's silence, followed by a strange rumbling sound. Merry Lou was laughing. She threw back her head and rocked with delight. Even George, unsure whether we were mocking his choice of restaurant, giggled. People at adjoining tables stared disapprovingly while Lillian smiled uncertainly.

She and Charlie had talked for a long time. He had persuaded her to change the suit for her party frock and helped her choose her brightest jewellery to set it off. She had experimented with Liz's make-up and topped the lot with her bird-of-paradise hat. They had come downstairs hand on arm like characters from *Gone with the Wind*, and Charlie had formally announced her entry to the sitting room.

"Ladies and gentleman," he'd said, "I give you the beautiful Miss Lillian Lord."

The look on her face defied description. I felt weak with pride. We all loved Lillian, we had each of us tried to help, but it was Charlie who'd brought her back to herself.

George broached the subject of Cedar Hall. He and Merry Lou were keen to go ahead with the conversion. In the first instance their architect would need to survey the house. Everything that happened thereafter would be subject to our agreement and confirmed in writing. Though it was George who spoke, the thinking was obviously Merry Lou's. Her discretion was impressive, she wouldn't undermine him in front of his family by implying that she was the boss.

"The gate-lodge could be extended," continued George. "It could be let as a separate unit or turned into staff accommodation."

"What about Tom? That's Tom's house." Charlie was shaking with anger.

"Absolutely," interjected Merry Lou. "It can't be touched unless your friend has another house to live in. Nothing is going to happen until you've had a chance to talk to him. Okay?"

"Promise?"

Merry Lou considered him. "Tell you what," she reached for a napkin and fished a fountain pen from her bag, "we'll give it to you in writing, right now, signed and witnessed."

The waiter glowered as she uncapped her pen and wrote on the linen. "Thees ees not papeur," he remarked in his best take on a French accent.

She didn't even look up. "Don't worry, we'll pay. Could you wait a moment?" She signed the napkin with a flourish.

"George too." Charlie was adamant.

George signed. The scowling waiter hovered.

"Could you witness these signatures? I'd be happy to remunerate you for the inconvenience."

He signed, returned the pen and palmed his cash in one fluid movement.

Charlie was in bed, with Boy draped across his feet like a throw. I lay down beside them.

"Tell me about the baby."

"Well," he paused, looking for the right words, "she's red. And wrinkled. And she has hair on her back. She's quite ugly, really. Maybe she'll improve."

"All babies are like that to start with. Give her a week."

"If she's my half-sister and I'm her half-brother, what are you?"

"To the baby? Nothing. I'm no relation."

"I thought you might be her half-mother, or mother once removed or something."

I had to smile. "Get some sleep. School tomorrow." I got up and turned out the light.

"Mum? Do you think I could see that tape, the one about Tom?"

"I'll see what I can do."

Nick's card was tacked to the kitchen noticeboard. I looked at the phone. All I had to do was lift the handset and punch in the numbers. No big deal, except that I was embarrassed and still a bit raw. I closed my eyes and counted to ten. I called the mobile number first. He answered on the second ring.

"Yes?"

"Nick?"

"Yes?" He sounded impatient.

"It's Ellie, Eleanor Pierce." I felt suddenly cold, pointless as a slug. I saw myself inching along the ground, my life on my back, leaving a sinuous, slimy trail in my wake.

"I can't talk now. Are you at home?"

"Well, yes . . ."

"I'll be there in half an hour."

I stared at the receiver, but he had rung off.

I lit the sitting room fire and set Liz's red wine to breathe. Then I ran to the bathroom, pulled a comb through my hair and brushed my teeth. My eyes – too bright, too eager – looked back at me from the mirror.

"What are you doing?" I asked my reflection. "The man is coming out of professional courtesy. This is not a date."

I recorked the wine as best I could and closed the sitting room door. Then I sat at the kitchen table and waited. Almost an hour passed before Nick showed up.

"Are you all right?"

No, I thought, not really. "Fine, thanks. But I need to ask a favour."

"Go on." His tone could only be described as neutral. This is for Charlie, I told myself, and plunged ahead. Nick heard me out with his usual courtesy. There was silence when I finished.

"Only," I blurted, "he's being terrific, but I know he feels abandoned. It might help him to know how much Tom's family miss him, how worried they've been."

"Yes," he said slowly. "I take your point."

There was another pause.

"Tell you what. If your son comes to the station after school I'll run the tape for him there. I'll be making a few calls in the morning and you never know, there might be something good to report."

"Would you? It's a lot to ask."

"Not at all. Consider it done."

CHAPTER THIRTY-ONE

"Steps!"

Paul and I ran out of the library as the first rattle sounded. Mrs Clark, resplendent in a new camel coat and tartan scarf, craned her neck to smile. A matching tartan beret perched on the back of her head. Close up I could see it was secured with four hatpins.

"Mrs Clark! Welcome home." I said the words without thinking, then realised they were apt. She needed the Blessed Oliver and the Blessed Oliver certainly needed her. Things had not been the same since she'd gone to her grandson's. "We missed you."

She grinned. "Oh I'm sure that's not the case at all. Take the old stick there, like a good girl."

Her throne was waiting. Martina had flicked her duster over it, Mrs Kelly had attacked it with non-slip polish and Miss Tuohy had brought in some extra cushions from home.

"My, my," she said, dropping Miss Tuohy's hand. "Haven't you been busy. That must be the smartest chair in Ireland."

We lifted her up. Unasked, Paul went to the office to check whether any new history periodicals had come in.

"Can you get this yoke off me? I'm half stabbed to death."

I slid out the pins and admired her new headgear.

"It's the young fella's wife, Deirdre. Always trying to smarten me up and you can't go hurting their feelings."

They had treated her like royalty, she said: breakfast in bed, a television set in her room, delicious hot meals and more tea than a person could drink. The house was warm and comfortable, the great-grandchildren civilised.

"But it wasn't home. They're lovely to visit, but I missed my own place."

"Mr Dixon was lonely without you."

"Was he now? Isn't that just like a man? Take no notice when you're under their nose and pine away the minute you're gone." She rocked on her chair, gratified.

Later, when I was doing the soup run, she grabbed my arm and hooked an arthritic finger to her ear. I leaned down.

"How's that fella of yours?" Her whisper echoed round the reading room.

I sighed. "Mrs Clark. We have to get this straight. I don't have a fella. He's just doing his job."

She dismissed that with a wave of the hand. "Even so." She waited expectantly.

"He's a good man," I conceded. She winked conspiratorially and took her soup.

Miss Tuohy had been wonderful about the fiasco at Michael's. I tried to apologise, but she was having none of it.

"We were all upset. I'd only be sorry if you'd felt unable to show it because I was there. And your friend Michael is delightful."

"So how do you feel, knowing about Tom's family and all?"

"Good lord," she said, "I'm just happy to know he has a home to go to."

"*If* that's where he's gone. Do you think he'll come back, Miss Tuohy?"

"I don't know, dear. I learned long ago that there's no point in trying to second-guess life."

Martina came in after lunch, exhausted from a morning's shopping in town.

"Savages, them women in the bargain basement. Knock you down as soon as look at you." She had the righteous mien of the truly organised. She would observe the rest of us as we rushed into town on Christmas Eve, with frantic, last-minute lists, secure in the superiority of her foresight.

Miss Tuohy was in the office, working on the accessions figures. The Blessed Oliver's budget was tiny, and even with our limited acquisitions the overspend caused by any fluctuation of the Irish pound against sterling was significant. In her place I wouldn't have bothered, I would have stuck it to the Library Committee with pleasure, but that wasn't Miss Tuohy's way. She would be meticulous to the moment she locked the building for the last time.

I was filing catalogue cards for her thrillers and romances when my nostrils started to tingle, assailed by the scent of musk. Ah-Ah-Tishoo. Once, twice, three times.

"Good afternoon, Mr Pender," said I, without looking round.

"Eleanor. Are you psychic along with your other talents?"

"Absolutely."

"Facilities!"

I glared at Mrs Clark. She was just being bold. To my amazement Billy the Kid was at her side in a flash. He lifted her to the floor as if she were porcelain.

"You'll have to do the rest, I'm afraid."

When you got beyond the dazzle he had a nice smile.

"You can bring me to the door. She'll take it from there."

They waltzed across the reading room, her head up to his elbow. Mr Dixon wiped his afflicted eye and gave them a dirty look. I went to the office and informed Miss Tuohy she had a visitor.

"He smells beautiful, don't you think?" said Mrs Clark in the loo. "Just like young Prince Charles."

"I wouldn't know about that."

"My Mam, God rest her, used to say perfume was for people who didn't wash. And that was before the men took to it."

"I think Mr Pender washes all right. Do you know he has a proper shower in his office?"

"Well fancy that. Why would you want a shower in the office? Doesn't he have a home to wash in?"

Paul helped me settle her back on the throne. Mr Dixon moved to her table, his expression Rottweiler-like. She certainly knew how to keep her men on their toes.

Half an hour later I was summoned to the office. Billy the Kid leaned against the fireplace. At least he had the manners to leave the leather chair to Miss Tuohy.

"Sit down, Ellie. Mr Pender has been . . ."

"William, please."

"Yes, well . . . has been telling me there's an emergency meeting of the Library Committee on Thursday."

"Will you be attending, Miss Tuohy?"

"Absolutely," said Billy. "As acting librarian that is her right."

The point was, he continued, he had some influence with a couple of members, and he wanted to know how we would like the Blessed Oliver's case argued. The meeting would be attended by a number of civil servants who wished to discuss the building and its future use. "Obviously, I have spoken to Agnes, but in the eventuality that she may opt for early retirement she feels your views are vital."

Between us, Miss Tuohy and I outlined our ideas. She filled him in on what had happened when the delegation went to the Department of Health. He tapped a finger against his lips, thoughtful.

"I don't know about the involvement of Social Services," he said, "but from a library angle I've had a few thoughts myself. Suppose the stock were to be modified. A lot of material could be cut back or thrown out. The reference section, for example, could be pared to basics. Non-fiction could be reduced to areas of active interest to your readers. Fiction could be expanded to match their requirements. In other words, the service would cater to a specific community group. It would not be a library in the fullest sense of the word, more an outreach branch responding to local needs."

We stared at him.

"Where would the funding come from?"

"The Council would never agree," added Miss Tuohy. The spirit of Mr Condor from Personnel wafted in, the spectre at our feast.

"The Blessed Oliver could be funded as a subsidiary extension of my own operation. The librarian would answer to me but would in fact have autonomy in the day-to-day running of the place, a real say in policy development and a separate budget."

"You've put a lot of thought into this," remarked Miss Tuohy. "William," she added generously.

Echoing her own philosophy, he said quietly, "We're here to serve the community. It seems to me you've been doing that better than most. I would be proud to have a part in it."

Mr Dixon scowled, Mrs Clark clicked her dentures and waved as he left.

"And of course it means you could stay on, Ellie, if you chose," said Miss Tuohy.

"I don't know. The Library Committee might veto his suggestion. There's a way to go yet. One thing's for sure, Miss Tuohy. If I do have to work with him the aftershave has to go."

Charlie ran into the office at quarter to six. "Nick's in the car. He can give us a lift if you're ready."

I looked at Miss Tuohy. She shut the door and sat me down.

"What you're going to do, Ellie, is leave slowly and calmly. If there's any news about Tom you might call me later."

I walked to the car like a person who'd recently had neck surgery. Nick opened the door and sat me in. Martina stood at the steps to wave us off.

"He's beautiful, like one of them choirboys," were the last words to reach me as we drove away. I turned to see if Charlie had heard, but he gave no sign. The journey was quick and quiet, each of us preoccupied. I was relieved to see that Charlie looked more thoughtful than upset.

I remembered the last time Nick had driven me home, the day he had summoned me to Divisional Headquarters to watch my reaction to the dominatrix photographs. That had been my first insight into the murky underworld of my boss's secret life. In truth I hadn't learned much since, but the details seemed irrelevant; whichever way you looked at it, it added up to shame and pain.

"How's his wife taking it?"

"Badly, but she's a fighter."

I realised there had been no need to tell him who I was asking about.

Nick dropped us at the cottage, saying he had to get back to work but would call me later.

There was a message on the answering machine from Matt, wondering whether we would like to come and see the baby after work. The old saw about giving people an inch sprang to mind. I could feel my anger rising. We needed to get this sorted, and fast. I was not available to play happy families. To have couched his suggestion in terms of meeting his baby was unforgivable. The fact that I no longer wanted to kill Bethany, and indeed himself, did not mean that we were buddies. If he wanted Charlie to go he could bloody say so. What was more, he could drive him.

I called up to Charlie. "Would you like to go to the hospital if your Dad can pick you up?"

"What, now?"

"After supper, maybe."

There was a pause. "I have maths tomorrow."

It didn't quite wash that Charlie would use house exams as a pretext for not doing something. Maybe he'd had enough at the weekend. I had no wish to prevent him going, but I wasn't going to force the issue either.

"I need to call Matt. What do I tell him?"

"Say I'll see them all on Saturday."

I called Matt's mobile number and gave him an earful. He asked me to hold on, presumably so he could move to another room. I had a vision of Bethany, her long hair spread over the pillows, face and nightgown perfect, glowing with the fulfilment of motherhood. Her stomach was probably flat as a board already. I hoped she had heard.

"Sorry about that, Bethany's parents . . ." His voice trailed off.

Even better, I thought. She could fill them in on the bitch of a wife who screamed and ranted and was unreasonable about every little thing.

Suddenly the fight went out of me. I was only hurting myself. What Bethany or her parents thought or said was immaterial. I needed to get a civilised handle on relations with my ex-husband for my own sake, for my son's, for my sanity.

"Matt. Your suggestion was not appropriate. You and I are not friends and we're no longer family. You need to think before you speak."

"I'm sorry. It seemed like a good idea . . . but you're right. Maybe it's a bit soon."

"I have to go now."

There was no getting through to him.

Charlie was subdued at supper. We agreed that he would walk Boy and get an early night. He was worn out from all he'd had to cope with since Friday. Only two days remained till the start of his Christmas holidays. He would probably need to sleep for a week.

I parked my feet on the kitchen table and lay back in my chair, listening to Bach's *St Matthew Passion*. I was half-asleep by the time Nick called.

Tom had not actually been found, he told me, but the Scottish police had come up with a contact number for his sister in Edinburgh. She was disbelieving at first, then relieved that Tom was safe and well, though since he hadn't been in touch she feared that might be overstating the case. She had promised to call if there was any word from him. Nick himself was not unduly worried that Tom had not yet shown up. After all, assuming that Tom was headed for Edinburgh, we didn't know what route he would take or how he would travel.

"Old habits die hard. He may be walking a good deal of the way."

It was said to reassure but I sensed an undercurrent of concern. Tom had been gone for almost four days. Whatever had prompted his leaving had all the appearance of being sudden and urgent. Why then would he be dawdling through the highways and byways of Britain?

"How on earth did you come up with that tape? Miss Tuohy says you have quite a library."

"Let's just say I'm attuned. I look through them every once in a while, keep the faces fresh."

"What, as a kind of mental exercise?"

There was a long pause. I wondered if he was still there.

"I lost someone myself, once. I know how it feels."

Then he rang off.

CHAPTER THIRTY-TWO

THE DAYS THAT followed were tense. The Library Committee meeting that would decide our fate hung over the Blessed Oliver. Miss Tuohy had decided to take Mr Carolan into her confidence but to say nothing to the elders until something definite emerged. There was no point in raising their hopes and Mr Dixon in particular would only become agitated and drive everyone mad.

We were waiting, too, for news of Tom. I knew Nick was actively liaising with the British police and had had a missing poster circulated to ports and railway stations. Incongruously, the photo used was a cropped version of the image Miss Tuohy and I had found so upsetting: Tom lying on the ground, laughing. It was unlikely that anyone seeing him now would make an immediate connection.

And Christmas was nearly upon us. Try as I might, I couldn't get my head around it. Not alone had I done nothing, I had no plan, no inspiration. It was a time I had always loved: the plotting, the secrecy, wrapping presents in the middle of the night, dressing the tree, cramming windows with Santas, reindeer and candles, even preparing the meal, knowing we would overindulge and live on sandwiches for a week afterwards. And this year, our first without husband and father, I had wanted everything to be special.

Young Dr Saul's Christmas Eve invitation, thoughtfully including myself and Charlie, had already been received and gloated over by the aunts. The day itself we would spend at Cedar Hall – after all, who could know how things might stand next year. The house might be a building site, or filled with foreigners in search of their Irish roots. Perhaps with this in mind May was considering hosting a small party on New Year's Eve. She was hoping to persuade George and Merry Lou to come over. Lillian was egging her on furiously. Dorothy conceded she was prepared to help if it went ahead.

On Thursday Miss Tuohy arrived at work looking even more efficient than usual. Her hair was sculpted to her head, her blouse starched. Billy had arranged to meet her for coffee before going to the Council offices. He would fill her in on any late developments and hopefully give her moral support. Mr Carolan had offered to drive her, which was unnecessary but considerate. We knew she felt the fate of the Blessed Oliver rested on her shoulders, that the case would be won or lost by the conviction with which she could argue it. The less time she had alone to become nervous the better.

I walked her to the front door.

"Wish me luck," she whispered.

"Feck it," called Martina from the counter, "you can only do your best."

"Amen," I said, giving her the thumbs up.

The afternoon dragged by. I had swapped my half-day

with Paul. This time yesterday I had been slaving my guts out for the Seaview management – the hotel was in crisis with every room booked for Christmas. Grateful guests left enormous tips and offered to fly me to exotic tropical locations should I ever feel in need of a break. Even the kitchen presses were sparkling. I had gone to bed early, smug in my exhaustion. Now I sat with Martina, watching the minutes tick by, wondering what stage the proceedings had reached. When the phone rang just after four we both rushed to the office. I got there first.

"Eleanor?"

"Nick?" I shook my head at Martina, hoping she would leave. She popped a fresh stick of gum and parked herself on the desk. "Counter," I mouthed. She ignored me. I turned away and faced the window.

"Tom's turned up. His sister called."

I offered a silent prayer of thanks. "Is he all right?"

"She didn't say much, just that he'd arrived and was sleeping. She'll call when she's had a chance to talk to him. It could be a couple of days."

"Will you let me know?"

"I'll be in touch."

I hauled Martina off the desk and swung her round the office.

"Me heels!" She tottered off, straightening her skirt. As she disappeared into the reading room she called over her shoulder. "For a grown woman you can act very fucking weird."

"Language!" chorused the elders.

I drove to Cedar Hall after work. There was still no word from Miss Tuohy. I wondered whether no news was good news. After all, if the Committee was not prepared even to countenance a reprieve the meeting would surely be over by now.

Beattie was in the kitchen, doing something suspicious to a stew.

"There you are," she beamed. "Sit down and have a fag."

I stuck my finger in the pot and licked it. Beattie slapped my hand away.

"Behave yourself. Nobody's asking you to eat it."

"You're a pet, we'd love to stay to supper. Where are the others?"

"Sitting room. There's a nice fire down."

"Come on then."

I dragged her along the corridor. We opened the door quietly and looked in. May and Lillian were reading, Charlie was writing at the table, stroking Boy with his foot, and Dorothy was embroidering a pillowslip with silk thread. You could hear the clock ticking. I tiptoed in and stood by Charlie's chair.

"Good news, everyone. Tom is safe."

They looked up, rudely wrenched from other worlds.

"He's at his sister's in Edinburgh."

Charlie clutched at Boy. Lillian's hand flew to her mouth.

"He is? He's safe?" Her eyes filled with tears. Charlie ran over and hugged her tightly.

"I told you, Lillian. I told you he'd be okay."

"You did, darling. Oh you did. This is the nicest Christmas present a person could wish for."

We stayed for Beattie's stew and ate in the kitchen where, whatever the food's shortcomings, it would at least be hot. The mood was upbeat and celebratory. Tom had been found, the future of Cedar Hall was secure and Christmas was coming. At last I felt it, a little niggle in my system, a pinprick of excitement. I looked around the table at these, the most important people in my life, and knew I was lucky: Beattie, big, generous Beattie, who had spent a lifetime holding together the fabric of the house and the lives it contained with her love and laughter; May, my warm, gifted mother, freed for the first time in decades from financial worries; and Dorothy and Lillian, exhilarated by the prospect of a whole new future working with Merry Lou. And there was Charlie, my thoughtful, talented boy, feeding illicit scraps to the mongrel under the table. He hadn't asked if Tom was coming back. He knew better than to ask too much.

We helped Beattie clear up and dropped her home. I was hoping to hear from Nick or Miss Tuohy, or both. Then I would turn my mind to Christmas, bearing in mind our new boiler and the state of my overdraft. It would have to be cheap and cheerful, but so what. A lot of imagination and a little cash could go a long way.

I was muffled against the cold on the old rope swing, having a quiet smoke and considering the night sky, when Charlie called out, "Mum, it's Miss Tuohy."

I ran inside, assuming she was on the phone, and nearly knocked her down in my haste.

"I hope this isn't inconvenient, Ellie." She held a tissue-wrapped bottle of what could only be champagne. She slid it self-consciously on to the table as if she couldn't imagine where it had come from. Her hair was still up, the library uniform immaculate. She must have come straight from the meeting. Her gaze was unusually shifty.

"You did it! Sainted Mother of God, you actually did it."

She shrugged. "With a lot of help."

I threw my arms around her and shouted to Charlie.

"What's going on?"

"I don't believe you've been formally introduced. Miss Tuohy, my son, Charlie. Charlie, I want you to meet my boss, the saviour of the Blessed Oliver Plunkett, Miss Agnes Tuohy."

"Oh really, Ellie. How do you do, Charlie. Your mother exaggerates."

Chapter Thirty-Two

"She's always on about how wonderful you are."

"For goodness sake." Miss Tuohy turned pink. "What a nice thing to say."

"Play something for us, Charlie. We're going to celebrate."

And we did. The meeting had been long and arduous. At various times she thought it was all over, but Billy the Kid would not give in. The Committee was besotted by him. He was young, articulate and good-looking. His was the vision they wanted for their library service. At one point he had hinted that the survival of the Blessed Oliver was the price they would have to pay to secure his ongoing services. Terrified that he was being headhunted, they had no option but to agree.

"Did he mean it? Would he have gone that far?"

"Who knows? It wasn't a risk they were prepared to take."

Fair play to him, I thought, he didn't do things by halves. He might just be a good man to work for if we could lose the labels and the musk.

First thing on Friday, Miss Tuohy took down the closure notices and replaced them with a huge sign that read:

The Blessed Oliver Plunkett branch of the municipal libraries will NOT now close on December 23rd as previously advised. We wish our readers a safe and happy Christmas, and look forward to serving you in the New Year.

We all signed and Martina did some fancy artwork in the corners.

The library was buzzing all day. There were the usual pensioners on their post office run, increased demand due to the upcoming holiday and then, as word spread, women from the Valley came down to wish us well. It was like an indoor street party. Mr Mulhern strutted, Mrs Clark presided on her throne, clapping her hands with delight, and Martina swore she even saw Mr Dixon smile.

Paul was sent out for mince pies. "Make sure they're boxed," called Miss Tuohy, as we made pots of tea and set up a buffet table in the reading room. The noise level was rising and Martina felt impelled to put manners on the counter queue.

"I think I'll call Mr Pender, let him see what he's bought into," said Miss Tuohy, heading for the office.

He arrived within the hour, accompanied by Pam, who hadn't thought to remove her label. She introduced herself to Martina, her sense of hierarchy scuppered by the lack of badges.

"I'm William's deputy."

"So I see," grunted Martina, staring at her chest.

"What a . . . lively operation."

Martina threw her a look and roared, "Get back in line, Mrs O'Toole. You're causing an obstruction." She turned her back on Pam and continued issuing loans.

Mrs Clark monopolised Billy, her pet. She summoned her cronies and presented him as her own creation. He looked around in wonder at all that he had saved, and at the people for whom he'd done it. I brought him a cup of tea and he shook his head, wordless.

"You're not the worst, Mr Pender," I sneezed. "We're very grateful."

He handed me a linen handkerchief. "You should do something about that cold."

"I will," I promised, pocketing his hanky. I figured he owed me.

Mrs Phelan came in, Bobby and the babies in tow. She looked tired and sad. Miss Tuohy propelled her into the office. They stayed there for quite some time. Bobby gorged himself on mince pies and the toddler resumed his circuit under the desks. When the baby started to cry a woman from the queue lifted him out of his buggy and slung him absently over her shoulder, talking all the while to her friend. Miss Tuohy opened the office door and beckoned me across.

"Would you give this to Robert, see if he can carry it home for his mother?"

I took the boxed set of Lavinia Mosse novels and looked around for Bobby. Mrs Phelan was beside me, taking her leave of Miss Tuohy. Suddenly it clicked. How had I never seen it? How had I misread her collection of romantic fiction at home, her encyclopaedic knowledge of publishing schedules and forthcoming titles?

"I hope these are signed, Miss Tuohy."

"Oh yes," she replied placidly. "They're personally inscribed."

It was several hours before I managed to get her alone. Billy and Pam were well gone – he, shell-shocked but gratified, she looking as if she intended to use the shower facility on her return. A steady stream of locals called in throughout the day. Rumours, tentative in the morning, had reached titanic proportions by late afternoon. The last version I heard had the police being called to restore order to the Committee meeting after Miss Tuohy decked Mr Condor from Personnel with a right hook. I saw no reason to put anything straight; after all, none of the stories was addressed to me and they held their own poetic justice.

Garda Murphy popped in for a cup of tea.

"With all the comings and goings I thought maybe the revolution had started. It's grand entirely to see things have worked out so well."

"No thanks to the pigs," shouted Mr Dixon.

"Ah hush, now," went Mrs Clark. "Where's the use in that kind of talk?"

Mr Dixon glowered but held his peace as Garda Murphy chatted to Mrs Clark, the Mammy's friend.

When I saw Miss Tuohy go into the office, probably for a break from the noise, I followed her. I stood with my back to the door to prevent anyone coming in.

"Why didn't you tell me?"

She shrugged. "As I said the evening you came round, I thought you'd have figured it out."

I jerked my head towards the reading room. "Are you going to tell them?"

"Absolutely not. And nor must you. It would be . . . cheap."

"For heaven's sake, why? They live for Lavinia Mosse. You give them their dreams."

"No. They make their own dreams. I just offer escape when reality overwhelms them. It's a very small, private thing. They can pretend to believe in that world if it gives them comfort. If they were to discover that it was nothing more than the fantasy of an old spinster, they would feel cheated. It would be tantamount to breaking faith."

CHAPTER THIRTY-THREE

O N THE DAY before Christmas Eve May received a letter from Scotland. It was our last day at work before the holiday break. I knew it was serious when she turned up at the Blessed Oliver in the Rover.

"Could I borrow Eleanor for a while?" she asked Miss Tuohy.

"Take as long as you like, Mrs St John. We're not exactly busy, as you can see."

Things were indeed quiet after Friday's stampede. Most of our readers had been issued their holiday loans and many of the elders, Mrs Clark among them, had gone to spend Christmas with family.

"I've been meaning to say, Miss Tuohy, that we're having a small celebration at Cedar Hall to see in the New Year. We'd be delighted if you could join us."

"How very kind. But I'm afraid my sister will be staying with me . . ."

"But you must bring her along. Isn't that so, Eleanor?"

"Absolutely. Do come, Miss Tuohy."

"Thank you," she smiled shyly. "We'd love to."

May and I went for coffee to the pub. There was nowhere else within walking distance. It smelled stalely of cigarette smoke and stout. When I had been there with Matt it had at least been busy with lunchtime trade. Now it was empty, dark, depressing.

May didn't seem to notice. She took the letter from her bag. "Read it."

It gave an Edinburgh address and telephone number, and went on:

> *Dear Mrs St John,*
> *I have to write for two reasons. One is to say I'm sorry that I upped and left so suddenly. There was a personal matter to deal with and I didn't stop to think.*
> *Two is to ask a favour. I'd like to come back if you'd have me. I can think on my own easier than here. I promise I would work hard and not leave again without telling you.*
> *Please reply soonest,*
> *Thomas Traherne (Tom)*
> *P.S. Please pass my respects to Miss Tuohy in the library, if she remembers me.*

"Uh-oh," I said.

"Indeed."

"Miss Tuohy. It's always Miss Tuohy."

"For goodness' sake, Eleanor. Can we deal with the matter in hand?"

"What's to deal with? He wants to come back. You want him back, and Charlie would give anything for him to be back. It's an answer to prayer."

"But I don't want to interfere between him and his family."

"That's not your decision, Mum."

She looked doubtful.

"Anyway," I pressed, "we're going to need someone to keep an eye on the builders and so on, make sure they don't wreck the garden. Merry Lou will be in a position to pay Tom properly, so he'll have the means to go home if and when he wants."

Still she seemed unconvinced.

"He's never asked for anything. He's asking now and you owe him."

"I suppose you're right," she said slowly.

That evening I was having my seasonal get-together with Liz. We did it every year, usually going for a meal, but since neither of us had thought to book, each assuming the other would have done so, we had to settle for the pub instead.

"You're joking," had been the response when I tried a couple of restaurants in the afternoon. They had been booked up with office parties for weeks.

Charlie was at Matt's until Christmas morning. I wasn't thrilled but Matt was keen that he spend time with the baby and I could hardly refuse. This way he got to spend the important part of Christmas at Cedar Hall.

Liz and I agreed to meet at a bar close to the cottage. If taxis were scarce, as was likely, she could spend the night with me.

I thought about Tom as I got ready. His sister had called Nick a couple of days after his return. She had been shocked at the change in him. He found it difficult to be around people and felt trapped in enclosed spaces. Even his language had altered.

Before coming to her place he had tracked down the elderly cyclist's daughter. Tom's sister could only guess at what had been said, but one thing was clear: Tom, burdened for so long by his sense of guilt, was having an equally hard time adjusting to the notion that he had not been to blame.

He came from a family of craftsmen, skilled in the restoration of musical instruments. Tom's reputation was legendary. Clients came to him from all over Britain, some from continental Europe. When the sister indicated that his place was with the family firm, doing what he loved, Tom had become agitated. She realised then it had been wrong to push him, that she must wait for him to feel his way back to normality and make his own decisions when he was good and ready.

On the night Tom came home, she told Nick finally, she had been sitting with her children watching television when Tom's Irish setter – old now, his sight failing – had started to whimper and scratch at the door. The sister thought he needed to go outside to do his business, but when her son headed for the back garden he wouldn't follow. Instead he lay in the hall, staring at the front door, whining. The family had heard nothing, there had been no knock or ring to alert them to a caller. Eventually, exasperated, Tom's sister had opened the door to shut the dog up and found herself face to face with her long-lost brother.

"Some things," she told Nick, "you just can't explain."

The pub was jammed to capacity. Liz beat a path to the bar only to have most of the drinks spilled by jostlers as she made her way back. The noise level was horrendous.

"This is hopeless," I roared. I could see Liz lip-reading to make sense of what I was saying. "Shall we go back to the house?"

She nodded. A woman standing near the Ladies' fainted. A couple of men tried to carry her through the crowd. People ignored them, refusing to make way. One of the punters became belligerent when he was poked in the back and took a swing at the man behind him. The crowd pressed back, creating a small space for a fight. The woman who had fainted dangled between her rescuers like a puppet without strings.

I looked around in desperation. All routes to the exits were blocked, people packed in like sardines. I scanned the far side of the room, frightened now, feeling dizzy and spaced as the heat and noise bore down on me. I hated crowds at the best of times. This was a nightmare. I was aware of Liz shouting in my ear, but not of what she was saying. The world receded in slow motion. I fixed my eyes on a point across the room where a man with an uncanny resemblance to Nick was talking to a blonde woman. The man looked over. I stared into his eyes, willing myself to stay on my feet. If I could just concentrate . . . But it was too hot, too noisy, too hard. Those eyes became my world and everything slid to black.

I came to on the pavement, with Nick bending over me in shirtsleeves.

"You shouldn't be out without a jacket," I scolded.

"You're lying on it," he pointed out reasonably.

It felt completely normal to be stretched out on a footpath with Liz watching anxiously while the blonde felt my pulse and smiled across at Nick.

I hate you, I thought, glaring at her.

"She'll be fine," she said pleasantly. "I don't think she should go back in, though. Rest and quiet would be helpful."

"Come on then," Nick hauled me to my feet. "Let's get you to the car. Can I drop anyone on my way?"

Liz shook her head. "I'm grand, thanks. Unless you'd like me to come with you, Ellie?"

"No way. Please don't make me feel worse than I do. I'm sorry for messing up your evening."

"Don't be a moron," said Liz. "I'll call you tomorrow."

Nick guided me to his car. I leaned on him rather more than was necessary, the blonde trailing behind us. To my surprise he handed me in to the front seat.

The blonde hunkered down beside me and held out her

hand. "Goodbye, Ellie. I hope we meet again under happier circumstances."

I slit my eyes at her. In your dreams, I thought.

She kissed Nick chastely on the forehead and disappeared. I was utterly confused. Was she going to follow in her own car? Meet him later? What?

"My sister Miriam," Nick replied to my unspoken question. "She's a doctor, so mind what she said. Quiet and rest."

And that's what I got. Nick made tea while I put on my striped pyjamas and climbed into bed. He leaned against the headboard and I snuggled down, my head on his chest, the dog between us. He stroked my hair as he told me about the child he'd had while still in his teens; about his girlfriend, the baby's mother, who had run away, taking the infant with her; about the months he'd spent searching for them, trailing them to Britain, then to Germany; about the scene when he'd finally found them, the abuse hurled at him by the new boyfriend, the girl screaming, the baby crying; about his long fight, and failure, to win custody of the child.

"He's nearly thirty now."

"Do you ever see him?"

"From time to time, but not when he was growing up. By the time he made contact it was almost too late."

"And you never married?"

He smiled. "I've yet to meet a woman who doesn't accuse me of being married to the job."

At some point I drifted off to sleep. I woke in the middle of the night and shot upright: something was wrong, but what? It took a few seconds for my brain to catch up. Nick had been here, now he was gone.

"Nick," I whispered, "you should have stayed." I thumped the pillow. "I wish you'd stayed."

I lay down. In the darkness a shadow detached itself from the rocking chair.

"I did," he said. "I'm here, Eleanor."

Acknowledgements
Warmest thanks to my early readers: Con Collins, Thomond Coogan,
Michael Good, Stanford Kingston, Trudi Mills and especially Una
Keating; the staff at Brandon/Mount Eagle; my agent, Faith O'Grady,
for her unfailing support; Hilary Kehoe and Martina Niland at
Samson Films for their endless patience; Paddy O'Doherty for proof-
reading; Pat McCartan, for filling me in on the legal niceties, any
errors being my own; Angela Rohan for editing, and Lia Mills for
help that was unstinting and went beyond editing, but did that too;
Sam, for the many cups of tea, and David, for being himself.

FICTION
from
BRANDON

KITTY FITZGERALD

Snapdragons

"A unique and extremely engaging story of two sisters, each of whom is looking for love and salvation in their different ways." *Irish Post*

"An original, daring book." *Books Ireland*

Sometimes shocking, frequently humorous, often surreal, *Snapdragons* is a unique and extremely engaging rites-of-passage novel about a young woman who grows up unhappily in rural Ireland after World War II. She is disliked – for reasons she cannot understand – by her parents, and has a running feud with her sister. Yet the mood of this story is strangely light-hearted, frequently comic and absolutely memorable.

She makes her escape to the English midlands, and works and lives in a pub in Digbeth, Birmingham, where her sister has settled with her husband. Her already difficult relationship with her sister is further strained when she discovers how she is living. She also learns the sad reason for her parents' hostility towards her.

A captivating story of a young girl in Birmingham and the North of England in the 1950s, its main protagonist, Bernadette, who carries on a constant angry dialogue with God, is one of the most delightfully drawn characters in recent Irish fiction.

ISBN 0 86322 258 7; Original Paperback £8.99

JOHN TROLAN

Slow Punctures

"Compelling. . . his writing, with its mix of brutal social realism, irony and humour, reads like a cross between Roddy Doyle and Irvine Welsh." *Sunday Independent*

"Three hundred manic, readable pages. . . *Slow Punctures* is grim, funny and bawdy in equal measure." *The Irish Times*

"Fast-moving and hilarious in the tradition of Roddy Doyle." *Sunday Business Post*

"Trolan writes in a crisp and consistent style. He handles the delicate subject of young suicide with a sensitive practicality and complete lack of sentiment. His novel is a brittle working-class rites of passage that tells a story about Dublin that probably should have been told a long time ago." *Irish Post*

ISBN 0 86322 252 8; Original Paperback £8.99

Any Other Time

"Trolan's portrayal of a hopeless underclass is both convincing and chilling . . . He has a rare and genuine gift for dialogue, and his characters' voices ring true. A relentlessly grim but undeniably powerful novel." *Sunday Tribune*

"Wonderfully written, and confirms Trolan's talent . . . Such is the power of Trolan's writing, and so skilful his descriptions and characterisation, that before long I was mesmerised by the seedy world I had landed in . . . Trolan writes from the inside, and it show." *Books Ireland*

John Trolan was born in a Dublin tenement in 1960, and lived for fifteen years in the high-rise flats of Ballymun. After a period of homelessness he studied at university in Bristol and took a degree. He now works as an addictions counsellor in Stroud and is actively involved in the performance poetry scene in Bristol.

ISBN 0 86322 265 X; Original Paperback £8.99

THE NOVELS OF J. M. O'NEILL

Duffy Is Dead

"A book written sparingly, with wit and without sentimentality, yet the effect can be like poetry . . . An exceptional novel." *Guardian*

"The atmosphere is indescribable but absolutely right: as if the world of Samuel Beckett had crossed with that of George V. Higgins." *Observer*

"Not a single word out of place . . . Every word of it rings true." *Daily Telegraph*

ISBN 0 86322 261 7; Paperback £6.99

Open Cut

"A hard and squalid world depicted economically and evocatively. . . the tension in the slang-spotted dialogue and the mean prose creates effective atmosphere." *Hampstead & Highgate Express*

"A powerful thriller." *Radio Times*

"O'Neill's prose, like the winter wind is cutting and sharp." *British Book News*

"Fascinating." *Yorkshire Post*

"An uncannily exacting and accomplished novelist." *Observer*

"Exciting and dangerous, with a touch of the poet." *Sunday Times*

ISBN 0 86322 264 1; Paperback £6.99

Rellighan, Undertaker

A dark, intriguing modern gothic tale. The final novel by a writer who was a master of his craft.

In a small rural town in Ireland, nothing is as it appears. Ester Machen brings with her a mystery, and death is stalking the young people of the town. Though 'the town is talking', the only person determined to get to the bottom of the mystery is the detective Coleman. He has few allies, but Rellighan the undertaker gradually assists him in attempting to reveal and rid the town of the terror that has grown within it. They both risk death but unfalteringly continue to unveil the mystery, becoming deeply embroiled in the dark world of the occult as they strive to eradicate evil.

ISBN 0 86322 260 9; Original Paperback £8.99

Bennett & Company

Winner of the 1999 Kerry Ingredients Book of the Year award

"O'Neill's world owes something to the sagas of Forsyte and Onedin, and his plotting has, at times, some of the pace and complexity of John Buchan, but the novel is, nonetheless, uniquely Irish with its sanctuary lamps, street-children, moving statues and bitter memories, and it is a contribution to an overdue examination of Irish conscience. The poor and the middle classes are indeed those of Frank McCourt and Kate O'Brien, but O'Neill's is a strictly modern and undeluded vision of the past. The writing is shockingly credible." *Times Literary Supplement*

"He is an exceptional writer, and one we must take very seriously." *Sunday Independent*

ISBN 1 90201 106 6; Original paperback £7.99

THE NOVELS OF WALTER MACKEN

I Am Alone

Banned in Ireland when it was first published, *I Am Alone* tells the story of a young Irishman, who leaves behind the grey stone and green fields of Galway for the bright lights of pre-war London.

ISBN 0 86322 266 8; hardback £12.99

Rain on the Wind

"It is a raw, savage story full of passion and drama set amongst the Galway fishing community . . . it is the story of romantic passion, a constant struggle with the sea, with poverty and with the political conservatism of post-independence Ireland." *Irish Independent*

ISBN 0 86322 185 8; paperback £6.99

Sunset on the Window-Panes

Careless of the hurt he inflicts, Bart O'Breen walks his own road, as proud as the devil and as lonely as hell.

ISBN 0 86322 254 4; paperback £6.99

The Bogman

"Macken captures the isolation and poverty of the village – its closed attitudes, its frozen social mores . . . and its deeply unforgiving nature." *Irish Independent*

ISBN 0 86322 184 X; paperback £6.99

Brown Lord of the Mountain

"Macken knows his people and his places, and his love of them shines through." *Examiner*

ISBN 0 86322 201 3; paperback £5.95

Quench the Moon

A romantic story of the wild, hard and beautiful land of Connemara.

ISBN 0 86322 202 1; paperback £5.95

CHET RAYMO

In The Falcon's Claw

"A metaphysical thriller comparable to Umberto Eco's *In the Name of the Rose,* but more poetic, more moving, and more sensual." *Lire*

"Raymo's gift is to bring to life that distant time, vividly but without straining the reader's credulity, in a brief 200 pages or so. There are many strands in this fine novel – love, religion, the stars and the nature of time, church politics, Latin and Irish verse – and they are skilfully put together in a vigorous language that invokes a fresh, unexplored Europe of 1,000 years ago." *Sunday Tribune*

"An astonishing text that reminds us of Umberto Eco's *In the Name of the Rose . . .* with Chet Raymo, this generation of American literature has found one of its most profound philosophers." *Dernieres Nouvelles d'Alsace*

"The French critics were right when they saw in Chet Raymo, author of *The Dork of Cork*, a writer of exceptional culture and erudition, which in no way diminishes the strength and originality of his wit, nor the vivacity of his novel . . . *In The Falcon's Claw* is a novel of never-ending pleasure . . . superbly innovative. It is a work of rare and irreverent intelligence." *Le Figaro Litteraire*

ISBN 0 86322 204 8

Original paperback £6.95

STEVE MacDONOGH (ed)

The Brandon Book of Irish Short Stories

"This impressive collection." *Times Literary Supplement*

"Ranges hugely in setting, style and tone. The confident internationalism of these mostly young writers reflects something of the spirit of the new Ireland but it is grounded in an undeceived realism . . . On the evidence here, the future of Irish fiction is in good hands."
Observer

"This exciting collection of short fiction."
The Irish Times

"A host of the best contemporary Irish writers."
Ireland on Sunday

ISBN 0 86322 237 4

Paperback £6.99